THE LANGUAGE OF CANNIBALS

A MONGO MYSTERY

GEORGE C. CHESBRO

THE MYSTERIOUS PRESS

New York • Tokyo • Sweden • Milan

Published by Warner Books

 A Time Warner Company

MYSTERIOUS PRESS EDITION

Copyright © 1990 by George C. Chesbro
All rights reserved.

Cover design by Tom McKeveny

The Mysterious Press name and logo are trademarks of
Warner Books, Inc.

Mysterious Press books are published by
Warner Books, Inc.
666 Fifth Avenue
New York, New York 10103

A Time Warner Company

Printed in the United States of America

Originally published in hardcover by The Mysterious Press.
First Mysterious Press Paperback Printing: March, 1991

10 9 8 7 6 5 4 3 2 1

CRITICAL ACCLAIM FOR

George C. Chesbro and Mongo

⚒

"The most engaging criminologist to appear in decades is a former circus star undaunted by his dwarfism."

—*Booklist*

⚒

"Mongo has a way of cutting brutes down to his size, the better to beat the whey out of them."

—*Los Angeles Times*

⚒

"Not-quite-science-fiction and suspense make a thrilling combination, and nobody works it better than Chesbro."

—*Playboy*

⚒

"Bloodcurdling adventure . . . Chesbro generates genuine suspense with the question of how, not if, his little hero with the giant's heart will triumph."

—*Publishers Weekly*

⚒

"Mongo is one of the successful challengers to the bruiser class of hard-boiled detective heroes."

—*Time*

⚒

"Chesbro's wild roller-coaster rides mix detection with science fiction and fantasy but keep a center of humanity and rationality in the amazing Mongo, one of the greatest characters of recent mystery fiction."

—*Ellery Queen's Mystery Magazine*

THE MONGO MYSTERIES

For Judi and Dick Ragone,
Krysten, Kara, and Michael,
and for all those
who respect language

CHAPTER ONE

In the purple distance neatly scripted alphabet vultures with Zs for eyes soared in the thermals swirling over and around an alphabet volcano spewing what appeared to be incomplete, fractured sentences and clustered gobs of words that were half submerged in a river of blood red lava. Block-letter trees formed an oppressive jungle that appeared like a great fungus growth that was an infection on, rather than a part of, the land. The exhausted, hapless soldier who had wandered into this eerie and alien landscape was hopelessly entangled in a web of punctuation-mark vines. His boyish features twisted in anguish and horror as crablike creatures—rendered, like everything else in the landscape except the soldier, of a profusion of single letters and half-formed words or sentences—dined on his left leg. The foot had already been consumed, and a gleaming white shaft of bone protruded from the ragged flesh of his ankle, which was spewing blood of red and blue. I looked for some pattern, complete sentences or phrases, in the maelstrom of letters and words but couldn't find any; in this haunted place, the twenty-six letters of the alphabet were just the skeletal matter of mindless creatures that existed to rend, consume, and infect, not make sense. The painting, titled *The Language of Cannibals*, was by a man named Jack Trex, and I rather liked it. I found the notion of these flesh-eating letter-creatures food for thought.

The hand-printed placard taped to the wall beneath the painting identified Trex as the commander of the Cairn chapter of Vietnam Veterans of America, whose members were the sole contributors to the exhibit of art and crafts.

For some time, I'd been reading and hearing good things about Cairn, a small town on the banks of the Hudson River a few miles north of New York City. Noted for its many art galleries, antique shops, and fine restaurants, as well as its thriving community of artists, Cairn is a mixed society of very rich, some poor blue-collar families, and assorted celebrities who like their yachts close at hand but have tired of Connecticut and the Hamptons. Bed-and-board establishments, most of them operated by the blue-collar families who once supplied man-power for the now-defunct stone quarry on a mountain at the edge of town, have proliferated, and of late tour buses operating out of New York City bring weekend day-trippers to Cairn to enjoy street fairs, antiquing, or simply the bucolic atmosphere, and perhaps catch a glimpse of the occasional rock or movie stars who eat, shop, or stroll on the narrow streets of the small business district. For longer than a year I'd been meaning to spend a weekend checking out Cairn with some lady friend, or maybe my brother, but simply had never gotten around to it. Now I was in Cairn, but definitely not under circumstances I would have chosen.

Four days before, a troubled friend of mine died in this area. Certain specifics in the news reports of his death, most of which focused primarily on his notoriety and disgrace of the past year, did not square with the Michael Burana I had known. I was in Cairn to supply information and ask a few questions, not necessarily in that order.

It was a Friday evening in early August, and it had been oppressively hot for more than two weeks. Since March, Garth and I had been working on a particularly Byzantine case of industrial espionage, commuting at least once a week to Silicon Valley, and using our weekends to try to deal with Frederickson and Frederickson's mounting mass of paperwork, mostly detailed reports that had to be filed with our client. We were still at it, and I had no time for an outing, but I'd figured that the business I had to take care of in Cairn should take no more than one or two hours, a morning at most, and I'd planned to drive up early Saturday. But when the air conditioner in my apartment in our brownstone on West Fifty-sixth Street broke down in late afternoon, I'd decided to immediately head for cooler climes, namely someplace with air-conditioning in or near Cairn. I'd left a message for Garth, who was out meeting with our client's battalion of attorneys as they prepared for the impending court trial, had hopped into my modified Volkswagen Rabbit, Beloved Too, and headed for the George Washington Bridge. Assuming that all the bed-and-board places in town would be full, I'd checked into a motel on Route 9W, which forms the western boundary of Cairn. I'd immediately turned the air conditioner on full blast, showered and changed into fresh clothes, then gone out to get something to eat and poke around town.

I'd enjoyed a fine, inexpensive meal in an exquisite Thai restaurant housed in a converted diner next to an old-fashioned ice cream parlor that really is old, then gone out and started down Cairn's Main Street toward the river. I'd passed through the business district without attracting more than a moderate number of stares from people standing outside the various rock and jazz bars, then angled off onto a side street to investigate what appeared to be some fine old houses that probably date back to the turn of the century. I'd gone about a block and a half when I saw something across the street that caught my attention and brought me to a stop. A modest frame house that, according to the bronze sign planted in the front yard, had been the childhood home of one of America's finest artists had been converted into an art gallery, and the red, white, and blue banner hanging across the front read *Art of Vietnam Veterans*. According to another sign on the lawn, this was the first day of the exhibition, and it looked to me like the doors had just opened. People were starting to go in, the majority of them pointedly ignoring the three young men who stood at the edge of the sidewalk in front of the gallery trying to pass out literature. The men, all of whom looked to be in their late twenties or early thirties, had longish hair and wore robin's-egg-blue T-shirts with the words *COMMUNITY OF CONCILIATION: GIVE PEACE A CHANCE* emblazoned in crimson across the front and back. Since the organization that called itself the Community of Conciliation was one of the reasons I was in Cairn, the presence of the three men on the sidewalk in front of the gallery had more than served to pique my curiosity.

I'd crossed the street, debating whether or not to try to engage the men in conversation. I'd taken a mimeographed flier from one of the men, then stepped back off the sidewalk to read it. The sheet, single-spaced, outlined the basic goals of the Community of Conciliation, a pacifist and environmental organization, and listed its activities, both worldwide and local. One of the local activities was crossed out, thus making it impossible for a reader's attention not to be drawn to it; a thin line had been drawn through the item, but the text beneath the ink was clearly visible. The deleted item, almost certainly meant to be noticed, read: "Wednesday night fellowship and counseling sessions with Vietnam Veterans of America."

It appeared that the Community of Conciliation was attempting to send a message to the people entering the exhibit, or the veterans themselves, but it hadn't seemed the proper time or place for me to try to pinpoint just what that message was. I'd folded the flier, put it in the back pocket of my jeans, and gone into the house—to almost immediately be confronted, surprised, and pleased by *The Language of Cannibals*.

I went looking for Jack Trex, to tell him how much I liked his painting. He wasn't hard to find. In the main viewing area, in what had been the house's living room, five men wearing flag-emblazoned name tags were standing in a tight circle near a fireplace filled with freshly cut flowers. The tallest of them was about Garth's size, six feet three or four, and solid. The man, dressed in khaki slacks, plaid shirt, and running shoes, seemed to be doing more listening than talking. When he stepped back to reach for his drink on a small table behind him he swung his left leg stiffly, moving in the slightly listing manner of someone who has either suffered a severe leg injury or is wearing an artificial limb. I walked closer, and a glimpse at the man's name tag confirmed that he was Jack Trex.

Standing near Trex's left elbow, just outside the circle, I waited patiently for someone to take polite notice of me. When nobody did I cleared my throat, twice. The second throat-clearing did the trick; the men stopped talking, loosened their circle slightly, and began looking around to see who was making all the guttural noises. I found myself looking up into five faces that reflected not so much hostility as irritation. Although the occasion was a celebration of their art and craft work, and thus they might be expected to act as unofficial hosts to the public, it was clear that they were not interested in talking to "civilians."

Jack Trex had thinning black hair that was graying at the temples, and a full mustache that was all gray. His pale green eyes shone with an intelligence and sensitivity that belied the rather vacant, remote expression on his face. Two of the other veterans wore camouflage vests over gray T-shirts; one of the men had hostile, mud-brown eyes, and wore his long, yellow hair in a ponytail held in place by a leather thong. The men in the camouflage vests were staring at me as if they'd never seen a dwarf before. The man directly to my left, a Hispanic, wore a heavy flannel shirt despite the heat. Directly across the circle was a spindly, emaciated-looking veteran who wore a blue polyester suit that was baggy on him and which only served to highlight the network of red, alcohol-ruptured veins in his nose and cheeks. Although they'd been carrying on an animated conversation before I came over, all the men were now silent, their expressions wooden as they stared at me.

"Excuse me," I said, addressing all of them, "I didn't mean to interrupt."

The emaciated man with the blue polyester suit and broken veins giggled nervously, an abrupt and grating sound. "I ain't seen anyone as small as this guy since I left 'Nam," he said in a high-pitched voice and giggled again. "Who let the VC in here?"

Under other circumstances his remark might have called for a razor-sharp rejoinder from my vast repertory of counter-putdowns, but I decided from the look of him that he already had enough problems; there was pain in his nervous giggle, the soul-ache of a man who must struggle at all times to try to speak and behave normally or risk falling into the scream I suspected was always lurking at the back of his throat, like the tickle of a cough. Certainly, a disproportionate number of our Vietnam veterans seemed to have more than their share of emotional and physical problems, and I hadn't come over to trade barbs with one of the nation's walking wounded.

Turning to Trex, I said evenly, "I just wanted to tell you that I admire your painting."

The big man's features softened somewhat, and he was obviously pleased. He nodded slightly and opened his mouth to speak, but he was interrupted by the braying laughter of the man with the hostile, mud-brown eyes and pony tail.

"Jesus, Jack," the man with the ponytail said, "you finally found somebody who likes the smell of all that shit in your head. That painting of yours is the creepiest fucking thing I've ever seen. It doesn't make any fucking sense."

Trex glanced sharply at the man with the ponytail, and then at the man in the polyester suit. They both abruptly fell silent, and the ponytailed man looked down at the floor.

"Thanks," Trex said simply as he glanced back down at me, "I appreciate the kind words."

I didn't much care for this crew; there was too much alienation, too much insularity, too much thinly veiled hostility radiating from the men like body odor. But I also knew that such feelings were by no means unique to this small group. I tried to make some small talk, in a manner of speaking, and my conversational gambits were met with a modicum of polite, mumbled answers. The tension in the air remained. I felt like the cop who had accidentally wandered into the local gambling den; everyone was covering his hands and chips and waiting for me to go away.

After complimenting Jack Trex once again on his painting, I went away.

I fortified myself with a glass of white wine and some Jarlsberg cheese from a buffet that had been set up, then wandered through the rest of the rooms on the ground floor, examining the rest of the display of crafts and artwork. I saw nothing else that interested me. Jack Trex, with his primitive technique and sketchy command of material, was in no danger of becoming a professional artist, but there was real passion radiating from his canvas, feeling that belied the wooden, remote manner he displayed when I had tried to talk to him. I saw no comparable display of emotion in any of the other paintings, wood carvings, macramé, and pottery that constituted the rest of the show; it all seemed to me rather *institutional*, like baskets woven by mental patients during art therapy. There were lots of land- and seascapes, but they all lacked depth and feeling, like paintings of paintings or works executed by artists whose minds were on other things—which, I thought, was quite likely the case with some of them. Post-traumatic stress syndrome, it was called. There was no group that suffered more stress-related emotional and physical problems than America's Vietnam veterans, but with the obvious exception of Jack Trex's painting, none of that inner conflict was reflected in the work I viewed.

A close friend of mine to whom I owed my life, a very mysterious and multigifted man by the name of Veil Kendry, was not only a Vietnam veteran but a world-class artist whose works now hung in private collections and museums all over the world. From Veil I had learned not only a great deal about the catastrophically rending effect the Vietnam War had had upon the men who fought there but also about the pain and potential in the human heart in general; from Veil I had learned of, and witnessed, the power of art to transcend—and, finally, to heal— that pain, sublimating rage, violence, and vague hurt. But the artist first had to be willing to communicate, to try to describe the shapes and colors of the maelstrom within. Again with the sole exception of Jack Trex, I saw no one in this place making such an effort—not judging by the flat, emotionless quality of the work I examined.

I decided that there was a great deal of emotional repression in the Cairn chapter of Vietnam Veterans of America. It depressed me.

Before leaving I decided to view *The Language of Cannibals* once more. I left the main viewing area, turned down the corridor where Trex's painting was hanging in its out-of-the-way, dimly lighted setting. I stopped a quarter of the way down the corridor and studied the man who was studying the painting. He was about five feet nine or ten, with the compact frame and erect bearing of a former athlete who was fastidious about remaining in good shape. He had a full head of chestnut-brown hair, razor-cut in a short, conservative style. He was wearing a finely tailored, brown seersucker suit, light blue shirt and brown tie, pale brown loafers with tassels. Seen in profile, he had small ears, high, pronounced cheekbones, a strong mouth and chin. I felt I'd seen him somewhere before and that I should know who he was.

The solid man in the seersucker suit seemed totally absorbed in the painting, unaware that I was studying him. I watched as he leaned forward, peering closely at individual sections, apparently trying, as I had done, to find some meaning in the strings and clots of the letters themselves. After a few moments he backed away a step, leaned to one side and then the other in order to view the painting from different angles.

He wasn't a movie or rock star; I was certain of that. And he wasn't a celebrity in the usual sense.

He was . . . the confidant of, an aide to, a celebrity.

Ah.

The man's name was Jay Acton, and I had seen him—very briefly, in an unguarded moment when he was unaware that he was being photographed—in a PBS documentary on extreme right-wing influences in America.

Jay Acton was an aide to—and, the documentary had strongly hinted, the intellect and strategist behind—a curious fellow by the name of Elysius Culhane, the self-styled "last of the conservative purists." Culhane's words in his syndicated newspaper column and over the air on the political television talk shows he regularly hosted or appeared on were sometimes insightful, but always abrasive, and were raptly absorbed by millions of Americans.

To me, the man was a baying full-mooner. I considered Elysius Culhane a not-so-subtle Nazi sympathizer, a shameless hypocrite, a zealous ideologue, and an aggressive intellectual thug. He was a master of language, despite a slight speech impediment that caused him to occasionally slur two or three words together, but this man's language was not a descriptive or analytic tool for carving truth. It was just one more weapon to be used against what Culhane perceived as America's enemies—"godless communism" in general and all Russians in particular, *glasnost* and *perestroika* and the crumbling of the Evil Empire or no, liberals, moderates, humanists, women who had abortions and doctors who performed them, the Supreme Court, unmarried people who did not practice chastity, homosexuals, and any nation, institution, or individual not reflecting or espousing "Christian values," as he defined them.

In his autobiography, *If You're Not Right You're Wrong,* rumored to have been ghostwritten by Jay Acton, Culhane described his upbringing as the "runt" in the rough-and-tumble world of a Roman Catholic, working-class family with eleven children headed by a hard-drinking father and a manic-depressive mother who spent more time in mental hospitals than her home. I'd thought his father sounded more than a bit abusive, single-handedly ruling his brood of children with fists and a leather strap, but Culhane had written glowingly of a childhood dominated by a father who "taught me what real values are, and wasn't afraid to lay on the leather when you got it wrong." He had been educated in Roman Catholic schools run by priests, nuns, and brothers who "brooked no nonsense when it came to the meaning of the blood of Christ and America's hallowed place in God's plan for the world." Near the end of the book, after coming perilously close, within a verb or two, to calling for a coordinated, preemptive nuclear attack on Russia, China, and the "Arab world," he lamented the fact that all American children had not had the benefit of his upbringing. Elysius Culhane was always looking to lay on the fists and leather, at home and abroad.

Culhane had cut his political teeth as a fund-raiser in the political twilight world of Lyndon Larouche, a fact he denied but which had been confirmed by a number of reporters, then left when Larouche's ship began to sink under the combined weight of too many preposterous conspiracy theories, charges of widespread mail and credit card fraud, and increasingly frequent visits from the IRS.

He landed on his feet, running, when, through powerful connections he'd made while working for Larouche, he was taken on board by successive conservative administrations that found him, at least for a time, useful as a bulwark against right-wing critics. Then Kevin Shannon was elected president—an event in which Garth and I played no small part, albeit by default, and through no choice of our own—and Culhane was out.

Out, maybe, but by no means down. Quite the contrary.

Within a short time after Shannon's inauguration, Culhane was signed for a syndicated column, and began popping up all over the place on various television news and talk shows as a "spokesman for the right." He certainly caught on in this post-Vietnam world among a segment of the population living in an America that no longer quite fit their notion of what America had once been, and should be. Culhane's was an "us against them" view of the planet—and by "us" he by no means meant all Americans, but only those who shared his views; those who perceived things differently were "dupes of the Russians" at best, and at worst traitors.

It was a song-and-dance revue that played very nicely in Peoria, and a good many other places as well. While I might consider Elysius Culhane a monumental pain in the ass, a national embarrassment, and a transparent demagogue dispensing apocalyptic visions that bore no relationship whatever with reality, a very large mass of people considered him little less than a potential savior of America.

According to the PBS documentary, stating an opinion reflected in a number of articles I'd read since then, the *éminence grise* behind Elysius Culhane's relatively rapid rise to his present position of celebrity, power, and wealth was none other than the mysterious, rarely seen Jay Acton. Acton was the strategist who'd found the right formula to successfully mix hot air, flaming oratory, flammatory ideas, and uncanny skill at obfuscation into a potent brew that fueled an increasingly powerful political infernal medicine of divisiveness and hatred.

I wondered what Jay Acton was doing in Cairn, at this art exhibition.

"Dr. Robert Frederickson, I presume?"

Ah, again. Jay Acton was in Cairn, at this art exhibition, because his boss was here.

I turned around to face Elysius Culhane, who was standing directly behind me. I was used to seeing him in close-up on a television screen, perspiration filming his high forehead and upper lip as he leaned forward to launch into one of his harangues about "cleaning up the soul of America." On television he always loomed large, and I was surprised to find that he was no more than five feet six or seven, stocky. He was wearing an expensive gray silk suit with a cream-colored shirt, patterned silk tie, and black alligator shoes. His graying black hair was combed straight back. He had piercing black eyes, a nose that looked as if it had been broken at least once and not properly set. There was a comma of scar tissue at the corner of his right eye. His deep tan nicely highlighted the unnatural white of his capped teeth. I thought he looked like a Hollywood version of a mobster, but then I was prejudiced.

"Elysius Culhane," I replied. When I shook the hand he extended I noted a slight tremor.

"I'm flattered that you recognize me," he said with a disingenuous smile that indicated he certainly wasn't surprised I'd recognized him.

"Do I detect a note of false modesty? You're the celebrity here, Mr. Culhane, not me."

"From what I've heard about you, I wouldn't think that you'd be one of my viewers."

"I don't know what you've heard about me," I said with a little bit of my own disingenuous smile, "but the fact of the matter is that you're pretty hard to avoid these days if you watch any news shows at all."

He smiled thinly and nodded, obviously pleased with my observation. "Well, you and your brother aren't exactly just faces in the crowd, are you? It seems to me that I've been reading and hearing about the exploits of Mongo the Magnificent, ex-circus headliner turned criminology professor and private investigator, for years. You're quite a colorful character, and I'm pleased to meet you."

"Likewise," I said, trying as best I could to mask my lack of enthusiasm.

"You're in partnership now with your brother, aren't you?"

"You're very well informed, Mr. Culhane."

"It's my business to be informed, Dr. Frederickson, especially as it concerns the waxing and waning of political fortunes in Washington."

"You must have the wrong dwarf, Mr. Culhane. Frederickson and Frederickson has nothing to do with politics or power in Washington."

Culhane narrowed his eyelids and pursed his lips. "Now I

think it's you who's displaying false modesty. It's well known in the circles I travel in that you and your brother are personal friends of the president, as well as of that aging, cagey old fellow who's director of the Defense Intelligence Agency."

Elysius Culhane's tendency to slur words together was becoming gradually more pronounced, and he seemed slightly nervous. It occurred to me that he was digging for something.

"You'd better get some new sources, Culhane. Kevin Shannon would probably be highly amused to hear me described as a friend of his. He knows how I feel about politics and politicians."

"Oh? How do you feel about politics and politicians?"

"Anybody who expresses a desire to run for any office should automatically be disqualified."

"An interesting notion."

"Not original. Power doesn't necessarily corrupt, but power always holds a fascination for people who are easily corrupted."

Culhane's highly polished manner was growing a coat of tarnish; his smile had wrinkled into something approaching a sneer, and something that looked very much like contempt was glowing like banked coals in his black eyes. "Come now, Frederickson. Would you deny that Frederickson and Frederickson has grown enormously wealthy and powerful because of business that has been steered your way by this administration?"

"If it has, I don't know about it. I assume that Mr. Shannon and his associates have better things to do than steer business our way. Sometimes they even make decisions I agree with."

"Surely you're aware that yours is the investigative agency of choice for those corporations and individuals who want to stay in the good graces of this administration."

"I'd like to think that Frederickson and Frederickson is the investigative agency of choice for corporations and individuals who want topflight investigatory work done."

His sneer was becoming even more pronounced. "I've offended you."

Ordinarily I would have considered it time for a tart exit line, but I continued to experience the feeling that Culhane was after more from me than casual conversation. I couldn't imagine what, but my curiosity was sufficiently strong to keep me toe-to-toe with him for a while longer. I glanced over my shoulder, found that Jay Acton was gone. "Not at all," I said, returning my gaze to the other man. "You were suffering from a misconception, which I hope I've corrected. I've observed that not many people ever get a chance to get a word in edgewise with you, much less enjoy the opportunity to try to straighten you out on some of your quaint notions."

He didn't much like that, and he flushed slightly. "I've even heard it said that you and your brother, with certain knowledge in your possession, could perhaps have prevented the election of this accursed administration; I have to assume that the same information could bring down this administration. It wouldn't be hard for a neutral observer like myself to conclude that more than natural market forces have been at work in your firm's huge and relatively recent success. There may be powerful people who don't want to see you or your brother . . . disgruntled."

I was going to have to try to ignore the gross insult, because the first part of his statement happened to be true, and Elysius Culhane was the last person in the world I wanted to know. The knowledge he'd referred to could not only topple an administration but send a lot of people, including Garth and me, to prison. The realization that Elysius Culhane, with his complex web of confidants, contacts, and rumor-mongers, was sniffing the shreds of flesh left on these particular political skeletons chilled me.

I smiled, said, "You've got to be kidding me."

"Is it true?" he asked in a flat tone. A bead of perspiration had appeared on his upper lip, just as if he were on television, and he quickly wiped it away.

I smiled even harder, baring my teeth. "If it was, would I tell you?"

"There might come a time when your sense of patriotism and duty to your country will—"

"What are you doing in Cairn, Culhane?"

The interruption seemed to throw him off balance. He stared at me for a few moments, obviously debating whether or not to pursue his examination of my sense of patriotism and duty to country, apparently thought better of it. "I live here," he said with a shrug. "I moved from Washington to Cairn just about a year ago."

"Oh. Nice town."

"And you? Would you, uh . . . be here on business? I can't imagine what there would be in Cairn that would require or test the keen investigative skills of the famed Mongo Frederickson."

"You're too kind. Actually I'm just visiting; I happened to be passing by here, saw there was an art show, and decided to check it out."

"See anything you like?"

"As a matter of fact, yes," I replied, turning around in the otherwise empty corridor and pointing toward Jack Trex's dimly lighted painting. "I was rather taken with that work over there."

Culhane grimaced, as if something he'd had for lunch or dinner had just repeated on him. "Really? I don't like it at all. It doesn't make any sense, and it's depressing. In fact, I recommended that it not be included in the exhibit, but since the artist is the commander of this particular chapter of Vietnam Veterans of America, I was overruled."

"*You* recommended that it not be included? What are you, the local censor?"

"No," he replied in what I may only have imagined was a wistful tone, perhaps missing my sarcasm. "I underwrite a good many activities of the Vietnam veterans; as a matter of fact, this exhibit was my idea, and I'm sponsoring it. That painting has no place in a show like this. It does nothing to improve the image of the Vietnam veterans; it gives people the wrong impression. I think it was Patrick Buchanan who wrote that the food you put in a man's mind is at least as important as the food you put in his stomach."

"By golly, that sounds almost Marxist. I think most people would rather have food in their bellies and be left alone."

"That painting is just garbage, and it's not good for people to eat garbage."

"You think image ranks high on the Vietnam veterans' list of problems?"

"Yes. I think their image ranks high on the nation's list of problems. They're perceived as a bunch of drug addicts, alcoholics, adulterers, and sissies who can't handle stress."

"I always thought they were perceived as a group of fighting men who have some special problems because they were unfortunate enough to have been caught up in a special kind of war we weren't really prepared to fight."

"They have problems because they fought in a war America *lost*, Frederickson," Culhane said with real emotion, his slur once again becoming pronounced. "America now has special problems because it fought a war and lost, a war that was lost because of fuzzy-headed thinking and cowardly actions by leaders like Kevin Shannon. The Vietnam veterans were betrayed; the country was betrayed. Many of these men don't really understand that to this day. When they do understand it, and when they, or men like them, can be unleashed to fight communists once again and win for a change, they'll feel better. The country will feel better. When people see a painting like Trex's, their image of the veterans is that they're a group of cowards who blame America for what happened to them. It's defeatist."

"An intriguing political and artistic analysis."

"You're patronizing me."

"What do you expect me to say, Culhane? You expect me to argue with you? I'm not interested in politics, and I'm even less interested in political discussions. Sometimes I suspect that strong political ideology, like religious fervor, has a genetic as well as a cultural basis. Maybe they're just two faces of the same psychological phenomenon."

"You don't believe in God? You don't believe in your country?"

"I believe in gravity, mathematics, and mystery, as a friend of mine once said. As far as my country is concerned, I'm constantly amazed that our institutions have enabled us, at least so far, to survive the band of fools we keep on elevating to positions of power, not to mention the dunces, liars, thieves, and hypocrites."

"You're naive."

"Hmm. Does that mean you don't agree with me?"

"What does that painting mean?"

"I wouldn't presume to try and second-guess the artist. You probably wouldn't see it the same way in any case."

"What does it mean to you, Frederickson?"

"It means Jack Trex probably wouldn't see it the same way as you either."

Elysius Culhane studied me for a few moments, looked down at the floor, then back at me. I had the impression that he was making an effort to calm himself. "I'm enjoying this conversation immensely, Frederickson," he said at last. "May I suggest that we continue it tomorrow? I have a rather nice home on the river. Why don't you join me tomorrow afternoon for cocktails?"

"I won't be here that long, Culhane, and I don't believe you're enjoying this conversation. What do you really want from me?"

Again Culhane flushed, and he averted his gaze. His smile had become a grimace. He took a deep breath, slowly let it out. "All right, that's blunt enough," he said. "What I'd like is to talk some more about your relationship with Kevin Shannon."

"You mean you want me to tell you what you think I know that could hurt the president and his administration."

"Some people say you and your brother know more about some of this country's vital secrets than the director of the CIA."

"You know, Culhane, I can never tell if you're putting me on. I read your columns and listen to you on television; *you're* the one who's the obvious recipient of leaks of classified information. Every time there's going to be a vote on the defense budget, you come up with some of the most wondrous information."

"You may not always feel as anti-American as you do now. You—"

"Who said I feel anti-American?"

"There may come a time when your opinions will change."

"Meaning that I'll see things your way?"

"If and when that time comes, you may want to make some moves that could help your country. If you'll share information about Shannon with me, I'll make it worth your while."

"You'd pay me?"

"Of course."

"I love it. Is betrayal high on that list of what you call 'Christian values'?"

"Supplying information that will hurt the enemies of this country isn't betrayal."

"Do you really believe that Kevin Shannon is an enemy of this country?"

"Unwittingly, perhaps, but his actions make him a dupe of the communists."

"Culhane, has it ever occurred to you that there are people in this country who believe that the American right wing has been, and continues to be, a greater threat to our personal liberties than the communists ever have been, or will be? You guys are always talking about getting government off the backs of the people, but what you really mean is that you want the government to get off the back of business. It doesn't bother you at all, in fact you like it, when the government goes snooping into our bedrooms and libraries. Total *social* control has always been a wet dream of the far right. I don't mind the government auditing my taxes, Culhane, but I sure as hell don't want it auditing my mind."

The color drained from Elysius Culhane's face. He shifted his weight slightly, like a prizefighter, raised a thick index finger, and stuck it in my face. "*You're* what's wrong with this country, you fucking dwarf communist! People like you are the reason this country is going down the toilet!"

I was studying the finger in front of my face, trying to decide just what I wanted to do with it, when there was a sudden loud screech of brakes from the street, then movement and shouts from the people in the other room. Culhane turned in the direction of the noise, and I decided it was better to leave his finger alone than risk a lawsuit for assault. I brushed past him in the narrow corridor, went into the main viewing area to see what all the excitement was about.

It looked as if the house had listed and thrown everyone to the front; people were crowded in the entranceway and at the windows, staring at something outside.

A woman shouted, "*Atta boy, Gregory! Way to clean up the sidewalk!*"

Being of diminutive stature occasionally has it advantages. I was able to slip, sidle, and squeeze through the clot of people in the entranceway and make my way out to the porch, where I maneuvered around more people until I was able to claim a spot at the railing.

The screech of tires I'd heard had, I assumed, come from the Jeep Wagoneer that was now resting half up over the curb with its nose on the sidewalk at about the spot where the three men from the Community of Conciliation had been passing out their fliers. One of the blue-shirted Community members was sitting on the ground, ashen-faced and stunned, his fliers scattered around him. The other two men were trying unsuccessfully to hold their ground against a heavyset man, presumably the driver of the wayward Jeep, who kept advancing on them, bumping first one Community member and then the other with his barrel chest as he snatched at the fliers in their hands. The big man wore camouflage fatigues and a khaki tank top. He wore his blond hair cut very short on the top and shaved on the sides. I decided he was too young, probably in his early twenties, to be a veteran of anything more serious than Grenada. Except for the black sneakers he wore, and the fact that MPs and commanding officers take a very dim view of servicemen driving up on sidewalks and bullying civilians, he looked as if he might have just stepped out of a Marine barracks or boot camp.

A woman from the Community of Conciliation had joined the group since I'd come in. She was now standing by herself on the other side of the sidewalk bisected by the nose of the Jeep, her back straight, head high, and chin thrust out as she held aloft a neatly lettered cardboard sign stapled to a wooden stick. Whatever message the three men had been trying to convey with their fliers, there was nothing subtle about the message on the woman's sign. It read: STOP THE DEATH SQUAD.

There was something vaguely familiar about the woman, and I moved a few steps to my left in an effort to get a better angle of her face. She was tall and slender in her jeans and blue T-shirt that outlined small but firm breasts. I put her in her mid-forties. She wore steel-rimmed glasses that glinted in the light from the streetlamps, which had just come on. The most striking feature about her was her long hair, a light blond that was almost white, dramatically streaked with gray and hanging almost to the small of her back. The hands that clutched the wooden stick seemed too large for the rest of her frame, with the nails unpolished and cut very short.

They were hands I'd seen before playing an acoustic guitar as well as or better than any of her equally famous contemporaries as she'd sung her protest songs in a dulcet, achingly beautiful soprano.

Shades of the 1960s: antiwar protests, sit-ins, civil rights marches, Pete Seeger, Harry Peal, Judy Collins, Dylan, Buffy Sainte-Marie, Baez. The middle-aged woman standing on the sidewalk, defiantly holding up her sign, was none other than Mary Tree, one time "Queen of Folk," and my brother Garth's all-time secret heartthrob for more than twenty-five years. Although Garth had always disagreed with her pacifism, and a good deal of her politics, he'd bought every one of her records as soon as they were released, and had attended all of her concerts throughout the sixties and seventies whenever she appeared in the New York area. Then the war ended, the "Me Generation" blossomed into adolescence and adulthood wearing hundred-dollar sneakers and pushing five-hundred-dollar baby carriages, and Mary Tree's popularity faded like Puff the Magic Dragon, along with most of the protest movements of which she had been such an integral part. Her concerts became rarer, in smaller and smaller arenas. The woman who had once been able to sell out Madison Square Garden ended in tiny coffeehouses similar to the ones in which she had begun her career. And then she disappeared from public view altogether, and no more records were released. Garth was heartbroken, and he finally got around to transferring all of her records to tape about one playing or two before the needle on his record player would have broken through the vinyl. We both wondered what had happened to her. Now I knew; she'd apparently been living in Cairn, working with the Community of Conciliation.

It appeared that Mary Tree was about to have her commitment to pacifism sorely tested.

The burly young man with the thick chest and potbelly had tired of bumping the two standing Community members around, had finally snatched their fliers out of their hands and shoved both of them to the ground, where they sat, hands to their faces as if to ward off blows. But their tormentor had lost interest in them and was stalking back across the lawn toward Mary Tree.

I glanced to my right, up the street toward the town's business district, expecting—hoping—to see an approaching police car. The street was empty.

To my left, Jack Trex had pushed his way out onto the porch and was about to go down the steps when Elysius Culhane caught up with him, grabbed his arm, and went up on his toes in order to whisper something in the veteran's ear. Trex angrily shook his head, and Culhane whispered some more. Trex appeared to hesitate, then abruptly pivoted on his undamaged right leg and pushed his way back into the house. Aside from the few people acting as an impromptu cheering section, it didn't look like anybody in the house or on the porch was inclined to do anything but watch.

The man in the camouflage fatigues and khaki tank top had reached Mary Tree and was crowding her. He stuck his flushed face close to hers and shouted obscenities. Mary Tree's response was to stand her ground and hold her sign even higher.

Suddenly the man stepped back three paces, did a little hop, then abruptly spun clockwise and leaped into the air. His right leg shot out, and he executed a near-perfect roundhouse high kick. The side of his foot caught the stick Mary Tree was holding at just the right point, with just the right velocity, snapping it cleanly an inch or two below the cardboard sign, which went flying through the air to land on the lawn about twenty feet in front of me.

The high aerial kick and clean breaking of the stick was an expert move, very difficult to do, and definitely not the kind of martial arts maneuver you expect to see executed by a heavy man with a gut. The young man had surprising speed and advanced expertise in either karate or tai kwan do. That made him a dangerous man—not only a loose cannon but a loaded one.

After her initial startled reaction, Mary Tree glared into the man's face, then turned and marched up the lawn. She threw aside the stick, then bent over to retrieve the sign. But the man was there a step ahead of her, and he'd planted his foot on the sign. When Mary Tree gripped the edge of the cardboard with both hands and tried to free it, the man shoved her shoulder with his stomach, pushing her to the ground and knocking her glasses askew. As she straightened her glasses and tried to get up, the man moved forward and planted his legs on either side of her body, forcing her down onto her back. Then, still straddling her, the man grabbed his crotch and began to grind his hips in her face, all the while continuing to scream obscenities. Mary Tree crabbed backward, trying to get out from between the man's legs, but he kept shuffling forward.

There was still no sign of the police and no indication that anyone else intended to do anything.

Ah, well; as it was, Garth was going to be very displeased with me for playing spectator for so long. I vaulted over the railing onto the lawn, strode forward, and picked up the picket stake Mary Tree had discarded.

"I think you've made your point, pal," I said to the man's back, and then goosed him hard with the jagged end of the stick.

He whooped and went about three feet straight up into the air, releasing his crotch and grabbing with both hands at his insulted anus. He landed and wheeled around to see whence had cometh his discomfort. I didn't like what I saw at all. The young man's eyes, one of which was slightly cast, were the color of milky green jade; I saw madness glittering there, along with murderous rage. His mouth was half open, revealing small, gapped teeth. He was alternately panting and growling like an animal.

He obviously hadn't enjoyed being goosed, and in a moment of absolute mental clarity, I understood that he intended, at the very least, to break things in me. This man with the milky green eyes and small teeth was definitely not a partner with whom I was going to spend a lot of time on the dance floor.

His right hand darted out and grabbed the end of the stick in my hands, and he yanked. I immediately released my grip so as not to be pulled to him, then ducked beneath a hard, straight side kick that would have bashed in my face and snapped my neck if it had landed. The man was definitely serious. The momentum of his kick carried him forward, and by the time he regained his balance, with his feet slightly apart, I was already behind him and launching my own aerial act. I sprang up and back, whipping my right foot up between his legs and burying the toe of my sneaker in his groin. I landed on my back on the grass, immediately kipped to my feet, and walked around to the front of the man to see what kind of damage I had done.

Not surprisingly, the young man's jade-colored eyes had gone wide with shock and pain. His face was almost the color of blood. His mouth opened in a wide O as he clutched his groin with intent, slowly sank to his knees, and doubled over until his forehead rested on the lawn. He was once again making loud whooping sounds as he struggled to suck air into his lungs.

I turned at the sound of brakes, saw not one but two white Cairn patrol cars, each with a single policeman, pull up on either side of the Jeep. The policeman got out, and one walked toward me while the other headed toward Mary Tree and the three other Community members, who had gathered together at the far end of the sidewalk.

When I turned back I found the man in the tank top on his hands and knees, crawling toward me and grabbing for my legs. I jumped back not a millisecond too soon, and his ham-size right hand grabbed empty air. He was obviously not greatly impressed by the presence of the two policemen, if he even knew they were there. With the two uniformed cops on the scene, I could have easily afforded to keep backing away, playing matador and bull, until one or both of them stopped him. But I simply didn't feel like it. With the memory of his foot flying through the air toward my head, I found I was feeling a tad resentful and out of sorts.

As the man on the ground continued to growl and crawl forward, swiping at my legs with one hand as he cupped his groin with the other, I studied his head with its shaved sides. It looked hard, and there was simply too much paperwork waiting for me on my desk to risk breaking my knuckles or hand. As the policeman came abreast of me, I stepped around him to the fallen man's side, squatted down, cocked my right arm and wrist, and then sprang upright, hitting him with the heel of my hand precisely at the juncture of neck and jaw. His head snapped back, and the rest of his body followed. He landed on his side, rolled over on his back, and lay there with his legs splayed and twitching. He was out.

I glanced up toward the porch, found myself gazing into a crowd of faces wearing thoroughly astonished expressions. The four veterans Jack Trex had been speaking with were there, at the foot of the steps, but Trex was nowhere in sight. I hadn't seen Jay Acton since he'd disappeared from the hallway where Trex's painting was displayed. Elysius Culhane was standing on the porch near the spot where I had been; his mouth was actually open, and he was slowly shaking his head. There was no sign of a friendly face.

I turned around to face the policeman, who had sad, almond-colored eyes and a droopy mustache to match. His name tag said McAlpin. He was looking back and forth between the unconscious man and me, disbelief clearly etched on his face.

McAlpin finally fixed his gaze on me. "Who the hell are you?" he asked, his tone more than a bit incredulous.

"My name's Robert Frederickson, Officer. I—"

"Wait over there," he said curtly, pointing to the patrol car parked to the left of the Jeep.

I dutifully strolled across the lawn to the patrol car, leaned against the hood, and cradled my right wrist, which I was afraid I'd sprained in my effort to avoid breaking my hand on the young man's head.

Elysius Culhane and the veteran with the yellow hair and ponytail had come down off the porch and were trying to help the conscious but obviously disoriented young man in fatigues and black sneakers to his feet. All the while, Culhane was talking rapidly to the patrolman named McAlpin, who was making notes on a pad. The man whose jaw had hurt my wrist finally made it to his feet and angrily shook off the hands that were supporting him. He swayed a bit, and his milky green eyes finally came into focus—on me. He lurched forward, but his way was immediately blocked by Culhane, the ponytailed veteran, and McAlpin, who reached for his nightstick. The heavyset man stood still, but he continued to glare at me, raw hatred in his eyes. I resisted the impulse to wave at him.

Twenty yards down the sidewalk, to my right, the second policeman was talking to Mary Tree and the three others from the Community of Conciliation. The folksinger and her companions looked distinctly more delighted and amused than upset. They kept glancing, nodding, and smiling in my direction, but when Mary Tree and one of the men tried to walk over to me they were stopped by the policeman. The woman laughed and blew me a kiss; thinking of how Garth would eat his heart out when I told him this story, I grinned and blew her one back.

The second policeman walked across the lawn to McAlpin, who was standing with the end of his nightstick pressed against the young man's chest while he listened to the fast-talking Culhane. The two policemen stepped away a few paces and conferred in whispers. Both men nodded, then returned to their respective groups.

The burly young man continued to glare at me, obviously

oblivious to whatever negotiations were being conducted on his behalf. He only had eyes for me.

Down the sidewalk, the second policeman was forcefully pointing the four members of the Community of Conciliation up the street, away from me. After some more waves and nods in my direction, they moved away. The policeman got in his car and drove off.

McAlpin seemed to be lecturing the young man in fatigues, occasionally tapping him on the shoulder with the nightstick for emphasis. When he finished, Culhane, the ponytailed veteran, and a few other people ushered the young man back up the steps and into the house—but not before he cast one last baleful glance over his shoulder in my direction.

McAlpin came back across the lawn to me, studied me for a few moments as he absently stroked his droopy mustache. He seemed vaguely surprised that I hadn't grown any taller during his brief absence.

"Nobody else wants to press charges, Frederickson."

"Really? What do you have to do in this town to be arrested?"

He wasn't offended. On the contrary, something that might have been amusement moved in his almond-colored eyes. "Those people picketing out here could have been charged with trespassing."

"They were standing on the sidewalk."

"I didn't hear any of them asking for you as his lawyer," McAlpin said, and shrugged. "Be that as it may, it was their decision not to press charges. They don't want to spend money for a lawyer. Besides, a lot of people around here would think those commie shitheads got what they deserved. And as far as they're concerned, the asshole got more than his comeuppance." He paused for a few moments and studied me some more, as if he was still waiting for me to grow larger. "You really put the wood to him, Frederickson. I'm sorry I wasn't here to see it from the beginning."

"Me too," I replied, rubbing my sore wrist. "Who is the asshole?"

"Nobody you ever want to mess with again. What about it?"

"What about what?"

"You satisfied with the arrangement? I need your consent,

since you were a party to the disagreement. Since you ended up the winner by a knockout, I figure you've got no charges to make. Right?"

"Right. It never even occurred to me."

"Okay," McAlpin said as he snapped his notebook shut, then stepped around me to open the door to his car.

"Officer?"

He opened the door, looked up. "Yeah?"

"Is your chief in?"

McAlpin hesitated, frowned slightly. "As a matter of fact, he is. But you said—"

"I know what I said. I was planning on stopping around to see him in the morning anyway, but I figure now's as good a time as any. Can you tell me where to find the station house?"

He thought about it, then held up his hand. "Wait a minute, Frederickson," he said, then got in the car, closed the door, and rolled up the window.

I watched him as he picked up the receiver of his car radio and signaled on it. There began a lengthy conversation, during which I could feel eyes watching me from inside the house. Almost five minutes later McAlpin finally replaced the receiver in its cradle, rolled down the window, and motioned to me. In addition to the continuing incredulity in his eyes and voice, there was now something new, and I thought it might be respect.

"The chief's heard of you, Frederickson," McAlpin said. "Get in. I'll drive you there."

I got in the front, and McAlpin pulled away from the curb. When I glanced back, I could see that Jay Acton had joined Elysius Culhane. The two expensively suited men were standing on the sidewalk, watching the departing patrol car. Jay Acton's rather handsome face was impassive, but Elysius Culhane looked positively dyspeptic, and perhaps worried.

CHAPTER TWO

The Cairn police station turned out to be a dispatching room, two-office and two-cell section of a town hall that was housed in a magnificent old stone building set down near the river a few blocks from the center of town. One of the offices was occupied by Cairn's chief of police, whose desk plaque identified him as Dan Mosely. Mosely, a dapper man who looked to be in his mid- to late forties, was dressed in a crisp, starched uniform that I suspected had been specially tailored for his wiry, six-foot frame. He had a thick head of curly steel-gray hair, and gray eyes to match. Ugly, puckered acne scars ringed his neck near the collar line, but the rest of his face was clear, with the kind of deep, even tan that comes from spending a lot of time on the water. His office was decorated with framed prints of old sailing ships. There was a case filled with sailing trophies and above it a photograph of a sleek, nineteen-foot Hoby catamaran with a power jib.

Mosely rose as I entered, extended a sinewy, bronzed hand, and flashed a grin that revealed even, white teeth. "Dr. Frederickson," he said in a deep, resonant voice. "It's a pleasure to meet you."

"Likewise, Chief," I said, shaking his hand and wincing when pain shot through my wrist.

"Sorry," Mosely said, quickly withdrawing his hand and grimacing in sympathy. "It looks like you hurt yourself."

"Just a slight sprain," I replied, sitting down in the chair next to his desk that he had motioned me into.

"Did you do that when you coldcocked Trex?"

"Trex?"

Mosely sank down into the chair behind his desk and nodded amiably. "Gregory Trex. McAlpin tells me you really rang his bell for him. That must have been some surprise for him, not to mention the people watching."

"Yeah, well, being a dwarf sometimes has its advantages; nasty people don't always take you seriously at first, and you make a small target when they finally do."

"I wasn't surprised," Mosely said evenly as he studied me with his steel-gray eyes. "Your reputation precedes you. Black belt in karate, right?"

"I take it this Gregory Trex is related to the Trex who heads the Vietnam Veterans?"

"Father and son. You couldn't meet two people who are more different. Jack seems to think it's his fault that Gregory is the way he is . . . but I don't want to get into town gossip. It's a sad story."

"I'll bet. Psychotics always make me sad, especially when they're pushing women around or trying to take off my head. It seems to me that you've got a town bully on your hands."

Mosely grimaced again, nodded slightly. "Gregory's got his problems, that's for sure. He's a pain in the ass, always full of piss and vinegar, and always looking for a fight. Town bully, yes, but when the town bully's father is a bona fide war hero, sometimes you have to tread lightly. Gregory's obsessed with the fact that he was too young for Vietnam. He thinks *he* could have been a war hero—and it doesn't help that his father has kind of soured on the whole war and Vietnam thing. Some people around here think Jack has lost his patriotism."

"It looked to me like he'd lost his leg."

"That too. But Gregory kind of feels cheated, like he's John

Wayne forced to act in a Shirley Temple movie, if you know what I mean."

"So why doesn't he enlist in the Marines or some other branch of the service? The Vietnam War may be over, but the last I heard, the armed forces were still in business."

Mosely's response was a thin smile and a slight shake of his head.

I asked, "More town gossip?"

He nodded.

"Let me guess," I continued. "They either wouldn't take him or they threw him out on a Section Eight. Mental problems."

"Column B. It's good that you know."

"Why? What difference does it make?

Mosely studied me for some time, then said: "I'm sure you've seen the movie where the sheriff says to some guy that trouble follows him wherever he goes."

"Ah, I think I've got it. You're the sheriff, and I'm the handsome, mysterious stranger who's just come to town."

"You're no stranger, Dr. Frederickson. And trouble *does* tend to follow you around, doesn't it? I'm trying to tell you that Gregory Trex is a very dangerous man, and he's not about to forget that you humiliated him in front of all his veteran buddies. The man's a PKA champion, and if you meet again, he may not be so easy to surprise. I don't want anybody hurt, but if I *did* try to warn you to get out of town, you'd be the one quoting old movies." He paused, leaned forward in his chair, and narrowed his eyelids. "I don't suppose you would consider going back to New York as soon as possible?"

"Thanks for the warning, Chief. Trex shouldn't be too hard to spot; I'll watch out for him."

He nodded, and grunted softly. He didn't seem too pleased with my answer. "How's Garth?"

"You know my brother?"

The man with the gray eyes and hair nodded again. "I don't know if he remembers me, but I remember him, all right. Good cop with a big rep—not only for doing his own work but for the way he handled himself when he'd get tangled up with all those cockamamie cases that used to come your way. We worked out of the same precinct; he was with homicide, and I was with safe and loft. I put in my twenty years in New York, applied for this job last year, and got it. I like it real well in Cairn. Pulling down a New York pension and being chief of police in a town like Cairn is what New York City police detectives dream of when they dream of heaven. But then, I guess Garth found his own heaven when he teamed up with you, didn't he? I hear you two guys are doing really well."

"Yeah. Garth has always considered me an angel."

"So, how is he?"

"He's fine."

Mosely frowned, leaned back in his chair, and glanced at the ceiling. "Didn't I hear something a couple of years back about him being the head of some kind of religious cult?"

"Garth is fine, Chief. I'll tell him you say hello."

Suddenly the intercom on Mosely's desk buzzed. Cairn's chief of police looked surprised. He waited until it buzzed a second time, then punched an orange button at its base. "What is it?"

A male voice, presumably the dispatcher's, came over a speakerphone on the side of the intercom. *"You've got a phone call, Chief."*

"Emergency?"

"Not exactly."

"Tell whoever it is to call back later. I'm in conference."

"It's Mr. Culhane, Chief."

Dan Mosely looked even more surprised, and then his gray eyes glinted with annoyance. "Tell him I'll get back to him," he said curtly, and punched a black button. He was just starting to turn back toward me when the intercom buzzed again. He punched the orange button. "I said—!"

"Mr. Culhane's pretty insistent, Chief. I just thought you should know."

Mosely's annoyance flashed to anger, and his face flushed, making the acne scars on his neck stand out like a necklace of flawed pearls. "I'll take it out there," he snapped and punched the black button again. Then he rose and strode stiffly from the room.

I waited, idly rubbing my sore wrist while I stared out the small window in his office at the river. There was a marina to the east, and a covey of sailboats gently bobbed in the wake of a passing powerboat. Under a full moon, the river shone like a great silver highway. Mosely was back in less than a minute. His anger had passed, and now he looked merely embarrassed. I felt a little sorry for him. It seemed there were a few shadowy, dank corners in the heaven he'd found, and Elysius Culhane lurked in one of them, obviously expecting the chief of police to be at his beck and call; in another corner lurked a murderous young thug the police were expected to ride herd on, while at the same time protecting him from the consequences of his actions.

"Like I said, Frederickson," Mosely said in a low voice as he sank back down into the leather swivel chair behind his desk, "your reputation precedes you. You make people nervous."

"Why should I make Elysius Culhane nervous?"

"Ah, you've met Mr. Culhane?"

"We exchanged a few unpleasantries at the art exhibit."

"Mmm. Culhane has sort of taken Gregory Trex under his wing, in a manner of speaking."

"That's a pretty big hawk wing, Chief."

"Yeah, well, Culhane seems to think that he can straighten the boy out by acting as the sort of strong father figure he thinks the boy needs."

"A father who's a war hero and who lost his leg in Vietnam isn't a strong enough figure?"

Mosely averted his gaze and once more seemed embarrassed. "Culhane saw you get in the squad car, and he thinks maybe you don't quite understand the situation here and what happened back at the gallery. I told him I was filling you in on some background—"

"Chief, I don't have the slightest interest any longer in what happened earlier or in town gossip. That's not what I'm here to talk about."

Now he returned his gaze to my face. He looked surprised and perhaps a little relieved. "Huh? But I thought . . ."

"I came to talk about a friend of mine who died here on Monday. Michael Burana."

Mosely again leaned back in his chair and again stared up at the ceiling as he ran the fingers of both hands through his thick, curly hair. He seemed to be trying to collect his thoughts. "The

FBI agent," he said at last. "The one who let the CIA defector slip away to the Russians."

"He didn't let anyone slip away to Russia. That escape took split-second timing, with help from someone who knew a whole lot about FBI surveillance procedures. Maybe Michael should have been on the scene, but he wasn't; even he had to sleep once in a while. He was the man in charge of the surveillance team, so he was the one who took the fall and all the bad publicity. But that's neither here nor there. He's dead now. Like I said, he was a close friend of mine."

"And you have questions about his death?"

"Uh-huh."

He took his gaze from the ceiling, leaned forward in his chair, folded his hands on top of his desk, and looked at me with a puzzled expression. "You read the news reports?"

"That's how I found out about it. Because of the defector business, his death made all the news reports. Lousy obituary for a fine man."

"I'm sorry about your friend's death, Frederickson, but the circumstances surrounding it certainly seemed straightforward enough. He drowned. They found the canoe he must have been using smashed up on the rocks over on the Westchester side. It looks like he went out Sunday night and never made it back. It happens in the riverfront towns; people go out on the Hudson in some light craft like a canoe or a kayak without realizing just how powerful and tricky that river is. The tide changes, or a wind whips up, and they can't get back; before you know it, they're gone. The river's three miles wide at this point, and the distance is deceptive; people have a lot of room to get into trouble out there. Considering your professional background and reputation, I'll be happy to show you the file on the case."

"I appreciate the courtesy, Chief, but that won't be necessary. I'm not here to look over your shoulder or question your work. I'm sure your inquest, or investigation, was thorough, considering the evidence and what you had to go on."

"Then what—?"

"I came here to offer you information I'm sure you didn't have when you conducted your investigation. It might raise some questions in your mind and cause you to reconsider your original finding."

"What information?"

"Michael wasn't exactly a boating enthusiast, Chief; he hated the water. He wouldn't have gone out on the Hudson or any other body of water on a battleship, much less paddling in a canoe."

Mosely thought about it, said, "That's interesting."

"Yeah. Interesting."

He thought about it some more as he absently tapped the fingers of his right hand on the top of the desk. "Sometimes people with phobias like that will purposely do something risky to force their fear out in the open in order to try to face it down," he said at last.

"Michael didn't have a phobia of water, Chief. He just hated it. As a matter of fact, he was a strong swimmer, and he'd done some ocean sailing at one point in his life. Fifteen years ago he was living on a houseboat in Island City with his wife and three small children. Some leftover garbage from the Symbionese Liberation Army, friends of people he'd helped put into prison, found out where he was living and decided to pay him a visit. They blew up his houseboat with a few pounds of *plastique*. Michael wasn't aboard at the time, but his wife and three children were. He got back just in time to watch the police and Coast Guard picking bloody chunks out of the water with fish nets."

"Oh, God," Mosely said softly.

"An experience like that tends to leave a mark on you, Chief. After that, he couldn't stand to be near any large body of water; I suppose he'd look at the surface and still see parts of his family there. So there's no way I see Michael happily paddling a canoe out on the Hudson."

Mosely continued to drum his fingers on the desktop. "I see your point, Frederickson."

"Uh-huh."

"You think he could have committed suicide, maybe chosen that way as a kind of symbolic means of rejoining his family?"

"No. I don't think he committed suicide."

Mosely fixed me with his steel-gray eyes. "You suspect some other explanation?"

"I'll let you handle the suspecting, Chief. The only reason I'm here is to pass on that bit of information about Michael loathing water. There's no way you could have known that when you found the canoe and Michael's body, but I thought you might like to know that now; not many people knew about it, but I did. If he *was* out on the water in a canoe, it wasn't for recreational purposes; he would have had to have a good reason. I'm absolutely certain there's more to Michael's death than just an accidental drowning."

Mosely took a notebook out of a drawer in his desk, made a few notes in it. "I appreciate the information, Frederickson."

"I thought you would. Have you heard from the FBI on this yet?"

He shook his head as he studied the notes he had made. "Not a word." He made another note, then looked up at me. "The Bureau may be conducting their own investigation; if they are, I'm not aware of it. But no matter what they're doing, Frederickson, I'm going to be doing some more checking into the matter."

"I'd hoped you would," I said, rising and extending my left hand. "Thanks for your time, Chief."

He stood, shook my hand, then smiled thinly. "And if I didn't check into it further, you would. Am I right?"

"Chief," I said, suppressing a sigh, "you have no idea how much of my own work I have waiting for me back home on my desk. I can't think of any reason why I'd want, or presume, to try to do your work for you."

"I'll be in touch, let you know what else I find out, if anything. Call it professional courtesy."

"Thanks, Chief." I took a business card out of my wallet and handed it to him. Then I walked back across the office and opened the door.

"Frederickson?"

I turned back toward Dan Mosely, who was tapping the eraser of his pencil on top of his notepad. "Yes, Chief?"

"A question. I don't doubt anything you've told me, and your sincere concern is obvious. But is it possible that you didn't know your friend as well as you think?"

"What are you getting at, Chief?"

"If Michael Burana hated water so much, why did he choose to vacation in a riverfront town, and why would he choose to room in a place that's practically on the water?"

I released my grip on the doorknob, took a step back into the room. "What gave you the idea that Michael was in Cairn on vacation?"

Mosely gave a broad shrug of his shoulders, as if the answer were obvious. "Why else would he be here?"

"Christ, Chief, he was here on assignment."

Mosely shook his head. "Assignment? You mean he came to Cairn on Bureau business?"

Suddenly I felt tense, slightly bewildered. I was no longer aware of the pain in my wrist. "You didn't know that?"

"No."

"It's standard procedure for an FBI agent to establish a liaison with local law enforcement officials as soon as he or she begins an assignment."

"That I'm fully aware of, Frederickson," Mosely replied evenly. "The first time I ever laid eyes on Michael Burana was when we responded to a call early Monday morning and fished his body out from between two pilings down by the Tappan Zee Bridge. We made him as FBI from the shield in his wallet. What was his assignment?"

My mouth had gone dry, and I licked my lips and swallowed. It didn't help. "I'm not supposed to know."

"But you do."

"He was supposed to install wiretaps and conduct a mail surveillance. The whole business was probably illegal, but Michael's boss was never much concerned with minor technicalities like that."

"Who was he supposed to be conducting this surveillance on?"

"The Community of Conciliation."

Mosely abruptly dropped his pencil on top of the pad, leaned forward on his desk, and shook his head. Just before he turned his face away, I saw him smile.

"What's so funny?" I asked tersely.

When he looked at me, his smile was almost—but not quite—gone. "Sorry, Frederickson," he said evenly. "I don't mean to seem insensitive, but your friend must have been one hell of an agent and had one sweet-talking silver tongue. Either that, or he told you some things that may not have been exactly true. The Community of Conciliation owns a donated mansion on the north side of town, right on the river. That's where Michael Burana was staying, and that's where the canoe the Westchester police found came from. Some surveillance. Our investigation showed that the first thing Michael Burana did when he arrived in town was go to that mansion. And they let him in. That's where he stayed from his very first night in town."

The muscles in my stomach and between my shoulder blades had begun to flutter. "What did the people at the Community have to say about all this?"

"Goddamn little. They described him as an old friend."

"That's all?"

"They verified what I just told you, but they didn't have much else to say. The Cairn Police Department and the Community of Conciliation don't exactly form a mutual admiration society. It was a woman there who described him as an old friend."

"What woman, Chief?"

"Mary Tree."

•   •   •

No one had ever said civic duty and loyalty to friends were always easy, I thought as I walked back up the steeply inclined streets of Cairn toward my motel on 9W. I'd come to the river hamlet to unload some information that I'd hoped might raise a question or two in the minds of the local authorities who'd originally investigated Michael Burana's death in a supposed boating accident. The chief of police had fielded my modest offering with a gracious thank-you and tip of the hat, and then proceeded to unload on me in return a whole barrelful of questions for me to ponder. Instead of easing, my dilemma had grown more complicated.

I had no reason to think that Dan Mosely was lying, since most of what he'd told me would be relatively easy to check out. However, Michael Burana's behavior from the day he arrived in Cairn to the time of his death, as described by Mosely, didn't begin to match the profile of the topflight FBI agent who had sat in my living room until three in the morning getting drunk while he poured out his disappointment, rage, and sense of shame at the same time as he poured down my Irish whiskey.

It had been two weeks before, one week before he was scheduled to set up shop in Cairn in order to spy on the Community of Conciliation. His superior, Edward J. Hendricks, was deliberately trying to humiliate him, he'd said, and there wasn't a damn thing he could do about it. I'd reluctantly agreed with him on both points. He hadn't mentioned anything about visiting an old friend, and he certainly hadn't seemed in any mood to set aside a soul-deep aversion to water in order to go paddling in a canoe on the Hudson River.

The RestEasy Motel was a horseshoe-shaped affair, three building units trisected by two narrow promenades lined with vending machines. Only two of the units were being used, and the area around the third unit, including its adjacent promenade, was only dimly lighted. I had a room on the second floor of the middle unit, with the entrance at the rear, off the parking lot. To get to it I cut across the lawn and headed up the second, dim promenade. With my mind thrumming along at a fairly rapid pace, distracted by the questions raised by Dan Mosely, I had virtually dismissed Gregory Trex from my mind—failing, of course, to take into account the fact that he might feel he had further business to discuss with me, and that it wouldn't take a lot of phone calls by a genius to find out where a certain dwarf was staying.

Trex caught me completely by surprise, stepping out behind me from the shadow within a shadow between an ice maker and a soda machine near the end of the promenade, and delivering a whack to my left arm, just above the elbow, with something that felt like an iron rod. The blow knocked me sideways, off my feet. There was an explosion of white-hot pain, and the whole arm went numb virtually before I'd hit the ground and rolled on my right side. Immediately I rolled again, this time forward, over the curb and into the parking lot. I came up in a crouch, right arm and foot forward to protect my damaged left arm, which was hanging limp at my side.

Gregory Trex, still dressed in his tank top, camouflage fatigues, and black sneakers, stepped down off the curb, stopped about five yards away. His too-bright jade-green eyes, the polished mahogany of the rock-hard *nunchaku* sticks he carried, and the foot-long steel chain connecting the sticks all gleamed in the light from a floodlamp set on the balcony of the second unit, just above my head. I backed up a step, tentatively shrugged my left shoulder; welcome pain stabbed through it. I could tell the arm wasn't broken—but the triceps had received a severe banging, and it was going to be some time before the arm would condescend to do anything for me.

Trex's puffy lips curled back, revealing his small, gapped teeth. He took another step forward, whirling his *nunchaku* sticks over his head and at his sides, apparently to demonstrate his expertise, and not incidentally to put a good scare into me.

What I had in me was a good mad, despite the fact that I had no one but myself to blame for Trex getting the drop on me. I had a mountain of paperwork to attend to, and, thanks to Gregory Trex, it was beginning to look like I was going to have to do it holding the pencil in my mouth. I glanced up and around. While there was no one in the darkened unit to my left, there were people in my unit and the one beyond that. Trex apparently wasn't concerned about being seen, since he didn't believe the police would do a damn thing. It occurred to me that in some dark corridor of his decidedly primitive mind he might prefer that there be witnesses, so that word would get around town that I'd gotten my comeuppance. He might even be satisfied now and walk away if somebody else arrived on the scene; he'd already accomplished what he'd come to do. I suspected that I might be able to rouse some attention if I started shouting, but I really wasn't interested in attention or help. I was interested in putting a good hurt on Gregory Trex, who was proving to be a real pain in the ass; he'd seriously inconvenienced me and managed to make me very angry.

How I was going to accomplish this particular feat of laying some serious hurt on the other man wasn't clear to me at the moment, but I was damn well determined to find a way to do it.

"How does that feel, dwarf?" Trex said in a piping voice that sounded surprisingly high-pitched for a man of his bulk.

"Actually, Gregory, it's kind of hard to tell," I replied, keeping my gaze fixed on the *nunchaku* sticks he held. "Right now, my arm doesn't have much feeling in it, but I suspect it's going to smart like hell. What kind of a chickenshit war hero are you, anyway, ambushing me from behind? Did you ever see Chuck Norris pick on someone smaller than he was?"

His expression changed slightly, and something that actually looked like hurt passed over his thick features; I'd bruised his feelings by bringing up the subject of our disproportionate sizes. It occurred to me then that Gregory Trex, in addition to being a murderous young thug, might be more than moderately retarded.

"You made a fool out of me," he said in a whiny tone. "You hit me from behind, so I hit you from behind."

"I goosed you, Gregory, for Christ's sake. You tried to take off my head back there, and you could've broken my arm here."

"I could have killed you," he said in the same whiny tone. "You suckered me. I can't let anybody get away with that."

I tested my left arm again, found that feeling was continuing to return. It hurt like hell, but I suspected I would at least be able to wag it in Trex's face in a pinch. I also suspected that Gregory Trex, who hadn't even been able to make it in the army, was totally ineffectual at virtually everything in life except beating up people, and I found I was actually beginning to feel a little sorry for the dunce standing in front of me. I overcame it.

"Now, now, Gregory. Don't you know that *nunchaku* sticks are illegal?"

"Nothing's going to happen to me, dwarf. People saw what you did to me; I got a right to pay you back. Maybe I'll get chewed out real good, but that's all. People will figure you got what you deserve, the same as they figure I was giving them fucking communists outside the art gallery what they deserve. Somebody's gotta stand up for this country and show the communists we're not all weirdos and fags."

"Still, Gregory, *nunchaku* sticks are provocative. You know what I mean? A man could get into trouble just by carrying them around."

"I told you, dwarf: the cops won't do anything but chew me out."

"Ooh, dear boy, I think you miss my point."

Now it was Trex who was looking around, apparently disappointed that nobody had come around to witness my left arm dangling at my side, his handiwork. I decided that if I was going to make a move, it had better be quick, before anybody arrived on the scene and gave Trex an excuse to walk away, or before he decided it was safe to take another whack at me. So I started to run, just to see what he would do.

Naturally he ran after me.

I'd already seen that Trex was quick, which is not the same as fast. He was not exactly fleet of foot, and, despite the fact that I was clutching my left arm to keep it from flopping and being further aggravated, I found that I had to slow down as I approached the end of the darkened third unit so that I wouldn't get too far ahead of him. I glanced back to make certain he wasn't becoming discouraged in his chase, then rounded the corner and sprinted on the grass in the gloom surrounding the third unit. I ran around the front, glancing back once more to assure myself that Gregory Trex was chugging along, then rounded the third corner and headed up the promenade. I sprinted to the end before Trex could catch sight of me again, ducked into the same space between the ice maker and soda machine where Trex had waited to ambush me.

The poor dunce never slowed as he came lumbering up the promenade. I stuck my foot out as he passed; he went flying through the air and landed flat on his face and stomach on the concrete, narrowly avoiding smashing his skull against a steel support post near the curb. His *nunchaku* sticks flew out of his grasp and skittered over the concrete into the parking lot, ending up next to a large green dumpster.

With Trex dazed and virtually helpless for the moment, I had a number of options open to me. The quickest and easiest thing to do, of course, would be to kill him, but that seemed a bit extreme. Mulling over other measures proved to be time-consuming, and before I knew it he had managed to get up on his hands and knees. Not wanting to delay things further, I walked around to his right side and smashed my knee into his ear. Down he went again, this time with me on his back. There was no hair to grab, so I raised his head with my left hand on his forehead, planted my right hand on the back of his head, and slammed his face into the sidewalk. That worked quite nicely. He twitched a couple of times, then lay still.

A car pulled into the parking lot of the first unit. Fearing that any sudden move would attract attention, I kept my perch on top of Gregory Trex, waited and watched as a couple and their three young children got out and walked into a room on the ground floor. Nobody glanced in my direction.

It would have been a nice touch to drop Trex into the dumpster, but my right wrist and left arm hurt too much to even drag him over to it, much less perform the Herculean task of lifting him up over the edge. I settled for retrieving the *nunchaku* sticks from beside the dumpster and draping them neatly over the back of his neck. Then I took a bucket of ice from the ice maker, went up to my room on the second floor of the second unit, and made an anonymous call to the Cairn Volunteer Ambulance Service to report an unconscious man in the parking lot of the RestEasy Motel.

I poured myself a generous drink from a bottle of Scotch I'd brought with me, then dumped the ice into the bathroom sink in order to soak my badly bruised left upper arm. The ambulance service was in the parking lot in less than four minutes. I took my drink out onto the balcony and stood back in the shadows, watching the commotion below me and to my right; attendants loaded the still-unconscious Trex into a waiting ambulance, and two police officers who'd arrived on the scene began interviewing guests who had emerged from their rooms in response to the sirens and flashing lights. It seemed no one had witnessed a dwarf perpetrator; I didn't get any visitors. After the ambulance and police cars pulled away, I went back into my room to soak my arm some more in the ice water and then to take a hot shower. I had another drink, took two aspirin, then went to bed and fell asleep almost immediately.

CHAPTER THREE

My right wrist was much better in the morning, but my left arm throbbed painfully and was stiff as a board. A hot shower helped some, but I still couldn't lift my arm past shoulder height without pain shooting through the upper arm, shoulder, and across my back. I dressed, then checked the local phone directory and my illustrated Chamber of Commerce map of Cairn. The donated mansion housing the Community of Conciliation was about two and a half miles from the motel, on Pave Avenue, a main thoroughfare running north from the center of town. Judging from the pictures on the map, Pave Avenue was lined on both sides by very old houses and mansions; the road ended to the north in a Y, with one arm leading down to a small state park on the banks of the Hudson, and the second arm leading up to the abandoned stone quarry that had, according to a sidebar on the map, given Cairn its name.

Thinking that a walk might be therapeutic for my arm, I again left Beloved Too in the parking lot of the RestEasy Motel and headed down into town. Mistake. I'd gone less than a half mile when I started to limp; I'd bruised my right knee banging it on Gregory Trex's stone-hard head. I bought a container of coffee in an Irish delicatessen, of all things, then called a taxi for the relatively short ride out Pave Avenue.

The world headquarters of the Community of Conciliation announced itself with a wooden sign bearing its name in English, Spanish, French, and German. I hobbled up the long gravel driveway past three simple wooden grave markers, which a small sign identified as the gravesites of the founders of the pacifist organization, an American and two Swedes. I climbed the steps up onto the porch of the old Colonial-style mansion, announced my presence with an anchor-shaped brass door knocker that must have weighed twenty pounds.

Mary Tree herself answered the door. She was dressed in a paint-spattered man's work shirt that fell to her knees, worn jeans, and sneakers. She carried a large paintbrush in her left hand, and there were spots of cream-colored paint at the end of her nose and in the center of her forehead. Her waist-length, light blond hair was pulled back in a ponytail that cascaded down her neck like a gold and gray waterfall. Her sky-colored eyes mirrored warmth and not a little bemusement as she peered down at me over the rims of her glasses, which I could now see were bifocals. She abruptly broke into a grin that revealed even, white teeth and a dimple in her chin that nicely complemented her finely sculpted features.

"My hero," she intoned in a sexy voice that was as dulcet clear as her singing voice.

I grinned back, shrugged. "I really didn't have any choice but to ride to your rescue, Miss Tree, since I knew I was eventually going to have to report the incident to my brother."

"'Miss Tree' sounds like a character in a fairy tale. My name is Mary. And what does your brother have to do with what you did for me?"

"My brother, Garth, is the world's most ardent Mary Tree fan, and he's been madly in love with you for twenty years. He has all your albums and close to a half-dozen bootleg tapes of concerts that he paid a small fortune for; a framed poster of you, an advertisement for one of your concerts in the late sixties, hangs over the fireplace in his living room. If he ever found out that you were being pushed around and I hadn't tried to stop it, he might actually do me physical harm." I stuck out my hand. "My name is Robert Frederickson."

Mary Tree extended her right hand and enveloped mine in her long, powerful fingers. "Can't I call you Mongo? I understand all your friends call you that, and I hope we're going to be friends."

"I'd say we're already friends, and famous, beautiful folksingers are allowed to call me anything they like."

The woman released my hand, raised her fine eyebrows slightly. "Dr. Robert Frederickson, Mongo the Magnificent—the show business name you carried when you were a headliner with the Statler Brothers Circus; Circus Hall of Fame, criminology professor, now apparently retired, private investigator *extraordinaire*." She paused, then again favored me with one of her radiant smiles, at once worldly and oddly childlike. "Human being *extraordinaire*. Oh, I've heard and read about you, Mongo—and what I don't, or didn't, know, my brothers and sisters filled me in on. Thank you for what you did last night."

"You're very welcome."

"I'm so glad you stopped around to say hello."

"Mary, this isn't exactly a social visit."

Her smile faded slightly, and curiosity filmed her pale blue eyes. "How can we help you, Mongo?"

"I'd like to talk to you about a friend of mine who drowned near here after supposedly taking one of your members' canoes out for a joyride."

Mary Tree's smile faded completely, and the curiosity in her incredibly expressive eyes was replaced by sadness. "Michael was a friend of yours?"

"A good one. We went back a lot of years. Our paths first crossed on a case I was working on."

"Please come in, Mongo," she said quietly, moving aside, gently putting her right hand on my shoulder and ushering me into a marble foyer decorated with marble statues in various states of disrepair and cracked, antique paintings.

She led me out of the foyer, down a narrow corridor, then through a large archway into a huge chamber that looked as if it had once been a ballroom. The room, which smelled of fresh paint, was bare except for a couch and three folding chairs set against one wall. The couch was covered with a plastic tarpaulin, as was the floor beneath a wall that was partially covered with cream-colored paint that matched the samples on Mary Tree's brush and face. The entire east wall of the room consisted of a bank of windows that offered a breathtaking view over a neatly manicured lawn that sloped down to the river. She dropped her paintbrush into a coffee can filled with turpentine, then led me over to the couch. She stripped off the plastic cover and motioned for me to sit down.

"Everyone else in the house will very much want to meet you, Mongo," she continued quietly, "but I know you want to talk first. We'll have some privacy in here. Would you like some coffee?"

"I'd love some, but not if it's any trouble."

"It's not any trouble, Mongo; it's already been brewed." She smiled again, but her smile had become wistful. "I'll be right back."

She went out through the archway, and I gazed out the bank of windows. As the rising sun passed behind the luxuriant green crown of a large elm tree, I could see a floating dock at the shoreline and a small sailboat anchored about thirty yards out. There were a number of dinghies tied to the dock, and nearby was a boat rack containing two canoes and a kayak, each intricately decorated with what appeared to be American Indian symbols, each exuding the almost sensual, palpable beauty that only lovingly handcrafted objects possess. One space in the rack was empty, and I wondered if it had held the canoe Michael had supposedly been using when he drowned.

Mary returned five minutes later with a wooden tray on which were arrayed a thermos jug, two coffee mugs, packets of sugar and a carton of Half and Half, and a plateful of bran muffins. She set the tray down on the seat of one of the folding chairs, which she placed in front of the couch. She poured me a mug of coffee, then sat down next to me on the couch. I declined milk and sugar, but did take one of the bran muffins; it was succulent, still warm from the oven.

"Good," I said as I finished off my muffin. "Thank you."

"You're welcome, Mongo," she replied, her tone matching her sad smile.

"Mary, I understand Michael was living here at the time of his death."

"Yes," she answered simply.

"How long had he been living here before he died?"

"About a week; six days, to be exact."

Exactly the length of time he would have been in Cairn from the starting date of his assignment. "How did he come to be living here?"

"We invited him."

"Did you know he was an FBI agent?"

"Uh-huh."

I drained off the coffee, which had a pleasant cinnamon aftertaste, then set the mug down on the floor. "Did you know he'd been sent here to Cairn specifically to spy on you people? Did you know he was supposed to tap your phones and monitor your mail?"

"Uh-huh," she replied in the same matter-of-fact tone as she picked up the thermos, then leaned over to refill my mug, which she handed to me. "He told us."

I almost spilled my coffee. "He *told* you?"

Mary held out the plate of bran muffins, and I absently shook my head. "What can I tell you, Mongo?" she said, a slight note of playfulness breaking through the sadness in her voice. "He decided he wanted to come over to work for the good guys for a change." She set the plate back down on the chair seat, then pointed to the half-painted wall to our right. "As a matter of fact, I'm now painting the section of wall he started. He liked to paint and fix things."

"You're saying Michael drove up here, knocked on your door, announced to whoever answered that he was Michael Burana, FBI agent, and that he was in town to spy on you?"

She leaned back on the couch, crossed her legs, and folded her large hands over her knees. "As a matter of fact," she said easily, "that's almost exactly what happened." She cocked her head, studying me, and obviously saw the consternation in my face. "Yeah, I know," she continued. "We were a little taken aback, too. Some of our people were more than a little taken aback; they were convinced it was a trick. But then, we figured that if it was a trick, it was a pretty good one. And who cared if he spied on us? It certainly wouldn't be anything new. We figured that the worst thing that could happen to us was that we'd get some work out of him while he was doing his spying. This place is really the ultimate white elephant, you know, a real bitch to maintain. But it wasn't a trick. Michael was sincere. He was going to wait until he got his next paycheck from the FBI, then submit his resignation and apply for his pension."

"Still, it wasn't as if he were coming into a houseful of strangers. You knew Michael."

Mary Tree shook her head. "Not before he showed up here."

"You told the police you were old friends."

This time her sad smile was tinged with a trace of bitterness, and she looked toward the ceiling in mock exasperation. "I was being facetious. I'm afraid the police aren't into my brand of humor."

"I'm sorry to report that I'm as dense as the police, Mary," I said carefully. "I don't get it either."

She looked at me, raised her palms, and shrugged broadly, as if the answer was obvious. "The FBI and a barefoot, pacifist folksinger of antiwar songs, a civil rights activist and war resister, Mongo? Old friends? Get it now? The FBI had been tapping my phones, monitoring my movements, opening my mail, planting phony stories in the press about me, and harassing my friends since I was seventeen years old and first walked onto a stage to sing one of Harry Peal's protest songs. In case you haven't noticed, this government takes a dim view of people who don't share its paranoid views of the world in general and communists in particular. All governments dislike citizens who protest, and different governments react in different ways. Over the years, this government has occasionally used the Gestapo and the KGB as role models for dealing with dissidents."

"Was Michael one of the agents who spied on you in the early days?"

"Yes—although I didn't know it at the time. He worked undercover then, and he told me that he traveled around the country, going to all my concerts and the protest rallies I was involved in." She paused, laughed lightly. "He told me he knew all my songs by heart."

"It sounds like the two of you got to know and like each other pretty well in the few days he was here."

"Yes. People can become good friends, or mortal enemies, in a lot less than six days."

"Indeed they can. Did you tell all this to the police?"

"No."

"Why not?"

"One thing didn't seem to have anything to do with the other. I answered their questions after they found Franz's canoe and traced it to here, but I didn't volunteer information. I saw no reason to tell the police anything unusual that might make it into the newspapers in addition to the stories that were already bound to appear. Michael had already had more than his share of bad publicity over that CIA defector thing—although I could never understand what all the fuss was about. I wish the whole damn Central Intelligence Agency would defect; the CIA and KGB deserve each other. With children starving and the planet virtually disintegrating under our feet, people still worry about the grown-up children who run our governments, and their children's games. I mean, who really gives a shit if a CIA agent defects to the Russians? The way this country has been run for the past forty years, the manner in which it's set its priorities, is enough to make you think the communists are really in charge, and constantly doing everything in their power to help us make fools of ourselves in the eyes of the world. Anyway, it seems Michael had come to share many of my views." She paused, perhaps again reacting to something she saw in my face. She bowed her head slightly, squinted at me over the tops of her bifocals. "You don't believe what I say about Michael, Mongo?"

I sipped at my coffee, which had gone cold. "Of course I believe you, Mary. I think Michael's change of heart had been coming on for a long time. I just never thought he would . . ."

"Turn traitor?" Mary asked wryly.

"Quit the FBI. Did he tell you about his troubles with his boss?"

She shook her head. "Aside from what he told us in order to introduce himself, he didn't talk about the FBI. He just said his spying days were over."

"The head of the Bureau's counterintelligence unit is a man by the name of Edward J. Hendricks, who could be described as an unreconstructed cold warrior. He could care less about what's happened in Russia and Eastern Europe because he's a man who desperately needs his old, familiar enemies to give his life meaning. He's a man with a visceral hatred of communists—and of anybody he thinks sides with the communists. That covers a pretty broad spectrum of people."

"I'm familiar with the type," Mary said in the same wry tone.

"Oh, I'm sure you are. Hendricks fancies himself a super-patriot—but super-patriots of his sort would also have been, and were, super-patriots in Nazi Germany. He finds it difficult, if not impossible, to distinguish between the country's critics and its enemies. Michael was probably pretty much like that in the early stages of his career; FBI recruits are chosen largely on the basis of ideology. As he told you, virtually all his assignments in the early part of his career involved surveillance of dissident groups, and there was a lot of illegal wiretapping and mail covers. Anyway, Michael mellowed, or got tired of it, whatever. He started arguing that the Bureau should stop wasting its time and manpower on peace groups, and should go after real spies as well as people in the violent right, like neo-Nazis and the Ku Klux Klan. This new attitude of Michael's didn't sit well with Hendricks, and their relationship deteriorated further, to say the least, when Michael became a kind of ombudsman and whistle-blower inside the Bureau regarding matters of racial discrimination in the hiring and promotion of agents. Then Michael's surveillance team blew the CIA defector thing, and Hendricks got his first real shot at Michael. First, Michael was demoted, and then Hendricks ordered him out here to do a spy number on you people. Hendricks knew Michael would hate the assignment; it was his way of getting revenge for all the grief Michael had been giving him."

"You're saying this Hendricks doesn't really believe that the Community of Conciliation is—oh, how I love this word—'subversive'?"

"Oh, he thinks you're subversive, all right, and he really does seem to believe that people like you pose a greater real danger to this country than the Klan or the neo-Nazis. He'd like to see just about every peace and civil rights activist in this country thrown out, or placed in some kind of internment camp, until, as he puts it, 'this thing with Russia is really over, and they're buried.'"

"Is he serious?"

"I've never met the man. Michael described the conversation to me, and Michael swears he was dead serious. But the point is that Hendricks has plenty of zealots under him who would have whistled 'The Star-Spangled Banner' all the time they were spying on you. Hendricks sent Michael here to humiliate him."

"Fools," Mary said tersely. "Damn fools."

"Did Michael tell you he hated being near water?"

She thought about it as she reached out for another bran muffin; she hesitated, then brought her hand back to her lap. "Yes," she said at last. "But he didn't put it that strongly. He said he didn't much care for water. I told him it was no problem, that he didn't have to stay in Cairn. We have chapters, stations, all over the world. I told him that if he really wanted to work for our cause we could send him to live on the top of a mountain, in the middle of a jungle—wherever he liked."

"Didn't it strike you as odd that a man who didn't like water would go out canoeing on the Hudson River at one of its widest points?"

"Not at the time, no," she replied distantly, her brows knitting into a frown. "People have changes of mood, sometimes do things they wouldn't normally do. . . . Mongo, do you think somebody killed Michael?"

"I haven't said that. I'm just trying to get a picture of what happened. I talked to the chief of police, and now I'm talking to you. Did Michael tell anyone he was going canoeing?"

"No," she answered in the same distant tone. "Not that I'm aware of. He didn't tell me."

"What about the man who owned the canoe? I think you said his name was Franz?"

"Franz Bauer."

"Did he ask Bauer's permission to use his canoe?"

Mary Tree slowly shook her head. "No."

"Building a canoe by hand must take a long time and cost some money. Each of those canoes I see down by the river would mean a lot to the man who made them."

"Yes. Franz made all of them."

"Do the people here normally take out any of the boats whenever they feel like it?"

Again, she shook her head. "The dinghies, yes, and the sailboat belongs to all of us. But not the canoes or the kayak; they're special."

"Did anybody see Michael go out in the canoe?"

"No. It had to have been in the evening, after dark, because all of the canoes were there when I went in to supper."

"Did Michael come to supper?"

"No." Now her brows were knitted even tighter, and tight lines of tension had appeared around her mouth as she thought back and remembered. "We all just assumed . . ."

"You assumed what, Mary?"

"There was a full moon Sunday night, and the river was very still. It can be very lovely and soothing out on the river at night when it's like that. Michael had seemed very distracted and tense after coming back from talking with Harry."

"Harry?"

"Harry Peal."

"Harry Peal lives around here?"

"About ten miles north of here. He has a house on a cliff overlooking the river."

"Did Michael tell you what he and Harry Peal talked about, or why he went to see him in the first place?"

The corners of her mouth drew back in a thin smile. "I know why Michael went up there. Harry was another of the FBI's 'old friends,' Mongo. Michael had spied on Harry, too." She paused, and her smile, while still tinged with sadness, grew broader. "At least, with Harry, Michael had himself a real, honest-to-goodness communist to deal with. Ex-communist, anyway. Michael said he wanted to pay his respects to the man who'd spent two terms in prison, first for refusing to answer questions before the House Un-American Activities Committee, and then for telling Joseph McCarthy—on live television—to go fuck himself. Harry was leaving that evening for Hungary to accept some award as part of President Shannon's cultural exchange program with the Russians and the Eastern Bloc countries. But he agreed to see Michael in the afternoon; if you knew Harry, you'd know what a hoot it was for him to have an FBI agent coming to visit him by the front door, as it were. Michael thought it was a real hoot, too. He was really high when he left here—but not so high when he got back. He was moody, distracted. He was in and out the rest of the day, and I know he went into town at least twice. I asked him if anything was wrong, and he said something . . ."

"What did he say, Mary?"

"Just one word: 'Unbelievable.' That's what he said. 'Unbelievable'; you know, like you say when you're just overwhelmed by something that's been said or done."

"He went into town twice?"

"Yes. I know, because he asked permission each time to use the pickup truck. He said he was in a hurry and didn't have the time to walk."

"He was in a hurry each time?"

"He said he was, yes."

"Do you know what he did in town or who he talked to either of those times?"

"No. Anyway, after we found out that he'd drowned, everyone here just assumed that he'd gone out canoeing to try to get rid of some tension."

"Uh-huh. Mary, is Harry Peal still out of the country?"

"As a matter of fact, I think he's scheduled to return sometime today."

"Can you get me an appointment to talk with him?"

She shrugged. "Sure. Harry's easy enough to see when he's around. I'll give him a chance to unpack and rest a little, and I'll call him later. I'm sure he'll be happy to talk with you."

I took a business card out of my wallet, wrote my unlisted apartment phone number and the number of the RestEasy Motel on the back, handed it to her. "After you speak to him, please give me a call. You should be able to reach me at one of these three numbers; if not, there's an answering service on the office phone."

Mary Tree's hand trembled slightly as she reached out and took the card. She suddenly looked very pale. "You do think somebody killed Michael, don't you?"

"Tell me about last night, Mary. What was that all about?"

Her knuckles were white where they were clasped around her

right knee, and her jaw was clenched tightly. She seemed now to be looking past, or through, me, at some private haunt.

"Mary . . . ?"

"If Michael was killed," she said in a low, tense voice, "they did it."

"Who, Mary? The death squad?"

Mary Tree looked away, then abruptly stood and walked across the empty ballroom to the bank of windows at the east end, where she stood stiffly, her arms wrapped around her.

There was still some coffee left in the thermos jug. I poured it into her mug, took it over to her. She glanced down at me, then took the mug in a hand that was still trembling, nodded her thanks.

"Are you afraid, Mary?" I asked quietly.

"No," she replied simply.

"Then what's wrong?"

"I . . . I don't want to be like them."

"Like who, Mary?"

She set the mug down on a small window ledge, then turned to face me. "I don't want to be like all the terrible people who've made such a mess of this country, Mongo. I've been accused of so many terrible things. The HUAC, the McCarthy hearings . . . Harry *was* a communist, and he made no bones about it, but he wouldn't name others he knew were communists. But so many people who *weren't* communists or subversive in any way had their lives destroyed just because of accusations. I don't want to be one of those people who just make accusations. Also, quite frankly, I don't want you to think I'm a fool or paranoid or both."

"Are you saying you don't really believe there's a death squad in Cairn?"

"I'm saying I don't have any proof."

"And yet, by holding up that sign, you were, in effect, accusing the Vietnam veterans."

"I know," she said in a voice so low I could hardly hear her. "I probably shouldn't have done that. I was just frustrated. Like I said, I don't want you to think I'm paranoid."

"Even paranoids have real enemies, Mary," I said with what I hoped was a disarming smile. I wanted to hear what she had to say. "What were you frustrated about?"

"You have to understand what's been happening in Cairn lately."

"Tell me."

"It used to be a pretty mellow place," she said, and shrugged. "It's always been an 'artsy' community, if you will—a refuge for artists, actors, and writers, and people who like to be around people like that. Cairn was inexpensive, easygoing. Then word got around in New York City that Cairn was a 'hot suburb.' All of a sudden we had an influx of yuppies, *nouveaux riches*, and all sorts of people who could never understand what Cairn is really all about. In my opinion, at least, these people began to destroy the very atmosphere that makes this town special."

"People like Elysius Culhane?"

"Yes," she said tersely, anger humming in her voice. She picked up her mug, stared down into its depths as she stirred the cold coffee with her finger, took a deep breath, and slowly exhaled. "For almost twenty years the Community of Conciliation has tried to reach out to veterans of all wars, and to fighting men everywhere. Some of these soldiers and veterans may hate us, but we don't hate them. They're not the enemy, just more victims, more casualties, of the disease called war. In fact, we've been trying to convince the Russians that they should allow us to set up similar programs there for their Afghan veterans, who are beginning to show the same kinds of severe, post-stress emotional disorders as our Vietnam vets. They don't think much of our setting up shop there."

"I hope that doesn't surprise you."

"Of course not. I never said our government had a monopoly on stupidity."

"What kind of programs are you talking about?"

"We had weekly fellowship meetings, and special counseling sessions led by volunteer therapists from around the county. We had good rapport with the vets, and I like to think we were doing some good for those men. Then Elysius Culhane moved here, and things began to change. I don't have to tell you he's a very powerful man—and he's a persuasive man, with a devil's tongue. He ingratiated himself with the veterans, primarily by throwing a lot of money around to sponsor events for them. Before long the fellowship meetings had to be canceled, because the veterans stopped coming. The same with the psychological and job counseling sessions. Culhane had convinced them that they were victims, all right—of, in his words, the left-wing politicians who used them as cannon fodder while they were selling out Vietnam to the communists. You know how that tune goes. He convinced them—or most of them—that it was unpatriotic to have anything to do with us, since we'd opposed the war. We oppose *all* wars. And Culhane hadn't been here more than a month before he got himself an emergency appointment as, of all things, a village trustee. There was a lot more money being spent in politics here, and before you knew it there were right-wing Republicans being elected to positions of power in all the riverfront communities that had once been considered liberal, like Cairn."

It was my turn to shrug. "Things like that happen in a democracy, Mary. It's the great American way."

"Yes, Mongo. But then people started to die."

"What people started to die? Political people? Leftists?"

She shook her head. "No, not yet." She paused, shuddered slightly. "Not unless Michael was a victim, which is what's so frightening. At first it was just a couple of drug dealers and then a vagrant who'd been accused of trying to molest some schoolchildren. All three men were shot in the back of the head."

"What makes you think these killings were the work of a death squad?"

"Because it was after the third death that the threats started coming, and the threats mentioned the execution-style killings."

"You've received threats?"

"Yes. The Community has, by letter and telephone. They say we're communists and deserve to be shot. And there's been repeated vandalism. A number of liberal organizations in the river communities have shut down because of the threats and vandalism. I wouldn't accuse Elysius Culhane of being behind it, because I don't think he's that stupid, but I certainly do accuse him of creating an atmosphere that supports that kind of vigilantism and terror. I've heard him defend and praise the

Salvadoran and Guatemalan death squads on a number of occasions."

"So have I, but right-wingers tend to talk like that. Have you reported these threats and the vandalism to the police?"

"Of course."

"And?"

"Nothing's happened."

"Do you think the police are choosing to do nothing about it?"

"I'm saying they haven't caught anybody."

"Do you think Chief Mosely is covering up something?"

She hesitated, then shook her head. "No, I'm not saying that. But I don't have a lot of faith in his passion for pursuit of equal justice for all. Mosely is a lackey of Elysius Culhane. It was Culhane who convinced his fellow town officials that Mosely was the perfect candidate for our chief of police."

"How do you know that?"

"I have a friend who's a village trustee. It's no secret that Dan Mosely was Culhane's choice. It doesn't mean that Mosely would cover up a crime, but I say it does mean that he's very tuned in to Culhane's sensibilities; I just don't believe he'd go out of his way to ease the problems of individuals or groups Culhane disapproves of. He seems a decent enough man, but I'm sure he feels grateful to Culhane for plucking him out of the jungles of New York City and plunking him down here in Cairn, where he can walk out of his office after work and sail off into the sunset on his catamaran."

"I've been waiting for you to mention Gregory Trex. I would think he'd be a prime suspect for threats, vandalism, and membership on a death squad."

"Vandalism and threats, sure," she replied matter-of-factly. "I'm not sure he has enough brains to be on a death squad."

"You don't need a lot of brains to pull a trigger, Mary."

She merely shrugged. "You're right, of course. It's just that I find it hard to get all that mad at Gregory."

"Really?" I said, making no effort to hide my surprise at her reaction—or lack of it. "That's funny; I didn't have any trouble at all getting mad at him."

"I noticed," she said, and smiled. "But then, you didn't watch him grow up. I've been a member of the Community of

Conciliation and lived here in Cairn for more than twenty years. Gregory's very limited, you know. He's the perfect example of the dull little fat boy everybody laughed at and picked on, and who grew up to be town bully. He was in a class for the educable retarded in school here, and he spent a year in a psychiatric hospital after he once tried to kill himself. They put him on some medication when he was there, and he seemed to be a lot mellower when he got out. His father's one of the nicest men you'll ever want to meet, and he blames himself for what's happened to Gregory. I don't want to go into a lot of detail, but that family has seen more than its share of tragedy."

"A lot of families have seen more than their share of tragedy. It's not an excuse."

"I know. But it was Culhane who got Gregory all worked up again with this war and patriotism business. Jesus, it was Culhane who suggested to Gregory that the poor boy enlist in the Marines. Can you imagine? He spent a week bragging all over town about what he was going to do before he actually did it. He did manage to get a recruiter to sign him up, but he was back from boot camp in less than two weeks. His story was that he was too good for the Marines, that he was showing everyone else up. He was discharged on a medical, of course. My point is that Gregory Trex is a victim. The real enemy of Gregory, you, me, and all the other people in the world is a man like Elysius Culhane. Men like Culhane can't stand the thought of living in a peaceful world."

"It's usually the Gregory Trexes of the world you have to deal with, Mary, not the Elysius Culhanes."

"No," she said, shaking her head adamantly. "That's treating the symptoms, not the disease."

"Gregory Trex is a symptom that will kill you."

"The only way to stop being manipulated by men like Elysius Culhane is to refuse to deal with, to fight, their surrogates— people like Gregory. When enough people refuse to fight, then the fighting will simply stop."

"Gandhi, Martin Luther King, and the Community of Conciliation would have lasted about five minutes in Nazi Germany or Pol Pot's Cambodia. Pacifism can only work in a basically just society, where the majority of people are basically just. The problem, Mary, is that it takes only one Gregory Trex with a machine gun to wipe out droves of pacifists, and Trex wouldn't give it a second thought if he thought he could get away with it. What do you do about that?"

"Wait for him to run out of ammunition."

"You're joking, of course."

"I am not," she said evenly, drawing herself up slightly. "He'll simply reload."

"Then we wait for the people who supply him with the ammunition to stop manufacturing it."

I had better things to do than debate pacifism with Mary Tree, and I didn't want our meeting to end on a sour note. I bowed slightly, extended my hand. "Thank you, Mary."

She took my hand in both of hers, smiled warmly. "I take it you don't think much of the pacifist philosophy."

"My philosophy is do unto others as you would have them do unto you, but keep a sharp lookout for the bad guys. There have always been bad guys, Mary, and there always will be. They'll roll right over you if you let them; first take everything you own and then take your life. If you're not prepared to fight and die for certain things, then you probably don't have much to live for."

"But you believe you also have to be prepared to kill for certain things."

"Yes."

"Then you're back to the danger of being manipulated by demagogues, cowards, bigots, and hypocrites like Elysius Culhane."

"No."

"Who tells the good guys from the bad guys?"

"I do."

"Only you?"

"Only me. Dying and killing are very personal things."

"Men should only, say, fight in wars they personally believe in, and refuse to fight in others?"

"Yep. And then accept the consequences of that decision if the government wants to throw you in jail, or even kill you. It's a hell of a lot better to die for what you believe in than to die—or kill—for something you don't believe in. Each individual must make his or her own decision."

"That makes you an anarchist."

"God, I hope Garth doesn't find out about it. He already has enough names to call me."

Mary Tree laughed lightly, then gripped me gently by the shoulders. "That reminds me of something I have to give you. Just wait here a minute."

I waited, kneading my sore left arm and gazing out the bank of windows at the river. She was back a few minutes later, looking slightly flushed. She was carrying a plastic shopping bag, which she handed to me. It felt heavy.

"This is just between you and me and your brother, Mongo," she said, her pale blue eyes bright with excitement and warmth. "I've been negotiating with a small record company in Los Angeles that wants to sign me to a new recording contract. These are copies of demo tapes I've been working on for the past year. They're not as clean as they should be, and a couple of rhythm tracks still have to be laid in, but, since you say your brother is such a fan of mine, I think he might enjoy listening to them. I've written a lot of the songs myself, which is a departure for me, but there are a number of new Harry Peal songs, and Dylan even gave me one. They're also doing some uncredited backup vocals. I've autographed the tape slipcases."

"Good grief, Mary," I said, hefting the plastic bag. "There must be enough music here for three or four albums. Talk about collectibles. I'll certainly enjoy listening to the tapes, but I'm going to be sure we're standing in Garth's apartment when I give these to him. He's going to lose control of his bodily functions when he hears what I've got here."

Mary Tree's smile grew even broader, warmer. "Also, I want you to bring him out for the day when this other business is behind you. We'll poke around the antique shops, have a picnic lunch up in the quarry, and maybe go sailing, if you'd like."

"I'd like. As for Garth, well, words cannot express."

"I've got everyone else lined up out in the foyer. They'd like to say hello. Okay with you?"

"Fine with me."

I followed her across the ballroom, stopped just before we reached the archway, and took her arm. She turned toward me, a puzzled expression on her face. "Mary," I continued quietly, "I don't want to frighten you, but I'd like you to be very careful for . . . a while. Until we get this matter of Michael's death cleared up, I want you to watch out for yourself. When you leave the house, even if it's just for a walk into town, always take somebody with you. Okay?"

She studied me for a few moments, and when she spoke her voice had grown slightly husky. "Mongo, you think Michael was murdered, don't you?"

"Yes," I said, feeling my stomach muscles flutter, "I do."

"You didn't seem so certain before."

"I got certain when you told me Michael had supposedly used the canoe without permission. There was a time when Michael loved boating and swimming, and I was willing to grant the possibility that he'd decided to celebrate the new life he was planning to start with you people by going back to doing the things he'd once enjoyed; if so, his being out in a canoe on the Hudson might be explainable. The river kicked up on him, he capsized and drowned."

"But now you don't believe that's what happened."

"No. What I'm not willing to grant is that he'd use somebody else's property—in this case a very special, handcrafted canoe—without asking permission. Michael was a gracious and rigorously courteous man, a stickler for respecting other people's privacy and property. He would never have taken that canoe without permission. I wasn't sure I wanted to tell you my suspicions, not only because I didn't want to frighten you but because somebody might think you know more than you do, and that could place you in danger. But then I realized that people are bound to find out that I've talked to you, and just that fact could be dangerous. That's why I want you to be careful. Yes, I believe Michael was murdered. Now the questions become who did it and why."

CHAPTER FOUR

I hung around in the huge foyer of the Community of Conciliation mansion for half an hour, chatting with Mary and fifteen other members of the pacifist organization, and then I was out the door and three quarters of the way down the driveway before I realized that I'd forgotten to call a taxi. I flexed my tender right knee, decided that I'd test it with the walk back into town and hope that it didn't stiffen up too badly on me.

I needn't have worried. I'd limped along only a half mile or so, occasionally reaching across my body to knead my throbbing left arm, when a white Cairn police car pulled up to the curb beside me and Dan Mosely rolled down the window.

"You look like you're hurting, Frederickson," Mosely said in his deep, resonant voice. "I think you need a lift."

I stopped, studied the impassive features of the man with the steel-colored hair and eyes. "Chief, that sounds to me like an official invitation."

"Semi-official. Get in, Frederickson. If you will."

I walked around to the other side of the car, got in, and fastened my seat belt, but Mosely didn't put the idling car into gear. He leaned forward, bowing his head slightly as he hooked his wrists over the steering wheel. "You must have hurt your leg while you were kicking the shit out of Gregory Trex again," Mosely said with a small sigh. "You really should be more careful; if you don't stop beating on that bonehead, you're going to cripple yourself."

"Pardon me?"

"It really is true what they say about you."

"What do they say about me, Chief?"

"That you're a goddamn holy terror."

"Who? Me? Wow. A goddamn holy terror. It has a ring to it."

"You might be interested in knowing that Gregory Trex is in the hospital with a concussion, a broken nose, lots of missing teeth, lots of abrasions, and a ruptured right eardrum. He may lose his hearing in that ear."

"Poor boy. Aside from my general concern for all humanity, why should I be interested in Trex's misfortune?"

"Because you did it to him. He was found virtually under your window."

"Who does Trex say did it to him?"

Mosely turned his head slightly to look at me, and his lips drew back in a thin smile that seemed to reflect respect along with his irritation. "He says he was coming around to talk to you and that he was mugged by four guys. He says three guys held him while the fourth worked him over with *nunchaku* sticks."

"It sounds terrible," I said, wincing. "Did he happen to mention what he wanted to discuss with me?"

"He never got around to explaining that. What the hell happened, Frederickson? Did that shit-for-brains make the mistake of coming after you again?"

"Chief, if Trex told you he was beaten up by four muggers, who am I to call him a liar? He might take offense."

Mosely grunted with disgust, then abruptly straightened up and slammed the car into reverse. The tires spun and spewed gravel as he backed into a driveway, and then he shifted again and we speeded away in the opposite direction, away from town. A decidedly captive audience, I figured I would find out soon enough where we were going and what he wanted, and so I remained silent as we reached the end of Pave Avenue. He took the left branch of the Y that led up to the abandoned stone quarry, then took a sharp right after a hundred yards or so onto another road. The pavement had ended abruptly, and we were on a winding, pitted, dirt road that had been carved right through the side of the mountain. He shifted into four-wheel drive to slowly maneuver around a truck-eating pothole, and then we continued on our way up. Viewed from a distance, the remains of the quarrying operation that had systematically devoured a good portion of the mountain appeared like an ocher and mauve scar across the face of the sky; seen up close, the naked, machine-washed face of the rock was starkly beautiful, cut in irregular, fluted patterns of rock shelves that made it seem as if we were traveling through the innards of some gigantic, petrified pipe organ of the gods.

"The whole mountain is trap rock," Mosely said in an easy, conversational tone as we reached a large, grass-covered plateau about three quarters of the way up the mountain. He shifted back to two-wheel drive and drove into a small parking lot that was virtually at the edge of a precipice overlooking the Hudson. Adjacent to the parking lot were a concrete and steel barbecue pit, a picnic table, and an overflowing trash can. There was a huge yellow building set back on the plateau, connected to the face of the mountain by flat umbilical cords of rusted steel that had once been conveyor belts. Two other wide conveyor belts emerged from the front of the building and plunged underground, presumably leading down to the river's edge. "Sixty to seventy years ago, this quarry supplied more than half of the crushed stone used in construction projects in New York City. They'd chop and shave the rock off the side of the mountain onto those conveyor belts, which would carry it to a rock crusher that was inside that building, which is now used for storage. The crushed rock would come out on those other conveyor belts and be carried down to the river, where it would be loaded onto barges that would take it downriver."

"Interesting," I said in a neutral tone.

Mosely parked in a corner of the lot, close to the picnic table, and got out. I followed him toward the table. There was a used condom draped over the edge of the trash can. Mosely picked up a stick, pushed the swollen rubber tube all the way into the can.

"Fucking kids can't even clean up after themselves," he said with disgust as he heaved the stick away.

Mosely eased his tall frame down on top of the picnic table, facing the river, rested his feet on the attached bench. I climbed up beside him, stared out over the breathtaking panorama before me—puffy cumulus clouds in a blue sky above me, sheer rock faces behind and on either side, and the broad, winding expanse of the Hudson below me. Closer to the Westchester side, a dozen sailboats were heeling nicely against a brisk wind blowing from the south. In the deep channel three quarters of the way across, three squat, muscular tugboats were shepherding a train of chain-connected barges loaded with what looked like concrete sewage pipes toward New York City.

I said, "Nice view."

"Frederickson," Mosely said in a slightly exasperated tone as he ran the fingers of both hands through his thick, curly hair, "I like it here in Cairn. I really do. I like the community, I like the atmosphere, I like the people, and most of all I like my job."

"And you feel that I somehow pose a threat to you, which is why you've been keeping track of my whereabouts."

Now he turned and looked at me, hard. When he spoke, his deep voice had developed a decided edge to it. "Cairn doesn't need a holy terror, Frederickson; we've already discussed how you attract trouble, and we've already seen evidence of it. You also attract publicity, and the kind of publicity you generate could definitely end up making me look bad."

"Are you trying to tell me it's high noon, Chief?"

"I thought we'd agreed that I was going to take another, closer look at this case, and that you were going to let me do my job."

"Chief, I had two stops on my schedule when I came to Cairn; you were the first stop, and the Community of Conciliation was the second. As a matter of fact, I was just on my way back to see you."

This caught him by surprise, and it showed in his steel-gray eyes. "Oh? Why?"

"To tell you that I'm now certain that Michael was murdered, and then let you get on with your job."

He shifted his weight around on the table so that he was facing me, crossed his arms over his chest, and narrowed his eyelids.

"What the hell makes you so sure now that your friend was murdered? What did those friendly, peace-loving folks in the Russian embassy down the road tell you that they didn't tell me?"

"They didn't tell you because they didn't think it was important."

"What didn't they think was important?"

"The fact that Michael didn't ask the owner's permission before he supposedly took that canoe out on the river."

"That's all?"

"It's enough. I've already told you that Michael hated even being near water, but that could have changed. His character wouldn't. He would never have taken that canoe without asking permission. It means somebody nabbed Michael and drowned him. Either before or after they killed him, they stole the canoe and set it adrift, knowing that the empty canoe, whenever and wherever it was found, would be connected to Michael's drowning; the police would naturally assume he'd been in it. Michael was murdered, Chief, and I wanted you to know it."

"And if I don't start looking real hard for this murderer, the famous Dr. Robert Frederickson will. Right?"

Dan Mosely and his apparent insecurity were starting to annoy me. I shifted my own position, turning to face him so that our knees were almost touching. "I think you may have an attitude problem, Chief," I said tersely. "I don't need any more of this 'holy terror' and 'famous Dr. Frederickson' shit from you. I came here because a friend of mine died under what I considered to be questionable circumstances. You were the first person I talked to about it, and I'm talking to you now. *I've* never suggested that you didn't do your job or that you won't continue to do it. Since you've indicated that you'll extend me the courtesy of letting me know whatever you may turn up, I'll be more than happy to get back to the city so I can get on with my own work. So get off my back."

Mosely continued to study me through narrowed lids for a few more moments, then abruptly turned away and resumed staring down at the river. "Who'd you talk to there?"

"I spoke to everyone who was in the house."

"Yeah, but who did the most talking over there?"

"What difference does it make? I assume you'll be talking to them again."

"Mary Tree."

"If you're going to answer your own questions, why bother asking me?"

"What else did she have to say?"

I shrugged. "More town gossip. I've given you the salient points of our discussion."

"Did she mention her notion that there's a death squad operating in the towns along the river?"

"The subject was touched upon."

Mosely dug out a splinter from the weathered wood of the tabletop, casually tossed it into the air; the wind caught it and carried it over the edge of the cliff. "You think I'm a crooked cop, Frederickson?" he asked in an even tone. "You think I'm letting killers operate right under my nose?"

"Chief, since you're the one I'm counting on to nab the man or men who murdered my friend, I certainly hope not."

He was silent for some time. Finally he nodded slightly, said, "I interpret that as a vote of confidence, Frederickson. I appreciate it. I know I'm an honest cop; I like to think I'm also a good one. Yes, there've been execution-style killings around here lately, and they're being investigated jointly by the police forces in all the river communities. I don't have to tell you that we're not immune to the problems you'll find in the rest of the country; we have drugs and drug dealers; we have crazy people living on the streets. Except for the vagrant, we think the deaths represent a struggle for turf among drug dealers. The vagrant may have just gotten in their way. Check it out, if you'd like."

"Chief, I didn't come here to investigate you. What about the vandalism and the threats to the leftist groups around here? I'm told that business started at about the same time as these execution-style killings."

"Those are being investigated too. The letters are almost impossible to trace, since they're mailed from outside the county. As far as the vandalism is concerned, we can't be everywhere at once. The place the Community of Conciliation owns covers four acres, much of it wooded, and with river frontage. It's easy to get at. We suggested that they hire private security guards, but so far they haven't done it." He paused, laughed without humor. "I think they're afraid that employing a security force will hurt their pacifist image."

"But what about the link—if there is a link—between the killings and the threats? Why would warring drug dealers concern themselves with a group like the Community of Conciliation?"

Mosely looked down at his hands. "I don't have an answer for that, Frederickson. I don't think there is an easy answer."

"What about a guess?"

"Okay, I'll give you a guess. There's been a change in the political makeup of Cairn and the other river towns, a rightward shift. Personally, I don't think there is a link between the deaths and the threats, at least not a direct one. There are some types around here who actually *like* the idea of a death squad to carry out political killings, even if there isn't such a group. They *like* the idea that drug dealers and child molesters are being taken care of without a lot of judicial fuss, and they'd like to see the same thing happen to people they consider communists or communist sympathizers. They weren't prepared to actually start killing people, of course, but they thought it was a neat idea, if you will, to kind of climb on the bandwagon and piggyback vandalism and heavy threats on top of the actual murders; they wanted—want—the Community and similar leftist groups to *think* there may be a death squad on their case. In short, the vandals and letter-writers are being opportunistic. They want the Community of Conciliation to set up headquarters someplace else, and they're trying to scare them out of town."

"Some people might trace the rightward shift and the start of a lot of these troubles to the arrival of Elysius Culhane," I said carefully, watching his face.

Mosely made a derisive gesture with his right hand. "That's Mary Tree talking again. You think Culhane's a fool, Frederickson? You think he'd risk his reputation, career, and maybe a fine or jail sentence by getting involved in a nasty letter-writing campaign?"

"The man's mind and real motivations are a mystery to me," I said even more carefully, "so I don't have the slightest idea what he would or wouldn't do. Some people think you might; some people think Elysius Culhane is the reason you're chief of police in Cairn."

He didn't like that at all. His jaw muscles clenched, and the acne scars ringing his neck stood out as blood rushed to his face. His head snapped around, and his gray eyes glinted with anger. He started to say something, then apparently thought better of it. He took a deep breath, turned away again. "Did that woman tell you I was in Culhane's pocket?" he asked in an even tone.

"No. But it was suggested that you might be a bit more sensitive to his views of law and order than to other points of view because you owe your job to him."

"I was appointed by the mayor after a vote of the town board and trustees."

"Sure," I said easily. "That's how democracy works."

He sighed again, studied the backs of his sinewy hands. "Look, Frederickson, I'm not going to try to bullshit you. You're goddamn right I pay attention to Culhane's opinions, the same as I pay attention to the opinions and views of the mayor, the trustees, the board, and the owners of all those mansions on the north side of town. They're the power structure in this town, and if I don't perform this job to their satisfaction, they'll get somebody else in here who will. I have to consider politics, yes, but that doesn't mean I don't enforce the laws in an evenhanded manner. There are politics involved in any job like this. In that sense Cairn is no different from New York City or East Podunk. It doesn't make me a crooked cop."

"A good, honest answer, Chief," I said, then paused to clear my throat. "But then, the question would remain as to why Elysius Culhane chose to sponsor you, and not someone else who was also honest and equally sensitive to the political dynamics of law enforcement."

"Now you're pushing it, Frederickson."

"You opened the subject when you insisted on hearing my version of the town gossip. Did you and Elysius Culhane know each other before you came here?"

Again, the man's jaw muscles clenched, but his tone remained even. "I'd never met the man before, Frederickson. I have to assume I was hired because I was the best candidate. Now, do you have anything else to tell me?"

70

"Nope."

"You have any more stops in Cairn?"

"No, Chief, I don't have any more stops in Cairn."

"Then, may I assume you'll be leaving town?" He paused, looked at me. His smile was thin, but not without warmth. "Before Gregory Trex gets out of the hospital, and before a '60 Minutes' crew shows up on the steps of Town Hall?"

"I'll be leaving town forthwith."

"I will be in touch, Frederickson."

"So you told me."

He nodded curtly, slid off the table onto the ground. "If you don't mind, there's somebody else who'd like to talk to you."

"Who?"

"Trex."

"Gregory Trex wants to talk to me, and you want me to talk to him?"

"Not the son, the father. Jack Trex."

• • •

Mosely drove me back through the center of town, and then south into an area of Cairn where the old, clapboard houses were undoubtedly worth much less than the land they sat on. He stopped the car at the side of the road, pointed to a dirt driveway that led in the direction of the river. I got out, and he drove away without a word. I limped down the tree-lined driveway, went around a corner, and found myself on a lawn beside a ramshackle, weather-beaten house sitting high on a stone foundation only two or three yards from the high-tide mark of the river. Two goats inside a large wire enclosure munched contentedly on the grass—cheap, perpetual lawn mowers. It seemed Jack Trex was a working fisherman; there was a battered dinghy and a Boston Whaler tied up at a floating dock that was missing half its planks. Nets for catching shad hung on drying racks, and there were a half dozen crab pots.

The goats brayed at me. I brayed back, went up to the front door, and knocked. The door was opened almost immediately by Jack Trex, who was leaning on crutches. The veteran was wearing baggy brown corduroy trousers and a faded green T-shirt that

71

almost matched the color of his eyes, and which emphasized the bulge of muscle in his chest, arms, and shoulders. He was not wearing his artificial limb, and the pants cuff where his left leg should have been was hanging loose and empty. His thinning black hair was unkempt, but he was clean-shaven, except for his gray mustache, and his pale green eyes were clear, reflecting no trace of hostility.

"Thank you for coming, Dr. Frederickson," Trex said warmly. He shifted his weight on his crutches in order to free his right arm, then extended a large, thickly callused hand, which I shook. "I appreciate it very much. How about some coffee?"

"Sure," I said in a somewhat tentative tone. I hadn't known quite what to expect from the father of the disturbed young man I'd twice beaten on and humiliated, and the genuine warmth and sincerity of his greeting took me by surprise.

Trex stood to one side and held the door open for me. I stepped into an enormous kitchen; judging from what I'd seen of the exterior, it had to be the largest room in the house. Trex stroked his gray mustache, studied me. There seemed to be a hint of amusement in his limpid, expressive eyes, and perhaps other things that I couldn't read.

"I don't wear the prosthesis around the house," he said in his deep, raspy voice. "It chafes. Does the sight of an amputee bother you?"

"No."

"It does some people."

"Well, Mr. Trex, there's no doubt in my mind that it bothers the amputee a lot more."

Jack Trex chuckled. "You've got that right." He pointed to a round wooden table ringed with wooden chairs in the center of the room. "Have yourself a seat. The coffee will be ready in a minute."

I sat down while Trex propelled himself across the kitchen to a counter where a coffee grinder was situated. He poured beans into the canister of the machine, turned it on, then busied himself preparing the pot and filter. Still not knowing what to expect, I contented myself with looking around the kitchen while the other man prepared the coffee.

To my left were two gas ranges and ceiling racks with an

assortment of pots and pans hanging from them. There was an overriding odor of fried fish; since shad, the only Hudson catch that could be commercially sold, only ran in the spring, I suspected that Jack Trex ate a good deal of what he caught during the rest of the year.

There was an easel in one corner, but there was nothing on it. Behind me, a scarred rolltop desk was set against the wall next to an open door that looked as if it led into a gloomy, poorly lit living room. The desk and the rickety card table set up next to it were overflowing with magazines, newspapers, clippings, books, jars of pens and pencils, and notepads. Hanging on the wall over the desk were two framed quotes. One was from George Orwell, referring to his definition of political language as the use of words to defend the indefensible. The second quote was from Lenin: "The fastest way to destroy a society is to corrupt language."

It had struck me when I viewed his painting that Jack Trex was not your average Vietnam veteran, or average anything, and nothing that I was seeing served to disabuse me of that notion.

The big man at the kitchen counter must have seen me looking at his work space. He leaned back on his crutches, cocked his head slightly, said, "This is a nation built on, and held together by, illusions."

"Aren't they all?" I replied in a neutral tone.

I waited for more, but it seemed there wasn't going to be any—at least not at the moment. Almost five minutes passed before the coffee finished brewing. I rose, helped Trex put the pot of coffee on a tray, along with mugs, cream, and sugar. I brought it back to the table, and we both sat down. Trex poured for both of us. The coffee was strong, good.

"But I believe that the United States is—or was—truly unique," he said, picking up the thread of conversation as though no time had passed. "How's your history, Frederickson?"

"Assuredly not as good as yours."

"Somehow I tend to doubt that."

"I have a revisionist mentality; I'm skeptical of any account of any event that happened more recently than five hundred years ago."

He smiled, nodded. "Still, I think you'd agree that this nation of ours emerged from the Second World War indisputably the greatest economic and military power that had ever existed."

"No illusion there, Mr. Trex."

"The illusion was that our transcendent power as a nation meant that we were the greatest *people*."

Resisting the impulse to shrug, still wondering what Jack Trex wanted with me and what I was doing there, I said, "A not uncommon trait of most people in most nations, Mr. Trex. American chauvinism pales in comparison to that of at least a half dozen nations I could mention."

"But I bought it," Trex said in a low voice that seemed to be growing even raspier as he spoke, as if he had a cold. "I *believed* America was not only the mightiest but the *greatest* and *finest* nation, and that we were the finest, most noble people in all the world. It really made me very angry when people in this country, and even people who were citizens of other countries, didn't acknowledge this. I mean, it just seemed so *obvious* to me."

He paused and raised his eyebrows, obviously extending an invitation to respond. My response was to sip at my coffee as I met his gaze over the rim of my mug. His pale green eyes had begun to glow, and it struck me that Mr. Jack Trex had caught himself an obsession. He'd experienced an epiphany of sorts and was still struggling to come to terms with the brightness of his vision.

"I grew up Roman Catholic, Frederickson," the other man continued when he saw that I had nothing to say. "I remember sitting in Sunday school classes and listening to tapes of various sermons by American priests, bishops, and cardinals informing us not only that Roman Catholicism was the one true faith but that America was the nation finally chosen by God to be His headquarters. We Americans were to show the correct path to other nations and individuals that didn't see the absolute correctness of Christ and capitalism—and not necessarily in that order. We were the Redeemer Nation, and communism was the great enemy of man and God. We had been given permission by God, we were *expected* by God, to impose our beliefs and our way of life on the rest of the world. We knew best, and it was for their benefit. We were the Messiah of Nations, the defender of the oppressed. That was our illusion, Frederickson; but that image of ourselves went down the tubes in Vietnam. That's where and when first the soldiers fighting over there, and then the people back home, learned that so much of what we'd been led to believe about ourselves and our government is a lie, conjured up with smoke and mirrors. This government *lies*, Frederickson!"

"Don't they all?" I said quietly. "Except that governments don't lie; people lie. The more powerful the person, the more people his or her lies affect. I'm getting the impression, Mr. Trex, that somewhere along the line you discovered that American political, business, and religious leaders can lie with the best of them, and that this came as somewhat of a shock to you."

He stared at me for some time, stroking his mustache with a hand that had begun to tremble slightly. He noticed the trembling, abruptly gripped his mug with both hands. "Some men find a kind of state of grace in war, Frederickson; they can kill, maim, rape, and brutalize, and still feel good about themselves— sometimes better than they've ever felt about themselves. Not me. I lost both my leg and my faith over there. And it was my own fault, because I never realized that the weapons my own countrymen, our leaders, were using against me were more deadly than bombs, hand grenades, or bullets."

"Words," I said. "Lies. It's the language of cannibals."

Trex bowed his head, nodded slightly, and grunted with approval, as if I was a particularly bright student. "Yeah, that's right. Their goddamn lies swallowed the lives of more than fifty thousand American servicemen, God knows how many Vietnamese, Cambodians, and Laotians, and they ate away my leg."

"Mr. Trex, you must be some politician to have managed to get yourself elected commander of the local chapter of Vietnam Veterans of America."

He looked up quickly, and color rose in his cheeks. "Are you mocking me, Frederickson?"

"No, sir, I am not. I'm saying that people who attend the same school don't always receive the same lesson."

He ran a hand through his thinning, unkempt hair, shook his head. "Up until a little more than a year ago, most of the men in our chapter agreed with me. Like me, they'd never much thought about it before. When they did, when they listened to what I had to say, a lot of them came around to see what I meant."

"And then Elysius Culhane came to town with a brand-new smoke machine and more mirrors," I said in a flat voice.

Jack Trex leaned back in his chair, blinked slowly as he stared at me. I suspected that my status as star pupil was rapidly deteriorating. "Am I boring you, Frederickson?"

"No."

"You don't seem all that interested. Or maybe you disagree. Maybe I misread you."

"I don't know what you read."

"But you understood what my picture meant."

"I knew what *I* thought your picture meant. It was a nice way of visualizing an idea, Mr. Trex, but it's not exactly a new idea. It wasn't new with Orwell, and it wasn't new with Lenin. It probably started with some caveman who finally came to realize that his shaman was bullshitting him, and went looking for a new cave."

"It was new to me!"

"I understand that, Mr. Trex, and I respect that. For you, this realization that so-called leaders in all walks of life have been blowing smoke up your ass, trying to manipulate you all your life, astonished you. You're still astonished. You're still trying to come to terms with the fact that people you trusted have been trying to jerk you around with the language of cannibals, mesmerizing you with symbols—things like flags and music. I even suspect you still can't really believe the depths of that deception; maybe you feel like a fool." I paused, used my thumb to point to the overflowing desk and card table behind me. "It looks to me like you're really getting into the subject. Are you collecting samples of doublespeak, phrases like Department of Defense, Peacekeeper missile, and preemptive counterattack?"

"Yes," he said softly.

"You know what I think, Mr. Trex? I think the reason you find all this smoke and mirrors business so deeply disturbing is that you still, in your own way, buy into the notion that America is somehow unique among nations. You were terribly hurt by this betrayal by your leaders and the country's institutions. You're *still* hurt. You should stop. You've identified the dog that bit you, and it's enough; it's a mean dog, so you should stop worrying it and get on with things."

"Aren't you proud to be an American?"

"I feel *lucky* to be an American, because being an American means that I have greater freedom than many to do things that I'm proud of. Sometimes I'm proud of what our elected leaders do, sometimes not. There are a lot of dogs in the world a hell of a lot meaner than the one that bit you. There are no equivalents in politics to the painter, writer, musician, or sculptor, Mr. Trex. What motivates people to try to gain power over other people is the same thing that drives them to use the language of cannibals. Understanding that won't bring your leg back, but it could ease your sense of betrayal and hurt."

Jack Trex picked up the coffeepot with a hand that continued to tremble slightly, refilled both our mugs. "I got married the month before I went to Vietnam, Frederickson," he said in a low voice. "My wife was an alcoholic—hell, I was probably an alcoholic, too, but just wouldn't admit to it. My son Gregory was born with what the doctors call infant alcohol syndrome."

"I'm familiar with it," I said evenly, watching pain and shame march across the other man's face.

"Gregory was diagnosed as being mildly retarded, Frederickson. I found out about it when I got back. He was only a little more than a year old at the time. I think he might have been all right under other circumstances, but what really messed him up were his messed-up parents. I didn't know it yet, because the term hadn't been invented, but I was suffering from post-traumatic stress syndrome. I was really fucked up, feeling terror one moment and rage the next. I couldn't work, couldn't sleep—couldn't do much of anything. I sure as hell couldn't manage to be any kind of father. I was drunk most of the time, and I did a lot of drugs. You know what? It was the meetings at the Community of Conciliation that first helped me start get myself together. That's when I began to get it clear in my head what had happened. I laid off the booze and drugs, but it was too late. My wife died of a drug overdose when Gregory was only four years old."

He paused and turned away, but not before I had seen tears glisten in his pale eyes. I shifted uncomfortably in my chair, averted my gaze.

"Gregory was eventually taken away from me," he finally

continued. "They put him in a home not far from here. They said he was emotionally disturbed as well as retarded. I vowed I was always going to stand by him, to help him in any way I could. I'd lost, or helped to destroy, everything else; I wasn't going to throw away my son."

"Mr. Trex," I said quietly, studying the wall to my right, "I'm no mental health expert, but in my opinion your son needs professional help badly. He needs intensive therapy, maybe medication, and maybe even hospitalization for a time."

"I know that, Frederickson," Trex said in a strong, flat voice.

I looked back at him, found him looking at me. Tears glistened on his cheeks, but his eyes were now dry. "Then why don't you do something about it?"

"I . . . can't. He's of age. He refuses to even talk about going to a therapist or taking medication again. In order to hospitalize him I'd have to get a court order, and there's no guarantee I'd succeed."

"You could try."

"Gregory would never forgive me if I did that, Frederickson. Somehow, I have to find some other way to bring him around. You see, he doesn't think there's anything wrong with him, and he's surrounded by people who don't think there's anything wrong with him. He thinks there's something wrong with me. The people he hangs around with all feed into his fantasies. Their words are going to . . ."

"Does Gregory live at home, Mr. Trex?"

Jack Trex slowly shook his head. "He did—up until a few months ago. Now he lives in an apartment that's subsidized by Elysius Culhane."

"Does he work?"

"Odd jobs for Culhane—mowing the lawn, raking leaves, that kind of thing. That's another reason I don't think I could get a court order for Gregory's hospitalization; Culhane would have it quashed. I just don't dare try."

"Mr. Trex," I said evenly, pushing my coffee mug away, "I don't understand why you're telling me all this. Just why did you want to see me?"

Trex pushed his mug across the table until it clicked up against mine. He wiped at his mustache, met my gaze. "I want to ask you please not to kill my son."

The words caught me so completely by surprise that I could do nothing but stare back dumbfounded into the anguished face of the man sitting across from me.

"I've found out some things about you, Frederickson," Trex continued quickly, his words now tumbling over one another. "I know about your reputation. People like my son who don't know you and don't take you seriously because you're a dwarf make a big mistake. Sometimes a fatal mistake. I know you've killed men; I think you've killed more men than I have, and I was in a combat unit. I know you could have killed Gregory last night. I can see that you're hurting, and I know Gregory did that to you. Maybe it would have served him right if you had killed him, but you didn't, and I thank you for that."

"Mr. Trex," I said when I finally managed to collect my thoughts and find my voice, "I don't plan on killing anybody."

"Please hear me out. Gregory's a very sick young man."

"He's not so sick that he doesn't know what he's doing, Mr. Trex. All of us have to be responsible for our own actions; that's the antidote to the language of cannibals."

"Gregory is a victim of Vietnam, Frederickson, just as surely as I am, and just as surely as the fifty-five thousand Americans who died over there. I was so busy with the smoke and mirrors that I couldn't be a proper father to him. I know Gregory. He won't be able to live with what you did to him last night. He'll come after you; he'll keep coming after you. That's why I'm asking— begging—you not to kill him, to try . . . to find some other way."

I sighed. "Will he come for me in New York?"

Jack Trex shook his head. "No. He's actually afraid to go into the city. Gregory never goes far from Cairn. This is his turf, if you will; he feels safe here, in control."

"Then your son is safe from me, Mr. Trex. You don't have to worry. I'm leaving Cairn."

Trex swallowed hard, nodded with relief. "Thank you. I didn't want to suggest . . . but I was hoping for that. May I, uh, ask when you're leaving?"

"As soon as I leave here," I said, rising to my feet. He pushed himself up, braced himself with his left hand on the table as he extended his right. "Thanks for the coffee, Mr. Trex. Good luck to you."

I walked to the door, hesitated with my hand on the knob, turned back. Jack Trex was staring at me, a drawn, haunted expression on his face. "Mr. Trex," I continued, "what do you think of the idea that there's some kind of death squad operating in the towns along the river?"

He thought about it, and his brows knitted in a puzzled frown. "Death squad? What do you mean, 'death squad'?"

"Never mind," I said, and left the house.

Walking back up the driveway, I found I was not only depressed by my strange conversation with the driven Jack Trex but also deeply disturbed for reasons I was not sure I fully understood.

CHAPTER FIVE

It was not quite noon, and it was an easy Saturday drive down the Palisades Parkway and across the George Washington Bridge into Manhattan. I drove down the West Side, then over to the brownstone on West Fifty-sixth, a block over from Carnegie Hall, where Frederickson and Frederickson's offices and living quarters were located. I parked Beloved Too in the brownstone's underground garage, retrieved the plastic shopping bag containing Mary Tree's demo tapes from the trunk, and went looking for my brother. I found him in our basement mini-gym laying out our softball uniforms and equipment. We both played on a team we sponsored in one league, as well as on another team in another league; Garth led one league in home runs, and I led both leagues in number of walks. We were supposed to play a doubleheader the next day.

My brother had changed greatly in the past few years, I thought as I watched him sit down on a weight bench and begin to oil a glove. And not without reason. We had both been hammered good, both physically and psychologically, in the course of investigating a string of related cases that had turned nasty and bizarre on us. But Garth had been hammered more, and a poisoning he suffered had bent both his body and his mind. He'd emerged from that searing experience a mellower man in many ways; but he was considerably harder in other ways, and quite different from the much-honored NYPD detective he'd been for almost two decades. I considered him an almost perfect empath, with an uncanny ability to understand and feel the suffering of other people, and then to reach out and soothe them.

Loonies loved my brother, as did people who were down and out, or on their way there. With life's losers and hurting, he was the gentlest of men. If, on the other hand, you happened to be a person who caused others to suffer, Garth was a good person to avoid. He brooked no nonsense, did not suffer fools at all gladly, and no longer bothered reading bad guys their rights; when really worked up, he took no prisoners.

He now wore his thinning, wheat-colored hair long, sometimes in a ponytail held in place by a thin leather thong. In addition, he had a full beard liberally streaked with silver and gray. The effect of all this hair was to frame his limpid hazel eyes, which could be startling in their gleaming expressiveness—of love, sorrow, or rage; when Garth was upset, you knew it. Fortunately, the occasions on which he really grew angry were rare, for his reactions could be astonishingly quick and brutal. He now seemed to me to be a kind of emotionally polarized human being who lit up brightly at both ends of the emotional spectrum, but could seem dull emotionally to many people when he was in the middle. He could seem virtually Christ-like when dealing with people in need; indeed, with his long hair and limpid eyes I thought he even resembled some pop artist's conception of Jesus—assuming the artist's Jesus was over six feet and upwards of a hundred and ninety pounds of finely toned muscle.

"Yo, brother," Garth said, looking up as I limped across the room toward him. "You look a bit stiff."

"How observant you are today. I look a bit stiff because I am a bit stiff."

"What happened?"

"Nothing earth-shattering; I'm just getting old. But I'm not going to be able to play tomorrow. Can you get Ratso or Willy to sub for me?"

He nodded. "So, did you get to ask your questions?"

"Yep."

"And?"

"I've got good news, and I've got bad news."

Garth set the glove and the jar of oil aside, looked at me, and frowned. "Are you all right, brother?"

"Yeah. Just stiff."

"In that case, give me the good news first."

"I met Mary Tree. Damned if the love of your life isn't a long-term member of the Community of Conciliation who lives in that mansion of theirs in Cairn. As a matter of fact, I spent the better part of an hour talking to her. I told her what a fan you are, and she sent something for you."

Garth stared at me for some time, his mouth hanging slightly open. He finally managed to say, "Huh? Are you serious?"

"Here," I said, handing him the plastic bag. "These are for you."

My brother took the bag, held it open by its plastic straps, and peered inside. "You really met Mary Tree?" His voice was almost childlike.

"Yes, Garth," I replied, smiling, "I really met Mary Tree. Why don't you ask me what you're looking at?"

"What am I looking at?"

"Demo tapes; all new songs by Mary Tree, Harry Peal, and Dylan, performed by the light and love of your life. She mentioned that she's preparing a new album, but I'd guess that there's enough music in there for three albums. She thought you might enjoy a sneak preview. Oh, and by the way, she's invited us both up for a day of picnicking and sailing. If you can refrain from trying to jump her bones the moment you lay eyes on her, I'll bet she can even be persuaded to take out her guitar for a little sing-along."

Garth looked up at me, his hazel eyes gleaming—a small boy on Christmas morning when he first sees the gifts under the tree. "Holy shit," he whispered.

"Close your mouth, Garth; it makes you look stupid. Also, try to remember to breathe; I don't think you're breathing."

He dismissed my helpful suggestions with a wave of his hand, then reached down into the bag and took out one of the cardboard-jacketed reels, lovingly turned it over in his fingers. "Mongo, she signed it. Mary Tree."

"Sure enough," I said, and broke into laughter. Unaffected joy radiated from my brother like fever heat, and it was impossible not to be affected by and share in it. "What, did you think I was bullshitting you?"

"Holy shit."

I watched him reverently place the one tape down on a folded towel on the bench, then reach into the bag and take out another one. "Are you ready for the bad news?"

"Huh?" he said in a distinctly absent tone of voice. "Yeah, sure."

"The bad news is that your fly is open, your dong is hanging out, and the tip is covered with a thick, green fungus. It looks like New York City jungle rot to me, incurable. I'd say the whole thing is going to fall off in three or four days."

Garth glanced up from the tape, blinked slowly, shook his head slightly. "I'm sorry, brother. What did you say?"

I threw a heavy sigh at him and rolled my eyes toward the ceiling. "That was just a test to see if you were paying attention. You're not. How the hell am I supposed to give you bad news when you're not paying attention?"

Garth grinned, then picked up the tape off the towel and carefully placed it back into the plastic bag. He rose, put one hand on the back of my neck, kissed me wetly and loudly on the forehead. "Fuck the bad news," he said as he stepped around me and headed for the door. "As long as you're not seriously hurting, you can handle the bad news. I've got some serious music listening to attend to."

Okay.

I spent the rest of the afternoon attending to my paperwork, analyzing and condensing crude private intelligence reports on some Arab potentates that a client of ours, an oil company, was thinking of trying to cut a deal with. Through all the hours, the music of Mary Tree wafted up from Garth's apartment on the floor below; the floorboards tended to wipe out the treble and boost the bass, but the music still sounded excellent, and by the third run-through of the tapes I found myself singing along with half the songs.

At seven I took a break, went out, and walked a few blocks in an effort to try to loosen up my stiff knee. I stopped at a deli for a roast beef sandwich and some salad, then returned to my desk.

Mary Tree called at 10:45. She apologized for the lateness of the hour, but said she thought that I would want to know right away that Harry Peal would be happy to meet with me the next day and had suggested that I come up around 11:30 for brunch. She gave me directions. I thanked her, told her that Garth was ecstatic over her gift, said I'd be in touch, and hung up.

I wanted to fill Garth in on what was happening, but the silence from the apartment below told me that he was surely sleeping, and I didn't think it was important enough to wake him. I set my alarm for eight, took two aspirin, and went to bed.

• • •

I stopped in Garth's apartment on my way out, found that he had already left for the softball games. I left a note explaining that I was going back upstate to take care of some unfinished business, and asking him to check with his NYPD buddies for impressions of and information on one Daniel Mosely, former NYPD cop, and now Cairn's chief of police. Then I rolled Beloved Too out of the garage and headed for the West Side Highway.

A lot of people, it seemed, were out for a little Sunday day-tripping. Traffic was heavy and slow-moving, and it gave me a lot of time to think; what I thought about mostly was the man I was going to see.

I'd lost a lot of heroes over the years, but two remained. The first was my brother. Garth had, both literally and figuratively, carried his dwarf brother on his broad shoulders throughout said dwarf brother's tormented childhood and adolescence, had, along with our mother and father, tenderly nurtured the fairly bright mind of a child and young man who could not understand, deep down in that part of him where rational thought ceases and explanations are useless, why his body would not grow as other people's bodies grew. As a child I learned a thing or two about human cruelty, and it was only because of the love and understanding of my parents and Garth that I reached adulthood and took control of my own life with mind and heart, if not exactly unscathed, at least not hopelessly crippled.

Harry Peal was a hero of another sort. In my opinion, he was a quintessential American, and he had carried the conscience and best ideals of an entire nation on his frail shoulders for more than five decades. A communist at a time when a good many decent people thought that communism offered the best hope for a nation being crushed in the coils of a merciless economic depression, Harry Peal had traveled the Dust Bowl with Woody Guthrie, gone down into the Pennsylvania coal mines with men who were dying of black-lung disease, stood on picket lines in teeming rain and freezing cold—all the while singing, and capturing in his songs not only pride in a magnificent land and its people, but also crying the need for social and economic change.

No pacifist, Harry Peal; he had fought in the Lincoln Brigade in Spain and was a combat veteran of World War II, having volunteered for the Marine Corps. When Stalin crawled into bed with Hitler, and news of the massive purges and the Gulag began to leak out of the East, Harry promptly and forthrightly severed his ties with the American Communist party. If his dream of a better America and a better world through communism had been shattered and brutally betrayed by Mother Russia, he would not betray his own ideals or his friends or his onetime political comrades; he cheerfully but firmly refused to cooperate with the HUAC and later refused to cooperate with the McCarthy committee, both times explaining that if he had a taste for trials, witch-hunts—even for real witches—and purges, he would have remained a communist. He'd said that he was not afraid of them, because they couldn't make him stop writing and singing songs, and that he didn't have much to lose because he never made that much money doing what he did anyway. And so this combat veteran, winner of two Silver Stars, had been sent to prison twice.

Harry Peal was one of the first to protest against the war in Vietnam, had laid his body as well as his songs on the line in the struggle for civil rights, and had been in the forefront of the fight for better working conditions for migrant workers. He was still tossed into jail on occasion in connection with some demonstration or another, but for the past fifteen years he had been devoting all his time, royalties, performance fees, and growing prestige to the problem of cleaning up America's polluted lakes, rivers, and landscapes.

At least a dozen of his songs had become classics; he had become a classic. The right wing, of course, still hated him almost as much as they hated Roosevelt, but this was perfectly understandable and only served to put Harry Peal in good company; along with Pete Seeger, who had made cleaning up the Hudson River his own personal crusade, Harry Peal had proved to be a durable thorn in the sides of the kinds of "conservative" businessmen and factory owners who considered it their God-given right, if not their patriotic duty, to pour acid over the face of America in the pursuit of greater profits. Garth and I had been at the White House dinner where President Kevin Shannon presented Harry Peal with the Medal of Freedom for his work in leading the fight to clean up the environment. Harry Peal's was a ferocious integrity. If, to my mind, his politics and loyalties had always tended just a bit toward the mushy-minded, he was still, to my mind, a great American patriot who loved the land of his birth far more than most of his detractors, with their star-spangled invective.

Following Mary Tree's precise directions, I turned off Route 9W about ten miles north of Cairn and drove down a winding dirt road that led toward the river. Virtually at the end of the road, there was a mailbox with the name PEAL scrawled on it in red paint. I turned in the driveway, came to a stop beside a modest, freshly painted clapboard house with an enormous screened-in porch that rested on a ledge overlooking the Hudson, three hundred feet below.

As soon as I got out of the car, Harry Peal emerged from the house and hurried across a small expanse of lawn toward me. Age had bowed his back slightly, but had not reached his legs; although he was close to eighty years old, his gait was springy, lithe. He had a full head of white hair that nicely complemented his pale blue eyes; as he rushed to greet me, his face was wreathed in the simple smile that always made him look to me like Santa Claus on a diet. He was dressed in a variation of what I thought of as his "uniform"—clothes he wore everywhere, whether singing for a group of migrant workers in a dusty field or on the stage of Carnegie Hall, eating a potluck supper with striking union workers or being honored with a state dinner at the White House. He wore baggy jeans, fine boots of supple Spanish leather, and a worn, faded flannel shirt with the sleeves rolled up just past his elbows. A hand-carved wooden flute stuck out of his shirt pocket. As he reached me, I extended my hand; he shook it, then gripped both my shoulders.

"Mongo Frederickson," Harry Peal said, his smile growing even broader. "It's a pleasure to meet you."

"And it's an honor to meet you, Mr. Peal."

The old man with the heart and spirit of a child laughed loudly and shook me by the shoulders; pain shot down through my left arm, but I tried my best not to show it. "*Mr.* Peal? Do I look like a banker? My name's Harry."

"Okay, Harry," I said, suppressing a sigh of relief when he finally released his grip on my shoulders. "I appreciate your willingness to see me. I know you just got back from Europe, and you must be suffering from jet lag."

He dismissed the suggestion with a wave of one liver-spotted hand. "I've got no time for jet lag; I leave for Africa in the morning. Come on, we'll have something to eat on the porch."

I followed him across the narrow expanse of lawn between the house and driveway, entered the porch through a screen door that he held open for me. A wooden table set flush against the screening had been covered with a red-and-white-checkered tablecloth. On the table were a basket of fruit, a wooden board displaying a variety of cheeses, a loaf of bread that smelled as if it had just come from the oven, a large earthenware jug, and two place settings. Harry Peal motioned for me to sit in the chair on his left, and I did. He poured me a glassful of an amber, sparkling liquid from the jug. It turned out to be hard—very hard—cider, tangy and aromatic, with a pleasant little kick.

"Good," I said, raising the glass in salute. "I assume you make it yourself?"

"Yep," he said proudly, sitting down beside me and pouring himself a glass. "I store it in an underground herb cellar at the side of the house. It sits there through the winter and spring and starts tasting pretty good about this time of year." He pushed the loaf of bread and cheeseboard in front of me. "Mary give you good directions?"

"Perfect," I replied, helping myself to a piece of Gruyère. I tore off a chunk of bread, put the cheese and bread down on my plate, turned to face the other man. "Harry, did she tell you why I wanted to see you?"

He sipped at his cider, then pointed to his left ear. "My hearing isn't what it used to be, and I'm not sure I got all of it clear. She said it had something to do with the death of that nice FBI fellow who came to visit me."

"Michael Burana. He was a friend of mine."

Harry Peal shook his head. "I didn't know about it until Mary told me. Drowned in the river, I think she said. That's a real tragedy. Like I said, I thought he was a real nice fellow. The FBI could use more nice fellows like him."

"Harry," I said carefully, watching his seamed face, "did Mary tell you that I think Michael was murdered?"

He had raised a cheese-topped hunk of bread halfway to his mouth; now he put the bread down on the plate, looked at me with pale blue eyes that reflected shock and what I was certain was fear. He had gone pale. "Murdered?"

"Yes. I'm certain somebody killed him."

"Oh, boy," he said, passing a hand that had begun to tremble across his forehead. He took the wooden flute from his pocket and began to absently roll it back and forth between his fingers. "Boy, oh boy."

I'd definitely struck a deep and responsive chord in Harry Peal, but I wasn't at all sure just what that chord was. To hear that a man he'd met and liked had been murdered had to be shocking, to a degree, but I read the man's reaction as considerably more than that. Still trembling, he abruptly rose, walked around the table, and stood at the screen, looking down at the river. He raised the flute to his lips, began to play. The tune was melancholy and haunting, and I recognized it from one of his many albums as a Russian folk song. The sense of fear radiating from the other man was even stronger now. Harry Peal was not a man easily frightened, and it suddenly struck me that he could be afraid for someone, or something, other than himself.

"Harry?"

The old man finished the tune, put the flute back into his shirt pocket, and turned to face me. He still looked deeply shaken. "I'm sorry, Mongo," he said quietly. "I didn't mean to be rude. What you said kind of shook me up; when I get shook up, I just naturally take a dose of music to calm me down."

"What is it, Harry? What's the matter?"

He shook his head. "Mongo, I . . . You're sure this FBI fellow was murdered?"

"In my own mind, yes. I have no doubt."

"And you think this . . . killing . . . could have something to do with me?"

That was it, I thought. What Harry Peal feared was the possibility that he might be responsible for another man's death. "It might have something to do with something you said to him when he came to visit you, Harry. I'm not sure." I paused as he again took his flute from his pocket and began to play, then continued, raising my voice slightly so as to be heard above the soft, lilting, breathy notes issuing from the instrument. "Michael Burana was killed sometime in the evening of the day he came to visit you, Harry, which was a week ago today. Mary told me he seemed very distracted when he came back from seeing you. She said he'd used the word *unbelievable* in describing the conversation he'd had with you, but he never told her what that conversation was about. I know it's none of my business, but I'd like you to tell me just what it was you talked about. It may have nothing at all to do with Michael's murder, but I'd like to hear about it so that I can try to judge."

Harry Peal returned to the table, slumped in his chair, placed the flute on the table next to his plate, and absently rolled it back and forth beneath his palm. "That FBI fellow and I had ourselves quite a chat," he said after a time, in a soft voice. "Back in the sixties, he used to spend a lot of time following me around, listening to my phone conversations, and opening my mail."

"I know," I replied evenly. I felt a rising impatience, but knew that I had to let the folksinger and peace activist tell his story in his own way, in his own time.

"He told me he was sick and tired of that kind of work—spying on people just because they don't like government policy, and say so. He told me he thought the FBI was wasting a lot of time, money, and manpower doing that sort of thing and that he'd prefer they just chase after crooks, spies, terrorists, and neo-Nazis. He also didn't care much for the Bureau's personnel policies, and he even suggested that sometimes it almost seemed like some people at the Bureau were intentionally hiring racists, doing things to lower morale and spread their forces thin."

"Michael had grown a little bitter, Harry. Why on earth would anyone at the FBI do that? Did you ask him?"

The old man shrugged. "He couldn't think of a reason; he was just fed up. The last straw was when he was assigned to spy on Mary's people down there in Cairn. He said it was just another waste of time and that he was tired of throwing away the taxpayers' money. He felt humiliated, and he said he was quitting the FBI. He didn't sound like much of a pacifist to me, but he said he wanted to go to work for the Community of Concilia-tion. It was the damnedest thing, Mongo. I found myself in the position of saying some kind words about the FBI, arguing that just because they sometimes picked the wrong targets didn't mean that they weren't needed. It was pretty strange. By this time we'd both had a pretty good ration of that cider, and here was Harry Peal, not exactly the darling of federal agencies, defending the FBI, while this FBI agent was telling me in no uncertain terms that the Bureau was nothing but a fascist outfit. I reminded him that I *had* been a communist, and so I knew what I was talking about when I said that the Russians, at least at the time when I was a party member, fully expected to set up a world government that they would control, and they hadn't much cared what means they used to create it. I never wanted to blow anything up, but at that time I was meeting a lot of fellow party members who did. Anyway, I'd had something on my mind for a time, and . . . I'm thinking now that I should have kept it to myself."

"Harry," I prompted gently, "what did you say to Michael that he might later have described as 'unbelievable'?"

The old man shook his head, picked up the bread and cheese he had set aside, and began nibbling at it as he stared off into space. I waited, and finally my patience was rewarded. He finished the food, took a long swallow of the cider, and then began speaking in a low voice.

"Back in the thirties, when I was still in the party, the Russians sent over a cadre officer, a woman, to help us reorganize our New York cell. Supposedly she was to help us to become more effective in recruiting, but she was really there to make sure we understood the Russian Communist party line and toed it. She was a propaganda and indoctrination specialist, and her job was to constantly remind us that we were communists first and foremost, and Americans second. Her name was Olga Koussevitsky." He paused, looked at me, and smiled tightly. "She may have been an ideologue, Mongo, and she was most certainly KGB, but she was a beautiful ideologue. Spoke perfect English, and she was one tough cookie. She and I ended up spending a lot of time together, probably because she felt I was in particular need of ideological guidance; I was always questioning the need for the Russians to be in charge of everything. I'd tell her I was an *American* communist, and then she'd take me for long walks so she could tell me how misguided and deviant I was. Anyway, damned if we didn't fall in love. We even moved into an apartment together. She got pregnant, and I asked her to marry me. She agreed, on the condition that the party give her permission. They didn't; her Russian bosses told her that she was too important to the movement to marry anyone and that they'd received reports that I was a suspect communist to boot. She was ordered to return to Russia, and she obeyed. She was eight months pregnant when she left. I never saw or heard from her again."

When he paused again and looked away, I reached out and touched his arm. "Harry, I'm sorry."

He nodded, turned back to me. "A couple of months ago—in May, maybe early June—I was sitting out here on the porch, noodling on my guitar and trying to come up with some new tunes, when I see this big yacht steam on by below. I found out later that the yacht belongs to that guy who sounds like a Nazi on radio and television, a nasty fellow with a funny first name."

"Elysius Culhane?"

"That's the one. Anyway, it was a pretty warm day, and one of the men on the yacht had his shirt off; he was lying on his stomach near the bow, sunning himself. I looked, and couldn't believe what I thought I saw, so I went and got my binoculars for a better look. Sure enough, this man had a big blue birthmark spreading across his left shoulder and down over his shoulder blade. I told the FBI fellow about what I saw—probably because I'd had too much cider to drink. Now I'm thinking maybe I should have kept my mouth shut, like I'd intended; now I'm thinking I may be responsible for that nice fellow's death."

"I'm sorry, Harry. I don't understand."

Harry Peal's response was to unbutton his flannel shirt, pull it down to his waist, and then turn his back to me. I stared, transfixed, at the discoloration of his skin; splashing across his left shoulder, bleeding down over the shoulder blade, was a huge, raised birthmark, almost as blue as the sky. Although the rest of his skin was dry, the puffy blue flesh of the birthmark was exuding droplets of perspiration.

"That mark's called a blue rubber bleb nevus," he said over his shoulder in a low voice. "It's a genetic trait that runs strong in the Peal family. Just about every Peal has one. Of course, it's not just the Peals, but a blue rubber bleb nevus is very rare. It can appear anywhere on the torso or even cover the whole torso. This man had his same place as mine, and it was the same size."

Suddenly my mouth was very dry. I swallowed hard, said, "Boy, oh boy."

He pulled his shirt back on and buttoned it up, then turned around to face me. "I was pretty upset when I saw that guy with the birthmark, Mongo. I didn't know what to do, and I sure as hell didn't think the government needed or wanted Harry Peal to tell them their business. I kept telling myself that I didn't know what it meant and that I had no business spreading information when I didn't know the whole story; when you've had as many people informing on you as I have, it's kind of hard to turn informer yourself. So I just kept it to myself—but it bothered me. I was still debating whether or not to say anything to anybody when this FBI friend of yours came to see me. I ended up telling him, because I finally decided that the FBI should know."

My mouth and throat were still dry. I cleared my throat, and when that didn't help took a long swallow of the hard cider. "Harry, do you know the name of the man with the birthmark that you saw on Elysius Culhane's boat?"

"Jay Acton. I found that out when I found out who the yacht

belonged to. But that can't be his real name, because he was certainly born in Russia."

I felt slightly light-headed, and I knew it had nothing to do with the cider. Now when I looked at Harry Peal, I could see the resemblance. Jay Acton would have gotten his dark eyes from his mother, but he shared with his father smallish ears, high cheekbones, a strong mouth and chin. I rose from the chair, extended my hand. "I have to go, Harry. I think I have some idea of what you felt when you saw that birthmark on Acton, and I think I have some idea of how it tore your guts to tell Michael and me. I thank you."

He took my hand in both of his, gripped it hard. "Mongo, do you think my son killed the FBI fellow? Do you think my boy is a murderer?"

"I'm sorry, Harry, but I wouldn't be at all surprised. Things are certainly starting to point in that direction. I intend to find out for sure."

"Don't go getting yourself killed, Mongo."

"I don't plan to, Harry."

CHAPTER SIX

I was back home by 2:30. The official offices of Frederickson and Frederickson occupy the first two floors of our brownstone, and I went directly to my office on the first floor. I sat down in front of my computer terminal, plugged in my modem, and went to work. We paid out close to three hundred dollars a month for subscriptions to various computer newsletters and services—most of them perfectly legitimate, with only a couple of questionable legality. We'd taken courses, and even had our own hack-on-call, a very young computer whiz who'd barely missed getting a ten-year prison sentence for breaking into a Defense Department network and leaving a series of "Have a nice day" messages in both English and Russian. It was an age of electronic snooping, and Frederickson and Frederickson had taken pains not to get caught with its PCs down. But there was nothing particularly arcane about what I was up to at the moment. As a licensed private investigator, I was legally entitled to use the DMV network. I entered the appropriate code, then punched up the name of Jay Acton. I was in luck; he had a driver's license, and he owned a car. Within a minute I had his Social Security number.

Next, I consulted one of my quasi-legal newsletters, found the appropriate code, and invited myself into a network used by most of the nation's health insurance companies. It turned out that Jay Acton had health insurance provided through a right-wing think tank with which Elysius Culhane was associated. According to his application form, Acton was born on October 23, 1939, in Dayton, Ohio.

Sure.

Curious as to what the FBI might have on Olga Koussevitsky, I tried tapping into a network used for counterintelligence historical files but got nowhere. They'd changed the pass code in Washington, and I was going to have to wait for next week's mail to find out what the new code was. And if I couldn't get into the file, I had contacts in both the FBI and CIA who could get me the data I needed. Given enough time, acting on the information Harry Peal had given me, I was certain I could piece together a scenario of how Harry Peal's son was born in Russia and then smuggled back into the United States with his English-speaking mom to grow up as Jay Acton, All-American Boy. Except that this all-American boy would have a KGB mother to constantly indoctrinate him in communist ideology and fill him with a special sense of purpose and mission—to be a spy.

Or something like that.

I turned off the computer, leaned back in my swivel chair, and considered what I would do next—assuming I wanted to—in order to prove that Jay Acton was a KGB officer. The first step would be to prove that his birth records were phony. There are any number of ways to construct a false identity, and they have grown increasingly sophisticated over the years. Presumably, I would actually have to go to Dayton to check hospital birth records, and then pore over death records and walk through graveyards, to search for a real Jay Acton who might have died at, or soon after, birth, on October 23, 1939. I would try to find out the address or addresses where the "Actons" had lived, look over school records, talk to his teachers, and so on.

The work of proving that Jay Acton was a KGB ringer would be time-consuming but fairly routine. It could also prove to be perilous. I was not exactly an inconspicuous personage, and even if I could go to Dayton and begin traipsing through Jay Acton's past without calling attention to myself it was quite possible that there were "trip wires" embedded in the matrix of false records I would have to untangle; request a certain file, or question the wrong person, and a warning signal could be flashed to Russia or to Cairn. By the time I'd gathered enough information to drive a stake through this particular vampire's heart, he might well have flown from his coffin and be safely ensconced in a dacha on the Black Sea while he tried to become accustomed to Russian culture. I didn't want to take that responsibility.

I knew I already had more than enough to get the attention and help of Mr. Lippitt, our ageless and trusted friend who was the director of the Defense Intelligence Agency. The problem was that this kind of counterintelligence activity was clearly the province of the FBI. Mr. Lippitt would eventually feel constrained to contact Edward J. Hendricks anyway, and then I would have put the man to whom both Garth and I owed our lives in the uncomfortable position of having stepped on some very big, sensitive, and powerful toes. I didn't want to do that, and I didn't feel that I had to. This was, after all, the FBI's job, not mine or Mr. Lippitt's.

In addition, I wanted to make certain that Michael Burana would catch some favorable publicity. He'd taken the heat and suffered disgrace for losing a CIA defector, and now I wanted to see that he received credit for unmasking the man who was most certainly his murderer.

I opened the bottom right drawer in my desk, rummaged around until I found what I was looking for—a manila folder containing a sheaf of papers that had been stapled together. It was a list that was not available from any subscription service, and that money could not buy. In its original form it was called the Green Sheet, a designation that had always mystified me since it was not a sheet, but a half-inch-thick directory, and its cover was not green but beige. It was a classified directory listing the private home numbers of virtually every important politician and bureaucrat in the federal government. My first copy of the directory had been delivered to me two Christmases before, by special messenger, with no information as to who might have sent it. I received an update every three months, hand-delivered in the same manner. Garth and I had a pretty good idea who was responsible for this rather nice gift, and it wasn't Mr. Lippitt, who would never be so vulgar as to send us a copy of a classified document. We were certain that it arrived through the auspices of President Kevin Shannon; a little token of appreciation from the man who knew that his election, and subsequent continuance in office, depended upon our mutual cooperation—a conspiracy of silence about events surrounding his initial choice for secretary of state, a man who had turned out to be a murderous psychopath.

So much for history and Green Sheets. I thumbed through the directory until I found the home telephone number of Edward J. Hendricks, picked up the phone, and dialed it.

Hendricks answered on the fourth ring. "Hello, Jerry," he said in a lazy, Sunday afternoon voice. "What's happening on the—"

"This isn't Jerry, Mr. Hendricks. My name is Dr. Robert Frederickson. I apologize for calling you at home on a Sun—"

"*Who* is this?" he snapped in a distinctly Monday morning voice.

"Robert Frederickson."

There was a pause, then a tentative, "The dwarf?"

"That's the one. I—"

"How did you get this number, Frederickson?"

"Mr. Hendricks, you've got a KGB officer advising the most influential conservative columnist and television talking head in this country, namely Elysius Culhane. Culhane is having notions whispered in his ear by a Russian spy, who, in turn, is probably privy to all the nation's secrets that we both know are leaked to Culhane by right-wing congressmen and disgruntled generals at the Pentagon. As head of the FBI's counterintelligence unit, I thought you would appreciate getting the information as soon as possible—that's assuming you don't already know about it."

The sound of wheels turning in Edward J. Hendrick's head transcribed as almost a half minute of heavy, rasping breathing. Finally he said, "What are you talking about, Frederickson?"

"Michael Burana wasn't in touch with you concerning a Russian spy operating out of Cairn?"

"No," he replied in the same breathy voice, as if he were out of wind. "Tell me what you're talking about."

"As I'm sure you're aware, Elysius Culhane's top aide and

advisor is a man by the name of Jay Acton. That isn't his real name. His mother is, or was, a KGB officer named Olga Koussevitsky, and he was born somewhere in Russia, not Dayton, Ohio, which is what's listed on his American passport. Incidentally, Agent Burana did all the preliminary field work on this. I accidentally found his notes while I was going through his effects for his family, and I came across this information. He must have been planning on getting it all down pat before he filed his report. Anyway, when I saw what he'd uncovered, I knew I should contact you right away. Also, Agent Burana's death wasn't an accident; Acton had to have murdered him. I'll get this information off to you by express mail first thing in the morning, but in the meantime I expect you'll want to put Acton on ice while—"

"Frederickson, have you been doing any investigation of this matter on your own?"

"No," I said, surprised and somewhat taken aback by his tone. The raspiness was gone from his voice, and his tone was firm, decisive. He sounded as if he'd made some kind of decision—one I suspected I wasn't going to like. "I just told you that I'm working from Michael Burana's field notes."

"Have you spoken to anyone else about this matter?"

"No, Mr. Hendricks," I replied evenly. "I immediately recognized that this was a serious matter for the FBI to handle and that you'd want to start working on it immediately. As for arresting Acton, the name of the chief of police in Cairn is—"

"What about your good friend Mr. Lippitt? Have you spoken to him about this?"

"No," I replied tersely. "If you'll check the file I'm sure the FBI keeps on me, I think you'll find I'm—"

"I know all I need to know about you, Frederickson, from reputation and from the company you keep in this liberal administration. I want you to listen to me very, very carefully. The FBI appreciates your cooperation, but as of this moment the matter is entirely out of your jurisdiction. Agent Burana obviously did good work, and you've done good work. We'll handle it from here."

"Sir, Agent Burana was a friend of mine, and he was murdered. May I ask—?"

"You may ask nothing, Frederickson. You will speak to no one else about this matter, and you will do absolutely no further investigation on your own. It could be dangerous; if this man is indeed a KGB operative, we could lose him."

"I'm aware of that, sir."

"Consider everything concerning this matter classified—which it will be as soon as we conclude our conversation. I'm sure you're aware of the penalties that could be involved if you don't handle yourself properly."

Edward J. Hendricks, director of the counterintelligence unit of the FBI, was beginning to try my patience. "You wait a goddamn minute, Hendricks," I said in a less than cheery tone. "Do you have a policy of threatening patriotic citizens who call to provide you with valuable information about Russian spies in this country?"

"I'm not the only person in Washington who has questions about your loyalty, Frederickson. But your patriotism, or lack of it, is irrelevant. What's important is that this is a matter of national security, and some things are just more important than the fact that Agent Burana may have been murdered. If what you say is true, then we may possibly want to try and turn this Acton, or use him to try to unmask his controller. Those decisions will be made in due time, and we certainly don't need a private citizen looking over our shoulders."

"You're not going to jail him while you do a preliminary investigation?"

"Let me make myself clear, Frederickson, so that there won't be any misunderstanding in the future. If it's determined that you've shared this information with anyone else or if you pursue the matter in any way, shape, or form on your own, you will be prosecuted to the fullest extent of the law."

"One mistake, even a little one, on your part, and he could be gone. There are ways you can hold him."

"Mind your own business, Frederickson, and bear in mind what I just told you."

"I can't believe you're threatening me, pal. I hand you a KGB agent on a silver platter, and you treat me like I'm the enemy. Are you aware that this kind of behavior could lead someone like me to have less than total confidence in some of our public servants?

You've been spending all your time glowering at your left flank, and a nasty old Red menace slipped under the bedcovers on your right. Isn't that a howler? He killed one of your agents, Hendricks. Put the son-of-a-bitch away."

"You have a reputation for being a disrespectful wise-ass, Frederickson, and I can see that it's deserved. Your sarcasm is wasted on me. But you also have a reputation as a loose cannon. Before you do anything that may not be in the best interests of this country, consider the prosecution I mentioned—and, of course, the fact that you would almost certainly lose your license. This conversation is the end of your involvement in this matter, Frederickson. Do I make myself clear?"

"Perfectly," I said. "Have a nice day."

I hung up, then immediately picked up the phone again and called our travel agent to make arrangements to get me on the first available flight that would take me to Dayton, Ohio.

Then I dialed the number of the Cairn Town Hall.

I understood, all right. Best interests of the country, indeed. Hendricks, I thought, was too accustomed to talking to freshly minted graduates of the FBI academy. If it was possible to be outraged but not surprised by someone's behavior, that was how I felt. I didn't regret calling Edward J. Hendricks, because it had been essentially a forced move. I'd hoped for a different reception and outcome from the one I'd gotten, but I wasn't really surprised by what had happened. Elysius Culhane and Edward J. Hendricks—two hard-liners who listed so far to the right that it was a wonder they didn't fall over when they walked—were undoubtedly the best of buddies, and Hendricks was undoubtedly one of Culhane's government sources. Asses and reputations had to be protected, and there was no doubt in my mind that at that very moment orders were going out to all sorts of people with different interests but a common ideology to begin circling their wagons. This was one little Indian who was determined to find a way to sneak into their camp before all the wagons were in place.

Dan Mosely was off duty. I told the dispatcher who I was and strongly suggested that Chief Mosely get back on duty and in his office, because that was where I was going to be in approximately one hour and ten minutes.

Garth wouldn't be home for hours. I considered leaving him another message, then decided that the first would suffice. Then, without really knowing why, I took my Beretta out of the safe, where it had sat for close to a year. I quickly cleaned and oiled it, loaded up, strapped it on, and headed down to the garage.

•   •   •

Dan Mosely was behind his desk in the police headquarters at Cairn Town Hall. He was not in uniform, but he looked freshly showered and shaved. He wore a white cotton polo shirt over pale blue sailcloth slacks, and weathered docksiders worn without socks. Draped over his desk was a navy-blue windbreaker with the Cairn Yacht Club logo emblazoned over the left breast. He rose when I entered his office, but did not extend his hand. His steel-colored eyes and manner reflected more than a hint of annoyance.

"You didn't tell the dispatcher why you wanted to see me, Frederickson," he said brusquely as he motioned for me to sit in the chair beside his desk. "I hope it's important. I race on Sundays, and I was just about to go out when Officer McAlpin came around to tell me you'd called and were on your way. What is it?"

"I thought you'd want to know who killed Michael Burana," I said evenly, "so I'm here to tell you."

Mosely slowly eased his six-foot frame down into his leather swivel chair, absently touched the scars around his neck. "Explain."

"Jay Acton, Elysius Culhane's right-hand man, as it were, good buddy and key advisor, is a KGB officer. He would have had a strong motive for killing Michael, because Michael had found out about him. Michael found out that the man who calls himself Jay Acton was born in Russia to an English-speaking mother who was a hard-line communist ideologue and a KGB officer. Michael must have confronted Acton with the information; I'm not sure why he'd do that, but after all the shit he caught after the CIA defector thing, he may have wanted to bag himself a KGB operative on his own. Acton must have gotten the drop on him. He knocked Michael unconscious, drowned him in the river, then stole one of the Community's canoes and set it adrift so that the death would look like a boating accident."

Mosely pursed his lips, narrowed his eyelids as he stared at me. Finally he said, "My God, you're serious, aren't you?"

"Oh, good. You noticed."

"You left Cairn not much more than twenty-four hours ago, and it's a weekend. What happened between yesterday and today to bring you to this conclusion of yours?"

"I got a tip."

"From whom?"

"I can't tell you that yet."

"Are you claiming this is some kind of privileged information?"

"I'm saying I can't tell you yet."

"You mean you won't."

"As you like. As long as Acton is walking around free, my informant's life is in danger."

"Don't play games with me, Frederickson. You can come all the way back to Cairn to accuse a man of murder, but you won't say how you got your information. Maybe you're not so serious after all. Where's your proof?"

"I don't have proof that Acton is a murderer, and I may never have; he certainly isn't likely to confess. I doubt I'll even be able to prove that he's working for the KGB."

"Then what the hell—?!"

"I intend to prove beyond any doubt that he can't be who and what he says he is. I intend to prove that his birth records are phony, which means that every ID and document he has, from his Social Security card to his passport, is also phony. Then I'll produce a witness who'll tie Acton to a Russian mother who came to the United States with her baby, or young son, because the KGB ordered her to. When I do that, it may be enough to make a murder charge stick. It will certainly show motive. Maybe things will just fall into place."

"If you think Jay Acton is a spy, you should have reported it to the FBI."

"I did report it to the FBI. I spoke to Edward J. Hendricks, the head of their counterintelligence division."

"What did he say?"

"He takes me seriously."

"Then let the FBI handle it."

"Listen to me, Chief, because I'm going to tell you the drill. Edward J. Hendricks and Elysius Culhane are the best of friends and ideological soulmates. Hendricks is going to feel it's not only his personal but his *patriotic* duty to protect the reputation and career of his friend and to save the harebrained political faction they represent from some serious embarrassment. If it ever comes out that the principal spokesman for the radical right wing in this country has spent upwards of the past ten years speaking and acting on the advice of a KGB agent, said American right wing will end up a laughingstock around the world. Hendricks isn't going to allow that to happen, not if he can help it. If you and I leave Mr. Hendricks to his own devices, I guarantee you that word will somehow leak to Acton, and he'll split. The fact of who and what he was will be clamped under a tight lid of secrecy in the name of national security. It's called a cover-up."

"In your *opinion,* that's what will happen."

"You've got it."

"You're a hell of a cynic, Frederickson. Even if what you say about Acton is true, and I find it almost impossible to believe, I find it almost equally impossible to believe that your FBI friend would have compromised a matter of national security by unnecessarily exposing himself to danger. And I find it impossible to believe that a high-ranking FBI official would compromise national security for reasons of personal friendship or political expediency."

I sighed, shook my head. "I get this shit from a man who spent twenty years in the NYPD? You must have been permanently assigned to pooper-scooper detail."

Mosely flushed. "You've got a bad mouth, Frederickson."

"Do I? Let me tell you something about national security and cover-ups, Chief. During the course of my somewhat problematic career, I've had occasion to rub shoulders with a number of your spy types. My experiences have convinced me that about ten percent of our nation's so-called secrets are really secret, and should be. The only people who don't know the other ninety percent are Americans, because if American citizens ever found out the truth about some of the jokers we allow to run our lives and the incredible mistakes they've made, a whole hell of a lot of politicians, generals, and bureaucrats would be thrown out on the street. Most of what these people like to call national security is really political damage control; they don't want to lose their jobs. You may recall that the whole Iran-Contra farce was originally reported in a Lebanese newspaper. Right now, Hendricks is checking out Acton, employing hundreds of times the resources I have, and it isn't going to take him very long at all to discover that I'm right, that Acton is a KGB plant. Hendricks may or may not tip off Culhane, but he'll sure as hell find a way to make sure that Acton hightails it back home to Russia before he's caught and newspaper and television reporters can have at him. That's how your vaunted FBI is going to handle it—at least that's how Hendricks is going to handle it. I wouldn't give a shit, and would probably find it all highly amusing, if not for the fact that Acton almost certainly killed a good friend of mine. *That* I don't find amusing. I want Acton nailed publicly for what he is, and I want Michael Burana to get the credit for nailing him. That's probably the best I can hope for, but it's better than nothing. And I'll take some comfort in the fact that I don't think Mr. Acton is going to much like life in Russia after spending most of his life here."

Dan Mosely crossed, then uncrossed, his legs. He picked up a pencil and started to doodle on a pad, realized what he was doing, and stopped. Despite his obvious nervousness, his voice was steady, low. "Frederickson, that reputation of yours that we discussed doesn't begin to do you justice. You're a wild man. You're crazy. You just can't do whatever it is you think you want to do."

"You're wrong; I can, and I will. The reason I came here was to tell you that. You've treated me with respect and courtesy up to this point, and I figured I owed it to you to make sure you were kept fully informed—by me, at least—of what's likely to be going down on your turf. I didn't, don't, want you to be embarrassed in any way. Also, quite frankly, there's something I want you to do; it's something I think you *should* do."

Mosely abruptly swiveled around in his chair, turning his back to me, and eased back in the chair. It was the equivalent of a roll-your-eyes-toward-the-ceiling gesture, but his tone remained even when he spoke. "And just what would that be, Frederickson?"

"I'm on my way to Dayton, Ohio. That's where Jay Acton was supposedly born; for openers, I'm going to gather evidence to prove otherwise. But the danger is that I may unknowingly set off some built-in warning signals when I start to snoop around, and these would serve to warn Acton that somebody else is on to him. I don't want to do Hendricks any favors; Acton has to be frozen in place. What I want you to do is jail the bastard right now and find a way to keep him in jail while I go to work on him."

Mosely slowly swiveled around to face me, then raised his eyebrows. "You'd like me to put a man in jail, and keep him in jail, so that *you* won't end up in jail. Is that right?"

"If you like. I don't want him to get away."

"What do you suggest I charge him with?"

"Start off with suspicion of murder. Then trot out your best prosecutor to argue against bail on the grounds that very serious espionage charges may be pending against Mr. Acton. Make sure the local press hears about that. Believe me, once he's canned and the press starts to sniff around him, you'll have lots of help. Once it looks to Hendricks like the commie is out of the bag, it will look and feel as if you're holding an FBI convention in Cairn. They'll want to grab the credit. But the first move has to be made, and then the rest will follow."

"You say."

"I say."

"Somehow, I can imagine a number of different scenarios as to how things could turn out, and I don't like any of them."

"Give me two days. That's all I'll need to get the ball rolling—and the FBI will be taking him off your hands long before that, if you'll do the other things I suggested."

"I'm not sure you're aware of what you're asking me to do, Frederickson, or what this could cost me. I'm not sure you're fully aware of what it could cost you. Not only is what you want to do of questionable legality, but you propose to duke it out with some very, very heavy people."

"Look, Mosely, I appreciate your feeling that I'm putting you in a box, but that's Jay Acton's fault, not mine. You're the chief of police in Cairn, and a man was murdered here."

"That hasn't been determined yet."

"You're not listening to me, Chief. The fact that the murderer is most probably a KGB agent is really beside the point, but it complicates matters in this case. I'm just trying to simplify things. The way I see it, you have a chance to be a hero; you're going to be the small-town cop who bagged a KGB operative. This is going to be a *very* big story, and you're going to be a part of it one way or another. It's Hendricks and the FBI you'll have to fight for credit, not me. You'll have to take my word for it when I tell you I've had enough publicity bullshit to last me a lifetime. My only interest is in nailing the man who murdered my friend."

"Damned if I don't believe you, Frederickson," Mosely said drily as he rocked slightly in his chair. "The problem is that in all the scenarios I can imagine, I get flushed right down the toilet along with you. In effect, you're asking me to aid and abet you in violating a man's legal rights, and possibly jeopardizing national security interests, while you pursue a personal vendetta."

"You've got it ass-backward, Chief, which is exactly how Hendricks—and Culhane, if he knew about it—would like you to have it. I'm trying to bag a murderer, and in doing so, I'll be removing a possible threat to national security."

"You're insane."

"That may well be, but bear in mind that if you *don't* do something to freeze Acton in place, and he skips, you could end up getting some decidedly negative publicity. If I do Hendricks's work for him and scare Acton away, the FBI is going to need a scapegoat. They may not stop with me. So help me, Chief. Be a hero. No gain without pain. Go for it."

Mosely's response was to grunt, abruptly rise from his chair, and head for the door. "Wait here for me, Frederickson."

"Where are you going, Chief?" I asked, half rising from my chair. "If you're going to pick up Acton now, you'd better take some men with you. He's probably armed."

"I'll only be a few minutes," he said over his shoulder as he walked out of the office, closing the door behind him.

It was thirty-two minutes, to be exact, and Mosely got back just as I was preparing to get up and leave. He opened the door and entered the office looking tense, decidedly sheepish, and more than a little embarrassed. The reason for his discomfort stormed into the office right on his heels, fairly flew across the room toward me, and stopped barely inches away, hovering over me and trembling with fury. He was dressed in a pair of floral-pattern Bermuda shorts with matching short-sleeve shirt. He'd apparently dressed in a pretty big hurry, because the cordovan shoes he was wearing were untied. The tremor in his right hand was now especially pronounced. His close-set black eyes gleamed with rage—but also, I thought, with fear. His graying black hair was uncombed and stuck out from the sides of his head. Sweat ran down both sides of his crooked nose. Elysius Culhane no longer looked like a well-dressed thug, but merely a sweaty, extremely upset thug.

"What are you *doing*, Frederickson?!" Culhane screamed as he pounded the desk beside me. "Just what the hell do you think you're *doing*?!"

"It looks like you got the bad news, Mr. Culhane," I said as I glanced across the room at Mosely, who was standing stiffly with his back to us as he pretended to study a painting of a sailboat. The scarred flesh of his neck around his collar was very red.

"You can't do this to me, Frederickson!" Culhane shouted, pounding his fist on the desk again for emphasis.

I was getting a lot of Culhane's saliva in my face. I rose from my chair, stepped behind it. "Do this to you, Mr. Culhane? Nobody's doing anything to you."

"You're irresponsible!"

"Irresponsible? I'm not the one who hired himself a KGB agent just because his rhetoric put him to the right of Genghis Khan. How many of this nation's secrets have been leaked to you, Culhane, secrets that the Russians are now privy to?"

Culhane's jaw muscles worked, and for a moment I thought he was going to spit in my face. He didn't. Instead, he clenched his trembling hands to his sides, took a step backward, and drew himself up very straight. "You've made some very serious accusations, Frederickson," he said thickly, his rage making him slur his words together.

"I'd call them shocking. But you're not accused of anything but poor judgment and gullibility. My only interest is in nailing the KGB agent on your staff."

"This is none of your business, Frederickson! I want you to know I've already spoken to a very high-ranking FBI official, and he informs me that you're endangering national security! He's considering issuing a warrant for your arrest!"

"It'll be a cold day in hell before Edward J. Hendricks issues a warrant for my arrest, Culhane. It was never a possibility. Would you like to see me on trial? You'd be my first witness. I'm sure there are no fewer than five thousand reporters in this country who'd love to hear the story of the spokesman for the far right who, for years, has been using a KGB officer as an advisor."

"Think about the *country*, Frederickson! Do you really think it's in the best interests of the United States to have a story like that made public? It will make the whole nation look foolish!"

"Spare me, Culhane. It's not hard to figure out who's going to look foolish."

"I'm warning you, Frederickson!"

"Don't waste your time, Culhane; I've been threatened by *really* scary people. Let's talk about the real issue here. I note that you haven't tried to defend Acton; you haven't even suggested that I could be wrong. After your talk with your buddy Hendricks, I think you know better. With nothing more than your aide's Social Security number, which I have, I can prove he isn't who he says he is and that he wasn't born where and when he says he was. I have evidence he was born in Russia. I told all this to Hendricks, and it looks like he told you. All you're concerned about right now is your own ass. If you want to minimize any damage to your reputation as a fire-breathing, clear-thinking, hard-nosed movement conservative who would never let the Russians pull the wool over *his* eyes, I suggest you get with my program. Tell your employee over there to slap the cuffs on Acton and haul him into one of the cells he's got here. And then tell your friend Hendricks that you will not stand for any cover-up, and you insist that justice be done. I want to see a little patriotic fervor on your part regarding this matter. Acton may have made a fool of you, but you'll have the last laugh by helping to get him locked up and brought to justice. How about it, Culhane? Want to help me catch a commie spy?"

Elysius Culhane's response was to change colors like a traffic light—red to yellow to green—and retch. He got his hands over his mouth just in time to stop the initial flow of vomit, which oozed out through his fingers. Then he spun around and dashed from the office. I heard the door to the men's room out in the corridor open, and slam shut.

"I can't believe you did what you did, Mosely," I said in a low, tense voice as I came out from behind the protective barrier of the chair and started across the room toward Cairn's chief of police. Contempt tasted sour in my mouth, and I wanted to make sure there was no doubt in the other man's mind just what I thought of him. "Did you think this would be like fixing a traffic ticket? Where the fuck are your brains?"

Mosely spun around on his heels. His face was even redder, and continued embarrassment swam in his eyes along with an uneasy mix of anger and shame. But there was nothing apologetic about his tone. "Where the fuck are *yours*, Frederickson?!" he snapped. "You're in way, way over your head on this, and you refuse to see it! What *you* want just isn't as important as you seem to think it is! Maybe *you're* not as important as you think you are! You're just one big, fucking headache. It's not the business of this police department to help you carry out a personal vendetta. There are other issues involved here, big issues involving the reputations of important people as well as the good of the country. I'm no right-winger, Frederickson, but I'm not an ideological neuter, a man without a country, like you, either. I care about this country, and I've heard enough from you to know that you don't really give a rat's ass about the United States. Maybe you don't really give a rat's ass about anything except what you want, which in this case is revenge. If Jay Acton is a spy, then it's going to be taken care of. What fucking right do you have to say that *you're* right, and Elysius Culhane and the whole FBI are wrong? What right do you have to ask *me* to put my career on the line just so you can go off sharpshooting on your own? You have *no* right, Frederickson! So fuck off!"

I took a deep breath and backed away a few steps, retreating from my own anger as well as from Chief of Police Dan Mosely. I knew now that I had wasted my time in returning to Cairn and certainly wasted my energy by getting angry at Mosely.

"Do you think Culhane is going to respect you for this?" I asked quietly. "Do you think he's going to reward you or that your job is safer now? Forget it. If he and his right-wing buddies can engineer a scoot by Acton before he's caught, you're just going to be a continuing embarrassment to Culhane. You're making a big mistake, and by the time you realize it, it will be too late. I suspect you're not going to be feeling too good about it."

Mosely shook his head. "The leaders of this country aren't as corrupt or incompetent as you think they are, Frederickson. I'm keeping *you* from making a big mistake. There'll come a time when you'll thank me for this."

"Did you call Culhane or go and pick him up?"

Mosely stared at me for a time, and I didn't think he was going to answer. But he finally said, "I called him."

"Was Acton there when you spoke to him?"

"He's out sailing."

"I guess we have to learn to be thankful for small favors."

"Get out of here, Frederickson. If you want to end up with your ass in a federal prison, do it on your own time. I don't want to see or hear from you again."

I was trying to select an appropriate response from my reservoir of witty repartee when Elysius Culhane, now looking merely very pale, came back into the office. His hair was wet, matted down and combed straight back. He'd done a fairly good job of cleaning himself up, but there was still a strand of moist vomit that he apparently wasn't aware of staining the front of his shirt. He walked to the middle of the room, stopped a few paces away from me.

"You listen to me, Frederickson," he said, calmer now, but still slurring his words together slightly. "I'm not going to waste any more time arguing with you. I will *not* allow you to trash my reputation and career, and I will *not* allow you to use this unfortunate matter to subject the good, God-fearing, and patriotic people of this great nation to ridicule—which is certainly what you would like to do. As you know, I have very powerful friends in Washington. So do you. But I suspect that I have *more* than you do, and if it starts making the rounds that you're a traitor, that left-wing, candy-ass Shannon is going to run from you like a stuck pig. A traitor's what you'd be, because damaging my reputation would be a victory for the communists, something they sorely need right now. The Russians would have the whole world laughing at us. You're perfectly willing to be used as a propaganda tool by this nation's enemies."

"Jesus Christ, Culhane, would you believe that you actually have the capacity to make me feel sorry for you? You really *do* believe all that shit you say you believe, don't you? You can actually make yourself believe anything you want, and reason has nothing to do with it. Elysius Culhane in Wonderland. And here I thought you were just a hypocritical con man who'd learned to make a good living spouting garbage and waving the flag."

"That's the communist in you talking, Frederickson; that's Russian propaganda. People like you are what's wrong with this country. And don't count on your friend, Mr. Lippitt, who everyone knows dotes on the Frederickson brothers like sons. The Defense Intelligence Agency is small potatoes compared with the FBI and CIA. If Jay Acton is a KGB spy like you say he is, then the proper authorities will take care of the matter. But if you try to interfere any longer in any way, if you dare to even whisper a word to anyone about a KGB agent on my staff, I will sue you for slander and libel for everything you and your big creep of a brother have. And those powerful friends of mine will make sure I win. Cross me on this, Frederickson, and I will see that you lose your licenses, as well as all your possessions. You and your brother will be ruined. You are definitely to take this as a threat. If you try to use the information you have to harm this country that I love, I will crush you. Do I make myself perfectly—?"

"Excuse me, Mr. Culhane," I said mildly. "You've got throw-up on the front of your shirt. It's really disgusting."

"Huh—?"

That seemed as good an exit line as any, and as Elysius Culhane looked down at the front of his shirt, I walked around him and out of the office. I gave the door at the entrance to the town hall a good kick on my way out, but only managed to hurt my toe. Still seething, I walked quickly to where Beloved Too was parked on the street, got in, started the motor, and popped the clutch. Beloved Too's tires spun, and I left twin swaths of rubber behind as I shot away from the curb.

I started calming down and feeling considerably better by the time I reached the Cairn town limits. It was close to 5:00, but my flight out of LaGuardia wasn't until 9:15. Figuring I had plenty of time to pack and brief Garth on what I was up to before leaving for the airport, I stopped in Nyack—in my opinion the finest, and certainly the funkiest, of the riverfront towns—to get a liquor-laced ice-cream cone at a small ice-cream shop called Temptations. Then I sat on one of the two wood-and-iron benches outside to eat my cone and watch the weekend day-trippers from the city wandering by while I considered my position. All in all, I decided, things were not going all that badly.

I had been outraged by what I considered a lack of profession-alism, cowardice, and a betrayal of my trust on the part of Dan Mosely. But on reflection, I decided that the policeman had probably done me a favor, albeit unwittingly; he'd certainly done Elysius Culhane no favor by informing him that his top aide was probably a KGB agent. In effect, Mosely's phone call had made Culhane a conscious, responsible player, and then Culhane, by confronting and threatening me, had dealt himself even deeper into the game. He now shared responsibility for what happened to Jay Acton. Despite all his bluster and self-delusion, I was fairly certain he knew that I was going to proceed apace. I was also fairly certain that Culhane, by the time he paused long enough to change his shirt, would realize that, under the circumstances, he really had no choice but to help catch the spy he had hired, and then try to capture as much of the credit as he could in order to defend himself against the ridicule and other hits he was certain to take. If anyone could pull strings to keep Acton safely behind bars for two or three days, it was Elysius Culhane; in the end Culhane, for his own reasons, could end up my strongest ally.

I finished my cone, climbed back into Beloved Too, and went south on Broadway to 9W, then headed for Exit 4 of the Palisades Parkway. To my left, the Tappan Zee Bridge bisected the Hudson River, which appeared unusually blue and sparkling in the slanting rays of the late afternoon sun. Farther on, the grand earthen dam that had given Piermont its name jutted halfway across the river, a relic of World War II. It had been a busy weekend, and I was starting to feel tired, lazy. That feeling didn't last long. I perked up considerably when I glanced in my rearview mirror and saw a bulky pickup truck with a heavy steel plate welded to its front end come zipping up behind me to settle in only inches from my rear bumper. The man behind the wheel was wearing a ski mask—a bright red one, with Ho Ho Ho embroidered in green across the forehead.

Tailgating truck drivers wearing ski masks in August tend to make me jittery. I snapped on my seat belt and shoulder harness, tightened the straps as far as they would go, then took my Beretta from the glove department and laid it on the seat beside my thigh before tromping on the accelerator. My abrupt acceleration saved me from the full force of impact as the steel plate welded to the truck's front end struck me in the rear, but it was still enough to send me into a slight power skid. I straightened out, floored the accelerator again. The man behind me obviously had a few horses under his hood, because he immediately started gaining on me again.

Route 9W along this section was two-laned, winding and very narrow, with virtually no shoulders; trees lined the highway to my right, and to my left was all steep, tree-covered embankment with small houses nestled in alcoves all the way down to the river. There just wasn't that much room to maneuver. The next town was perhaps five or six miles ahead; there I could power slide off the highway into the parking lot of a restaurant or service station. But I was going to have to get there first, before I was shoved off the road into a tree.

Hoping to give my oversized partner in bumper tag something else to think about besides the fun of ramming me, I picked up my Beretta, switched it to my left hand, reached around, and winged a shot over my right shoulder. The rear window shattered, but when I looked into my rearview mirror I could see that I had missed the truck's windshield entirely. The driver was once again coming up on me fast.

There was a car coming the other way. I furiously honked my horn and flashed my headlights; the driver of the other car, apparently thinking that I was warning him of a speed trap ahead of him, honked and flashed back, waved cheerily as he sped past. I fired again, this time half turning in my seat and taking my eyes off the road for an instant in an effort to get off a better shot.

I turned back just in time to see the armored front end of a huge semi-trailer cab easing out into my lane from a side road. The driver of the second truck wore no ski mask, either because it would have hurt his heavily bandaged face or because he saw no need to hide his features from the man he intended to see dead. The grimly leering, bruised and bandaged, but clearly recognizable face of Gregory Trex was visible in the truck cab's side window. Crashing into the cab meant certain death for me and probably wouldn't do more than slightly addle the granite-headed Trex. My options were the ultimate in slim pickings.

I whipped the steering wheel to the left, then released my grip on the wheel and locked my hands behind my neck, bracing as the car hit the slight shoulder on the left and went airborne. This, I thought as I waited for the impending crash and darkness, was the last car I was going to name Beloved.

I didn't have long to wait.

CHAPTER SEVEN

I regained consciousness—in what I assumed was a hospital bed—with a skull that felt like someone had tried to split it down the center with a chisel, a mouth that felt and tasted like it was filled with steel wool soaked in dirty turpentine, and the terrible fear that I'd been partially blinded. I lay in a dim pool of pale yellow light cast by a bulb set somewhere in the wall above my head. Virtually everything beyond a three-foot radius was impenetrable darkness; what I could see out of my left eye was blurred and milky, and I could see nothing at all out of my right eye. I grabbed for the blind eye. Pain shot through my head and right shoulder, but I was rewarded, if that was the proper term, with the feel of a heavy bandage covering the right side of my face. Maybe I hadn't been blinded after all. I groaned, closed my good eye against the pain. When I opened it, a blurred but instantly recognizable shape, complete with full beard and shoulder-length hair, was leaning over me.

"Why do I have the distinct feeling that I should have stuck around Saturday to listen to your bad news?" Garth said in a voice that was wry, yet heavily laden with emotion.

"A comedian is just what I need, Garth. Ha ha."

"Sorry about that. Just my way of showing how happy I am to find you alive. I passed your wreck on the way here, and it gave me a few anxious moments."

"What's the news on me? Did I lose an eye?"

Garth laid one of his large, powerful hands on my left shoulder, squeezed it very gently. "No. You're going to be all right, brother. For a time they thought you'd fractured your skull, but X rays show otherwise. Mild concussion, lots of cuts, scrapes, and bruises to keep the other bruises you had company, but you'll live. You've got a twelve-stitch gash over your right eye, but the eye itself is undamaged; they just found it easier to bandage it the way they did. You've lost a little scalp and hair on the right side of your head, but you were thinking of getting a haircut this week anyway, right?"

"There you go again with another real knee-slapper."

"How do you feel, Mongo?"

"Garth, my physical and mental states of being lend the term 'feeling like shit' new depths of meaning."

He began to gently knead my shoulder in a way that relaxed my muscles, and somehow began to ease the twin suns of white-hot pain that were blazing behind my eyes. "That was some job of flying you did in the Volkswagen, brother," he said softly, his tone soothing, almost hypnotic. "You must have sailed better than a hundred feet through the air going down that hillside; you flew right between the eaves of two houses, rolled over, and landed on top of a tree beside some guy's deck. You made him spill his drink. When the paramedics finally managed to climb the tree, they found you hanging upside down in your harness. You're a hell of an advertisement for seat belts and harnesses." He stopped the kneading, eased himself carefully down on the side of the bed. When he spoke again, all traces of warmth and humor were gone from his voice. "What the hell happened, Mongo? What's going on here?"

I worked my tongue over my gummy lips, tried to clear my throat. "Get me some water, will you?"

"Watch your eye," Garth said as he rose from the bed.

He turned on the light, came back, and poured me a glass of

water from a plastic carafe on a table beside the bed. Then he sat down again, gently raised me up, and handed me the glass. As I sipped the water, he gently rubbed my back between the shoulder blades, then kneaded the back of my neck. Incredibly, my nausea and pain began to ease, and the vision in my uncovered left eye began to clear somewhat. If I was ever to bet on the healing power of the laying on of hands, it would be Garth's hands I'd bet on. They were hands that, more than a few times in the past, since his poisoning with nitrophenyldienal, had been ready to kill—never inappropriately, but often prematurely, at least in my opinion. But they were also, most definitely, a healer's hands.

"So," I said as I drained off the water and handed him back the glass, "where am I?"

"Cairn Hospital. I'm told it's a very good one."

"What time it it?"

"Three o'clock in the morning, Monday. I got home around six yesterday, found your note. When you weren't home by nine, I picked up the phone and called the police and the hospital. Bingo. That's how I found out you'd been in an accident."

"It was no accident; it was an on-purpose. Two guys ran me off the road."

Garth grunted, as if he wasn't surprised. The knotted muscles in his jaw and neck were the only sign of his anger and concern. He refilled the water glass, then pulled a chair over to the bed and sat down in it. When he spoke, his voice was low, but humming with tension. "What was the bad news you wanted to give me on Saturday, Mongo?"

"Oh, that," I said, rolling over on my side and propping myself up on a very sore elbow. "You mean the bad news you said I should take care of?"

"Come on, Mongo."

"The bad news on Saturday was that I'd become convinced Michael was murdered. Today's bad news is that the KGB agent who probably murdered Michael works for Elysius Culhane. Naturally, Culhane isn't too eager for this fact to become public knowledge, and the FBI seems perfectly willing to help him cover it up. Cairn has a chickenshit police chief who doesn't seem inclined to do anything about it, and then there's the minor matter of the possible existence of a death squad in Cairn, which may be responsible for me being here."

"Whoa, Mongo. I feel I've done sufficient groveling, so stop trying to be clever and just start from the beginning."

I did, relating what I'd learned and everything that had happened from the time I arrived in Cairn on Friday afternoon to the moment on Sunday afternoon when I yanked on Beloved Too's steering wheel and went soaring off into space. Garth listened in silence, the steady, bright gleam in his limpid eyes his only display of emotion. When I finished I was exhausted, once again in pain, and with increasingly blurred vision in my good eye. Garth seemed to sense this; he leaned forward in his chair and once again began to knead the muscles in my back and neck with his powerful but incredibly gentle hands.

"Okay," Garth said softly. "First, let's try to sort out this attempt to kill you. Trex and one of his buddies ran you off the road. The problem is that nobody seems to have seen it happen."

"Who reported the accident?"

"The guy who spilled his drink when you landed in the tree next to his deck. He just saw the car come sailing out of nowhere and land on top of the tree; he didn't see what happened up on the road, and no other witnesses have come forward. Do you think the ambush was Trex's idea?"

"He sure as hell had a powerful itch to kill me."

"And he was waiting for you in ambush. He knew you'd probably be using 9W to get to the Palisades Parkway. How did he know you were in Cairn? Could he have been following you?"

I shook my head. "He couldn't have been out of the hospital himself for more than a short time before he came at me. Besides, Gregory Trex wasn't interested in following me, only killing me—and, if he'd been following me, he'd have had a lot better places to kill me than on 9W. Even if they weren't in trucks, that shithead and his friends wouldn't be good enough to tail me without my knowing it. He must have seen my car parked outside Town Hall, or seen me go in. He figured I'd be going home eventually, so he rounded up a buddy and set up the ambush."

"Maybe Culhane put Trex and his buddy on to you."

I thought about it, nodded. "Could be; it would be enough simply to drop a hint to Trex that I was in town, and Trex would take it from there. After Mosely called him, Culhane had time to call Hendricks at the FBI before he came to confront me. Maybe he also took the time to call Trex."

"There's another possibility, Mongo. There is indeed a death squad operating here, with Gregory Trex and his masked buddy being two of its members and Jay Acton controlling it."

"Acton shouldn't have a clue that I'm breathing down his neck. Supposedly he was out sailing when Mosely called Culhane."

"Mosely could have reported to Culhane on the conversation you had with him on Friday evening. If Culhane mentioned to Acton that you had questions about Burana's death, it would have put Acton on his guard."

There was something odd in Garth's tone that made me nervous. "Okay, Garth," I said, watching his face, "that's a possibility. But I really can't see a clever KGB agent having anything to do with a loose cannon like Gregory Trex. Like I said, Trex didn't need anyone to goad him into trying to kill me. The ambush may be totally unrelated to the other matters."

"I think it is related."

"What's the matter, Garth? What is it?"

"Somebody has been following you, Mongo—and I agree that it had to have been a pro, or you'd have picked up on it."

"How the hell do you know somebody's been following me? You didn't even know I was in the hospital until a few hours ago, and you didn't know what's been happening until a few minutes ago."

Garth bowed his head slightly, sighed as he ran the fingers of both hands through his long hair. "Harry Peal's dead, Mongo."

"Oh, God," I said, turning my face away and clenching my fists against the new pain that suddenly shot through my heart. "*Shit*. How?"

"He died in a fall off the cliff outside his home sometime Sunday afternoon."

"That was yesterday; I told you I went up to see him yesterday afternoon."

"I know. Supposedly there was a witness to his death. This witness claims there was a struggle between Peal and a very small man—'dwarf' is the word he used, I'm told—and the dwarf pushed Peal off the cliff."

I kept my fists clenched and face turned away, fighting back tears of grief, frustration, and rage. Mosely had been dead on target when he labeled me, in so many words, a kind of pariah, but that wasn't news to me. A grand old man of folk song, conservation, and fierce *real* patriotism had survived more than eight decades of severe trials to body and soul; he'd survived everything but one Sunday afternoon conversation with Robert Frederickson. "Why didn't you tell me this at the beginning?" I asked in a voice that I hardly recognized as my own.

"To what purpose? I knew you didn't kill some old man. I wanted to hear what you had to say so that maybe I could get some clue as to who did kill him. My money's on your KGB plant."

"For Christ's sake, Garth, Harry Peal was Jay Acton's father."

"He'd never met the man. Harry Peal would have been just one more threat, like Burana, who had to be removed; we're talking KGB here, not the Junior Chamber of Commerce. And he figured he'd try to take you out along the way."

"That's fucking absurd," I said, turning back to face Garth. "It doesn't make any sense at all. If Acton wants me out of the way because I know he's probably KGB, why didn't he just kill me, instead of trying to frame me on some bullshit murder charge that can't hold up? Arranging for me to be charged with murder isn't going to keep me from talking."

"You have a point," Garth said evenly, staring thoughtfully at the palms of his hands. "Except that he couldn't be in two places at once. He took care of Peal himself, and he was counting on Trex and his buddy to take care of you."

"And they muffed it; I end up alive and in the hospital. So what's to be gained by this stupid murder charge? Who's this witness?"

"An anonymous phone tip."

"An anonymous *phone tip?*"

"What the hell; it did the job. You're currently under arrest, dear brother, on the charge of suspicion of murder. There's a guard sitting outside your door right now. He was looking real bored when I came in, so I managed to find him a newspaper."

"How did you get in here?"

"My old NYPD courtesy card and a little courtesy from a former comrade-in-arms."

"Mosely?"

"Uh-huh. That's where I got my information."

"I take it he failed to mention all the other shit that's been going down around here."

"It must have slipped his mind," Garth said absently.

"You remember Mosely from the good old days?"

Garth nodded. "Vaguely. Our paths used to occasionally cross at the station house, and I remember seeing his name on the duty list. He spent some years in safe and loft, then was transferred to full-time U.N. detail. The word on him was that he was a straight arrow—probably a lot straighter than most of the other cops in that precinct."

"Except you."

"There are a lot of honest cops, Mongo. You know that."

"And you're saying Mosely was an honest cop?"

"I never heard otherwise—and I would have."

"Well, he's a real . . . he's something else now."

"But not necessarily dishonest," Garth said distantly. I suspected he was thinking about the same thing that was troubling me, namely what my enemy or enemies hoped to accomplish by maneuvering Mosely into arresting me. "He's got a political job now."

"I still don't understand this move, Garth. What's the point of trying to pin Harry Peal's murder on me, especially when the witness is nothing but an anonymous phone tip? It can't stop me from talking about the KGB officer on Elysius Culhane's staff. I've already told you, and—oh, shit." Suddenly I understood. I sat bolt upright in bed, ignoring the pain that shot through my skull and back. "It's just a holding action, Garth. Acton had counted on Trex to kill me, and Trex blew it. Now Acton needs time to figure out how to get at me. I wanted to freeze him in place by having him arrested, and that's precisely what he's done to me. I have to die, same as Michael and Harry Peal, because of what Harry told me. Now you'll be marked too."

"Why wasn't Peal killed the same time as Burana?"

"There wasn't time. Harry left for Eastern Europe within hours after he talked to Michael. The KGB didn't want Harry to die in a communist country, because it would have been an embarrassment to the Russians and their allies. Harry had just returned from that trip when I talked to him on Sunday."

Garth rose, looked over his shoulder to make sure the door was closed, then reached into his jacket pocket and took out his old Colt automatic. Garth no longer liked guns and didn't even bother practicing on a firing range. I hadn't seen the old Colt in years, and yet from the way he held the weapon as he checked the firing chamber and magazine I suspected he remained the deadly accurate shooter he had once been.

He looked up, reacted to the surprise he must have seen on my face. "I noticed your gun was missing from the safe, so I figured I'd better bring mine along. I assume you lost the Beretta?"

"Yeah," I replied curtly. I felt very tense and anxious. Now that it had finally dawned on me why I was under arrest for the murder of Harry Peal, I hoped I wasn't too late to prevent another killing. "Listen, there has to be a pay phone around here someplace. Go find it and call Mary Tree; get the number for the Community of Conciliation from Information. Whoever's been following me must know that she and I talked, which means that her life is probably in danger; she's the one who steered me to Harry Peal in the first place. She has to be warned. Her organization has offices all over the world. She has to split, and she has to do it right now. Tell her to find some other Community residence to hole up in, preferably one that's a long ways from here. Tell her to pack her bags in a hurry, and you'll take her to the airport."

Garth grunted, clicked on the Colt's safety catch, then stepped forward and slipped the gun under the sheet, next to my thigh. "Hang on to that until I get back," he said, then turned and left the room.

I gripped the taped butt of the Colt and waited, my heart pounding. Hours had passed since Harry Peal had been killed and the attempt made on my life. Everything indicated that Jay Acton, whoever he really was, was in a hurry to clean house, to eliminate everyone he thought could connect him to his Russian mother and birthplace and membership in the KGB, which meant that Mary Tree might already be dead. I would not like that at all. It would be my fault.

Garth returned twenty minutes later. "Did you reach her?" I asked as soon as he stepped into the room and closed the door behind him.

"Yeah," Garth replied easily as he walked over to the bed, took the gun from my hand, and put it back into his jacket pocket. Then he went to the window, looked down. "No problem."

"What the hell does that mean? Does the Community have some other residence that's secure, and where she can hide?"

"I suppose so," he said in a tone of voice that I thought sounded oddly distracted under the circumstances.

"What the hell do you mean, you suppose so? Are you taking her to the airport?"

"No," he said evenly as he turned away from the window. "As a matter of fact, you and I are going to the Community residence here for an indefinite stay."

"What?"

"We both agree that your arrest is somebody's idea of a holding action, and we agree that said holding action isn't going to serve any purpose unless you're taken out before you can start talking to the media. Your police guard doesn't exactly remind me of Wyatt Earp to begin with, and when I came back from using the phone I found him down the hall trying to make time with one of the night nurses. I don't think you're safe here, brother, and I wonder how safe you'd be in police custody. If I were a KGB killer, I don't think I'd lose much sleep worrying about the prowess of the Cairn Police Department."

"I can't say I'm overjoyed with my situation, but I don't much care for the idea of putting you and Mary in the position of aiding and abetting a fugitive."

"I discussed that with Mary, and she and I agreed that the two of us have more serious things to worry about. As you pointed out, I'll be marked for death now that I've come to see you, so the three of us are all in this together. Even if she did want to fly out of the country, there's no guarantee that the KGB wouldn't be able to trace her. But I doubt we'd even make it to the airport; by now my car has been identified, and somebody is probably keeping an eye on it. Mary says she can sneak us into that mansion and find a place for us to hide in there without anyone else knowing about it. We'll have sanctuary there and time to figure out our next moves." He paused, turned back to the window, continued, "I checked again with your night nurse, and she said you definitely don't have a fractured skull. You're under observation, and she figures you'll be released from the hospital into police custody in two or three days. I'm kind of hoping that means your head won't fall off if you're moved."

"It's all well and good for you to say things like that, since it's not your head that's likely to fall off. What's so interesting out the window?"

"Mary should be here in about ten or fifteen minutes to pick us up; she told me she could sneak out in one of the Community's cars that isn't used too much and shouldn't be recognized." He turned back to me, raised his right hand. "How many fingers?"

I squinted my unbandaged left eye in an attempt to focus on the blurred figure across the room. "Four," I said.

"Be serious."

"I *am* being serious. I can count four fingers when I see them."

"Two," Garth said with a sigh as he lowered his hand. "It looks like you've got a good case of double vision, but it can't be helped. You've been hurt worse. Just divide everything you see by two."

"Thanks a lot, Garth. There are times when I can't imagine what I'd do without your sage advice. What floor are we on?"

"The third."

"Great. I like all your thinking and planning up to this point except for one very minor little detail. Even assuming I can walk without a serious wobble, which I don't assume at all, how the hell do you plan to spirit me out of here without us being seen? The guard may not be Wyatt Earp, but he's obviously not blind either."

"Tsk, tsk. You've always been such a worrywart."

"Garth? What the hell are you planning to do?"

Garth smiled sweetly, always a bad sign, and walked toward me. "You let me worry about spiriting you out of here, baby brother. It's as good as done."

CHAPTER EIGHT

Being lowered from the third story of a building by a rope of bedsheets, blankets, pillowcases, and towels knotted together and fashioned into a sling under my arms made for what I considered an ignominious exit. On the other hand, it occurred to me that a short flight in a car and a good knock on the noggin had done wonders for my sprained wrist, sore knee, and bruised left arm, since the stabbing pain in my head had made me forget all about the other injuries sustained while I was bouncing off and being bounced by Gregory Trex, the current scourge of my existence.

The window of my hospital room conveniently looked out over a wide alleyway used for deliveries and garbage pickup; Mary Tree, driving with her lights out, had backed into the alley just as I finished dressing and just as Garth was putting the finishing touches on my improvised escape route—remarking, with another of his ominously sweet smiles, that he hoped it would reach all the way to the ground.

As I continued my descent, with Mary craning her neck and peering anxiously up at me, I tried to improve on my undignified position by crossing my arms over my chest and proudly thrusting out my chin, posturing as if I were totally accustomed to this sort of royal transport. My vamping got a muffled laugh out of the woman. However, there was nothing but shock and concern in her face and eyes by the time I reached the ground and she managed to get a better look at me. She wrapped her left arm around me, used her right hand to undo the sling from under my arms.

"Mongo!" she said in a low, tense whisper. "Oh, my God, your head—!"

"It's okay," I said, gently pushing her arm away and taking a couple of tentative steps. I felt dizzy. "It looks worse than it is. You know how hospitals love to waste bandages."

I glanced up, found Garth half leaning out the window and looking down at me. I gave him a thumbs-up sign. He returned it, let loose of his end of the knotted linens, then stepped back out of sight. Mary gathered the tangle of linens and blankets together in both arms, dropped it all into a dumpster off to one side of the alley. Then she opened the back door of the car for me, supported me around the waist as I eased myself down across the back seat. She closed the door, hurried around to the other side of the car, and slid in behind the wheel. I noted with satisfaction that the interior lights had been disconnected; Garth had briefed her well. And the woman had more than her share of guts.

"What happens now, Mary?"

"Your brother said to wait here," she replied in a low voice that was breathy with tension. She twisted around in her seat to peer out the back window, then squinted down at me over the tops of her bifocals. "He said he's going to go down to the lobby, then try to find a way to sneak out the back without anyone seeing him. God, the way he acts and talks you'd think he does this kind of thing every day."

"Garth's a very good man to have around in a pinch, Mary. Or any other time, for that matter. He doesn't know the meaning of panic." I paused for a moment, then continued, "Mary, I'm really sorry about all of this. I hope you know that I'd never have contacted you if I'd known it was going to involve you like this."

Her response was to reach back across the seat and squeeze my thigh; the gentleness and affection in her touch were belied by the anger in her voice. "Harry Peal never hurt a soul in his whole life. I can't believe some bastard killed him. I told you there was a death squad in Cairn, Mongo."

"In this case, I think the murderer is Elysius Culhane's good buddy Jay Acton."

She grunted softly. "So your brother told me—but it wasn't that cold-blooded, preening son-of-a-bitch who ran you off the road."

"Right."

"Acton may be the mastermind; I'm still convinced there's a death squad operating here."

"You could be right."

The figure of Garth suddenly loomed out of the darkness, appearing outside the windows on the passenger's side. He opened the door, slid onto the front seat beside Mary, quickly closed the door. "Sorry I took so long," he said tersely as he looked back over the seat to inspect me. "The guard wanted to chat with me after I left the room." He paused, turned to Mary, extended his hand. "It's nice to meet you, Miss Tree. You are one gutsy lady. Thank you for helping us get out of there."

Mary pushed Garth's hand away, leaned across the seat, and kissed him on the lips. "Miss Tree—who never wants you to call her that again, since, as I told Mongo, it makes me sound like a character in a nursery rhyme—thinks that it's she who should be thanking you, since it's also her life you're undoubtedly saving. It's nice to meet you too, Garth Frederickson."

Under any other circumstances I would have half expected my brother to faint dead away after being kissed on the lips by Mary Tree, but now he was tightly focused on the matter at hand, all business. "Let's get out of here," he said curtly.

I sat up as Mary turned on the engine and, still leaving her lights off, eased forward out of the alley into a parking lot by the emergency room entrance, then proceeded to the street. Garth motioned for me to lie down again, which I did, and he ducked out of sight.

"Drive around awhile, Mary," he continued, his voice muffled by the seat between us. "We want to make sure we're not being followed."

"Right," Mary replied, and made a left turn. She switched on her lights, drove a block, and made another left turn, then started up a hill. I saw her shift her head to look down at Garth and heard a sharp intake of breath. "Garth, is that a gun?" she asked tightly.

"It most certainly is."

"Garth, do you really think it's necessary to—?"

"Mary, listen to me," Garth said in a firm voice that had a touch of coldness in it. "I know you're a pacifist. For the life of me, I've never understood how a person who lives on this planet could be a pacifist, but that's neither here nor there. I suppose it's a perfectly workable philosophy, just as long as some soldier in an opposing army doesn't have you lined up in his sights. Right now it looks like there are people who mean to see us dead; unfortunately they're not pacifists. I don't intend to cooperate. If I so much as get a glimpse of this Gregory Trex or Jay Acton or anybody else who means to harm you or my brother, I am going to put a bullet through that man's brain. I'm telling you this up front, just so there'll be no misunderstanding on your part if we meet up with any of these men. If the idea of killing or the sight of blood offends you, look away. I will kill them. Clear?"

Garth had never had any problems in making himself understood; there was no need for Mary to reply, and she didn't. However, judging from the stiff angle at which she held her head, she was now considerably more tense as she continued to drive through Cairn's night streets, occasionally going around a block, and once even abruptly making a U-turn and reversing direction. After one right turn she accelerated. The car kept going in a straight line, and I guessed that we were up on 9W. Not knowing how much Garth had told her over the phone, I used the time to fill Mary in on the details of what I'd learned at the meeting with Harry Peal, the fruits of my preliminary computer search, what had happened at the police station later Sunday afternoon, and the subsequent ambush. She listened without interrupting, an occasional, sibilant hiss her only show of emotion.

"How does it look, Mary?" Garth asked quietly when I finished.

I watched as she craned her neck to again glance in the rearview mirror. "I think we're in the clear," she replied evenly.

"All right," Garth said, "let's head for your place." He sat up, looked back at me. "How's the head holding up, brother?"

I sat up, groaned. "Don't ask."

Mary turned around and headed back toward Cairn. Ten minutes later we were at the Community of Conciliation mansion. Just before she pulled into the long driveway, Mary turned off her lights. As we approached the looming, gabled structure she pulled off the gravel drive, drove on the lawn around to the back of the mansion, then turned off the engine. The digital display on the dashboard clock read 4:08. To the right, sixty or seventy yards down the sloping lawn, the Hudson gleamed silver in the moonlight.

Mary got out, then motioned for us to do the same. We stepped out onto the lawn, and with Garth supporting me with a large, strong hand under my left armpit, we followed her the short distance from the car to the mansion. She opened a screen door, which led into a pantry area off a huge kitchen. To our left, barely visible in the moonlight that spilled in through the doorway, was a cobweb-covered door that creaked on its hinges as she opened it. Placing our hands on the wall to our right to guide us in the darkness, we started up a narrow, winding flight of stairs that, judging from the thick curtains of cobwebs that brushed across my face and clung to my flesh, hadn't been used since sometime around the Revolutionary War. After two flights of this I was beginning to feel nauseous and dizzy, but I concentrated on taking deep, measured breaths and placing one foot after the other on the stairs.

On the fourth floor Mary pushed open another door, led us out of the staircase into a musty-smelling corridor that was dimly, eerily illuminated by moonlight streaming in through a large stained-glass window at the opposite end. She led us into the third room on the right, closed the door, and turned on the light. I looked around, saw piles of broken furniture, steamer trunks, dozens of standing lamps without bulbs, assorted bric-a-brac. Everything was covered with a thick layer of dust. I turned to Mary, found her staring at me; her face was ashen, her eyes filled with alarm. I felt the warm blood on the lid of my left eye a moment before it oozed into the eye itself. Suddenly I was in total darkness.

"Mongo, you're bleeding!"

"Mmm," I replied as Garth grabbed me under the arms, marched me back a few steps, and planted me in the depths of an overstuffed armchair. A cloud of dust rose up around me, and I sneezed.

Garth wiped the blood away from my eye with his handkerchief, then began carefully unwrapping the bandage from my head. "I'll need fresh bandages, alcohol, and lots of cotton swabbing," he said over his shoulder to Mary, who continued to look very pale. "Do you think you can find those things around here?"

Mary swallowed hard, nodded. "Yes. We have medical supplies. I'll get them."

But she didn't move.

"Don't panic, Mary," Garth said in the same quiet, soothing tone as he continued to unwrap my bandages. "And don't worry. The hardest part of Mongo is his head, and we know there's no fracture. Just get the bandages and alcohol, and try not to be seen. Okay?"

"Okay," Mary replied in a small voice, and then hurried from the room.

Garth, who was kneeling on the floor in front of me, finished his unwrapping job. He dropped the blood-soaked bandages on the floor, then wrinkled his nose as he studied the gash above my right eye.

"How does it look?" I asked.

"Gory. Want to see?"

"Why not? I've never seen my own brains, and I need something to cheer me up."

Garth got to his feet and rummaged around in the surrounding piles of junk until he found a cracked hand mirror, which he brought back to me. I looked at myself in the mirror, decided that, all in all, my head didn't look as bad as I had expected. The right eye was swollen shut, which was no surprise. Scalp wounds are notoriously bloody, and all the blood was coming from an area above my right eye where two or three of the dozen or so stitches closing the gash had torn loose. There was also a shaved area the size of a pancake on the right side of my head, just above the ear, and another cut; I counted eight stitches there, and they had held firm.

"No sign of any brains," I said.

"I can't believe you actually said that. You're stealing my best lines."

A few minutes later Mary came back into the attic storage room, quickly and quietly closing the door behind her. She carried a paper bag, which she set down beside her as she knelt on the floor in front of me. Her face was still ashen, but she didn't flinch when she saw my wounds, and her voice was steady when she spoke.

"I'm afraid this is going to hurt a bit, Mongo," she said as she removed a bottle of hydrogen peroxide, a thick roll of bandages, and cotton swabbing from the bag. "There's nobody living on these two upper floors, so you can yell a little bit if you want to."

"I'll take care of it, Mary," Garth said evenly but firmly as he took the bottle of hydrogen peroxide from her hand. "I like to hear Mongo squeal."

"But—"

"I'll take care of it. Now, I don't know about you two, but I'm hungry. We have to keep our energy levels up. Mary, do you suppose you can sneak us all up something to eat?"

"I think so," she replied distantly. She studied Garth intently for a few moments, then abruptly got to her feet and once again slipped out through the door.

I leaned back in the chair and closed my good eye as Garth began his ministrations. He daubed more blood away from my eye and cleansed the wound with peroxide, then fashioned an effective pressure bandage from cotton wadding held in place by surgical tape. As his fingers moved, he had an almost blank stare, and he was humming some tune in a voice so low it was nearly inaudible. His touch and the humming had a near-hypnotic effect, and for the first time since I had awoken in the hospital I was virtually free of pain. When I opened my eye, I was startled to see Mary sitting on the floor a few feet away, staring at Garth as he worked on me. I had not heard the door open or close.

Beside her was a silver tray containing a loaf of bread, cold cuts, silverware, a tall pitcher of orange juice, and glasses. It seemed Garth's usual calming influence had also worked its powers on the woman, for some color had returned to Mary's face, and she no longer seemed as tense and nervous.

"It's not serious, Mary," Garth said softly, tilting his head back in her direction as he began to quickly and expertly rebandage my head, this time leaving both eyes uncovered. "Just messy. You have to understand my brother. The man craves constant attention, and he's not past flying his car through the air, banging up his head, and bleeding all over the place just to get sympathy."

I tried to think of an appropriate reply, but I didn't feel I knew Mary Tree well enough yet to employ the obscenities required; besides, I was too tired, if now pleasantly so, to engage in a lot of bantering. I satisfied myself with an exaggerated roll of my good eye.

The woman removed her bifocals and set them on the floor beside the tray, then brushed her hands back through her long, fine, graying golden hair. She cocked her head slightly and continued to stare at Garth's profile as he worked on me. There was a strange light in her eyes. "Garth Frederickson," she said at last in a low, husky, decidedly sexy voice, "we've only just met, and yet I have this odd feeling that I've known you a very long time. Maybe it's just that I've wanted to know someone like you. I don't really understand it. There's no artifice or sham in you, and yet I think you're the strangest man I've ever met."

I mumbled, "You've got that right, Mary."

But the folksinger had eyes only for Garth and no time for my piquant observations. I wasn't even sure she'd heard me.

"There's such a strange mix in you," she said, still staring at Garth. "There's no cruelty in you, and yet I sense a great capacity for violence . . . even brutality. At the same time there's this incredible gentleness in you, which is what I'm seeing right now. You're like some great jungle cat, ready to either purr or pounce at any given moment. I suspect that with some people you display infinite patience, and no patience at all with others. A half hour ago you were prepared to kill two men on sight."

"Oh, I'm still prepared to kill those two particular men on sight," Garth said mildly.

"I don't understand how you can live with those kinds of emotional extremes, two personalities which are contradictory, and at war in you."

Garth merely shrugged. "I don't see, or feel, any contradiction. Different types of people elicit different reactions and require different handling."

I said, "Garth has never hurt anyone who wasn't truly deserving, Mary."

"Violence begets violence," the woman said quietly, her tone slightly accusatory, but also uncertain.

"There's nothing complicated about me, Mary," Garth said evenly. "I am what you feel I am."

"But what I feel you are would be—is—quite different from what Gregory Trex or Jay Acton would feel if they met up with you."

Garth finished bandaging my head, using thin strips of surgical tape to secure the end of the bandage just behind my left ear. It was an excellent job, much better than had been done at the hospital; I felt considerably less pressure on the gash over my right eye and on the wound on the side of my head. Garth studied his handiwork for a few moments, grunted with satisfaction, then turned to face Mary and resumed speaking as if no time had passed between her words and his.

"Mary, you're a person who would sacrifice her life to save the life of another. But there are people who would gladly accept your sacrifice and laugh at you as they spat on your corpse. Dying for those kinds of people makes no sense to someone like me; you'll save far more lives if you just kill them and be done with it. It's what's called for, and it's what they really deserve. To me, your way of thinking is hopelessly complicated, like your behavior. I don't understand it. But it doesn't matter, because you've more than earned the right to think and behave as you like. I think we're about the same age. At a time long ago when my biggest concerns were pimples and finding ways to get girls to go out with me, you were already a world-class performer, singing on stages around the world and using your music to try to get nations to stop wasting their money on arms and use it to feed their people. You'd fight evil with a song, and that makes you the bravest person I know. I've always loved your music, and I've always thought you were just about the sexiest woman alive. Those tapes you gave Mongo to give me were a very fine gift, and I thank you."

Mary blushed—but she did not take her eyes away from Garth's. It certainly looked to me like the beginning of a mutual admiration society.

I said, "Let's eat."

The three of us sat cross-legged on the floor around the tray, making sandwiches from the bread and cold cuts and drinking the fresh-squeezed orange juice. With some food in my stomach, and my swollen right eye beginning to open, I felt a little better; my vision was not quite so blurred, and my headache was no worse than what I might suffer from a serious hangover—pesky, but not hopelessly debilitating.

"Well, Mongo," Garth said when we finished eating, "now I think it's time to evaluate our situation. I'd say we're in a peck of trouble. What do you say?"

I looked at Mary, grinned. "That brother of mine is such a perceptive analyst. Some of his insights will take your breath away."

Garth smiled benignly at me. "A local loony wants you dead because you embarrassed him. The KGB wants you dead because you can unmask one of their top agents. A very powerful right-winger and his FBI buddy would probably be just as happy if either the KGB or the local loony succeeds in getting you dead, because then you won't be in a position to embarrass *them*. The police around here turn out to be local errand boys who are willing to lock you up on a trumped-up murder charge, which has probably been engineered so that some sniper will know where to find you in order to put a bullet through your head. The FBI could probably guarantee your—our—safety, but Culhane's buddy Hendricks will make sure the FBI doesn't touch you—us—with a ten-mile-long pole. You're a fugitive from justice, and a warrant for my arrest is going to be issued just as soon as the police find out you're missing. Having talked to you means that both Mary and I are marked for death. The FBI will almost certainly ignore what we have to say, the local police can't guarantee our safety, and there are no good guys in the local vicinity; it seems all the guys around here are bad, hopelessly biased, blind, buffaloed, or simply don't want to be bothered. Have I left anything out?"

"No, I think that about covers it."

"Now, what's our next move?"

"Surely you jest," I said with a shrug. "Our next move is obvious; we call in the very old, very bald cavalry."

"My thinking exactly," Garth said, and turned to Mary. "Where's the nearest phone?"

"There are three, but they're all down on the first floor—two in our offices, and one for personal use in our recreation room."

"You don't have one in your room?"

"No."

"Can I get down there and use the phone without anyone seeing me?"

Mary grimaced. "I'm not sure, Garth. We have some early risers here. You'd have to go through the main living areas to get to any of the phones, and you'd have to stand out in the open to use them."

Garth grunted, then pushed himself to his feet and began searching through the dusty rubble in the storage room. In an old rolltop desk he found yellowed paper and a stub of a pencil. He wrote on the paper, then came back across the room and handed the slip to Mary.

"This is a number where you can reach a friend of ours," he said, smiling reassuringly. "His name is Mr. Lippitt. It isn't necessary that you know who he is or what he does. He's a heavyweight, and he can guarantee our safety until we get this business all straightened out. When you call that number, somebody will answer by repeating the number. Identify yourself as a friend of Robert and Garth Frederickson, say you want to talk to Mr. Lippitt, and state that it's a 'Valhalla priority.'"

Mary studied the name and number on the slip of paper, then looked up at Garth and me. "Valhalla priority? What does that mean?"

"It's not important," Garth said curtly, shaking his head. "After you make the call, you'll forget those words, Mr. Lippitt's name, and the number. Also, please destroy the paper immediately. What will happen is that you'll get through to Mr. Lippitt at once, with no questions asked, no matter where he is. He won't have much to say, and he'll probably be suspicious because he doesn't know you. Just tell him what's happened; tell him everything Mongo told you. Tell him where we are, and why we need him to help us get out of here. There should be men here within the hour to take us out, maybe by helicopter."

"Wow," Mary said softly as she once again looked at the slip of paper in her hand.

"Everything's going to be all right, Mary," Garth said evenly as he helped her to her feet. "Just make the call. Try not to be seen, but if you are just act as if nothing is wrong."

"I'll be right back," Mary said, and once more slipped out of the room.

"There's going to be a lot of nasty fallout from this, Garth," I said. "Hendricks and everyone else at the FBI are going to go apeshit when they find out Lippitt has muddied up their turf. Gregory Trex and Jay Acton and Dan Mosely's buddy-buddy relationship with Elysius Culhane notwithstanding, it's going to be hard to explain why I felt it necessary to skip away from police custody, and why you felt it was necessary to aid and abet me. You had to be there. They're going to say we overreacted."

"As long as we all get out of Cairn alive, anybody can say anything he likes."

"I'm thinking of Mr. Lippitt; he's not exactly a favorite son of the right wing. He could be accused of helping two of his friends elude justice, at considerable expense to the taxpayers. You know the right wing controls a lot of newspaper space and airtime. We don't want Mr. Lippitt hurt."

Garth shook his head. "Mr. Lippitt can take care of himself in any war, bureaucratic or otherwise. If he's smart, and we know he is, he'll send a second team to snatch Acton. With Elysius Culhane's KGB staff member on ice and ready to be trotted out for public show-and-tell, nobody on the right is going to touch a hair on Lippitt's head."

"A hair on Lippitt's head?"

"I was speaking figuratively, of course."

"That's good."

The door opened, and Mary stepped in. She still held the slip of paper Garth had given her in a hand that trembled noticeably. Her face was ashen again, but her voice was steady. "The phones don't work," she said, looking back and forth between Garth and me. "I can't get a dial tone on any of them."

"We waited too long," I said as I watched Garth take the Colt from his jacket pocket and remove the safety catch. "Somebody's cut the goddamn phone lines. They found out I was gone, saw that your car was still in the parking lot, and guessed where we'd go. Or maybe Mary's car was spotted after all."

Garth nodded tersely, then turned to Mary, who was staring at the gun in his hand. "Mary, you must do exactly as I say, and you must do it quickly. I don't know how much time we have. Right now there are men, maybe your death squad, watching this house, waiting for Mongo, you, and me to show ourselves. When we don't, they're likely to get impatient and come in after us. You have to get everyone else out of here; tell them to go jogging or take a walk into town, or whatever, but get them out."

Mary, who was still staring wide-eyed at the Colt in Garth's right hand, shook her head absently. "What reason am I supposed to give them, Garth?"

"I don't know; anything. Just get them out. I don't think the men will hassle the others; they want us."

"I'll send someone for the police."

Garth shook his head impatiently. "I doubt you'll find any cops in this part of town right now, but even if you did, it wouldn't do any good. Both Mongo and I, and maybe you, would be right back in the situation we just got Mongo out of."

Mary started to leave, and I grabbed her arm. "Mary, I know you don't have guns in the house, but do you have *anything* I might be able to use to defend myself? A knife, maybe? The people who are after us will kill us in cold blood if they get the chance."

"I believe you," she replied in a hoarse voice. "I'll see what I can find."

"Go," Garth said, and gently pushed her out of the room.

Garth turned off the light, left the door open a crack, and

listened. I moved closer, listened with him. I said, "Unless they actually saw us in the car, they can't be certain we're here. They're just guessing."

"Unless they saw us in the car."

"Right."

We waited by the door, listening. The air in the room suddenly felt musty and heavy in my lungs. From below I thought I heard a knock, and then the sound of muffled voices, but I couldn't be sure. Then there was silence. Footsteps, another knock, more voices.

And then gunfire—a short burst of automatic weapons fire from the ground or second floor. Shouts. Screams.

"Shit!" I said, and reached for the doorknob.

"Wait," Garth said, pushing me back.

"Jesus Christ, Garth, they were already in the house. They must have seen or heard Mary trying to move the others out and decided they'd waited long enough. We can't just let them kill those people down there."

Garth shook his head. "Wait. I don't think they're going to gun down a bunch of pacifists. That shooting was just to get their attention—and ours. They still may not be certain we're here; Mary may be able to bluff them."

Suddenly there was another burst of gunfire and then the sound of running feet. There were more shouts, but from where we were it was impossible to tell what was happening or being said.

"Christ, Garth, can we take that chance?!"

Garth held up the Colt. "Walking down there is the same as committing suicide. They have at least one automatic weapon, and this thing isn't going to be much use against it."

I couldn't argue with that.

We waited some more. There was no further gunfire, but muffled shouts continued to drift up from below. Then there was silence, which lasted for three or four minutes. Both Garth and I strained to hear some sound; what we finally heard was what sounded like heavy, booted footsteps on the main staircase, slowly ascending. The footsteps came closer, finally stopped at the top of the stairs on our floor, perhaps twenty feet to our right.

"*We know the two of you are in here someplace!*" a man shouted. I'd half expected the gunman coming up the stairs to be Gregory Trex, but this was not a voice I recognized. "*We've got everybody downstairs in the big room! If you two aren't down there in five minutes, those people are going to start to die! We'll shoot the folksinger first!*"

Somewhere below a woman screamed, the agonized sound penetrating clearly, harrowingly, up through the hardwood floors and thick plaster ceilings of the old mansion. I thought it might have been Mary, but I wasn't sure. I swallowed hard, glanced at the luminous dial of my wristwatch.

"They may plan to kill everybody anyway," I said in a voice that had gone hoarse. "Ten to one they're local boys, and masks aren't going to keep them from being recognized."

"Uh-huh," Garth said. From the light seeping in from the hallway, I could see that he was staring at the gun in his hand.

"If we go down there, we'll be walking right into an ambush. They certainly mean to kill us, and they probably won't waste any time doing it."

"Uh-huh."

"But we don't have much choice, do we?"

"Nope," Garth said as he turned me around and pulled up my shirt. He stuck the gun into the waistband of my jeans, pulled my shirt back down over it. "This Colt isn't going to do us much good in a straight shoot-out, but on the other hand, they don't know we have a gun at all. We're just going to have to rely on the Fredericksons' natural talents for stealth and cunning to get us through this. If we can get close enough to them, catch them off guard before they cut us down, I just might be able to relieve them of duty. You do the talking, I'll do the shooting. Bail out when you feel me grab the gun."

"That's the stupidest plan you've ever had, brother. What makes you think they're going to let either of us do any talking? They're probably going to cut us in half the moment we step into the ballroom downstairs, which is where they must be."

"You'll just have to talk very fast. Say something instantly hypnotic."

"Instantly hypnotic. I see." I removed the gun from my waistband, stepped around behind Garth, and stuck it into his.

"What the hell do you think you're doing?"

"It makes more sense for me to grab the gun off you; for one thing, I won't have to bend over to get at it. Don't *you* forget to drop to the floor. If you entertain any thoughts of trying to shield me after I grab the gun, forget them. You'll only interfere with my line of fire."

Garth reached back for the gun, but I grabbed his wrist.

"Mongo, you can't even *see,* for Christ's sake!"

"What's the matter? You afraid I won't remember to divide by two before I shoot?"

"Can you walk?"

"After all the other scrapes we've gotten into and survived, I find the prospect of being gunned down by a bunch of local shitheads in a place owned by a group of pacifists not only terribly ironic but tremendously stimulating to my nervous system. I can walk, and I'll shoot straight if I get the chance."

Garth sucked in a deep breath, slowly let it out. "Luck," he said softly.

"Luck," I said, then walked with my brother out of the room and into the corridor, which was now dimly awash with the light of dawn.

We'd reached the third-floor landing when a woman—this time definitely identifiable as Mary—screamed again.

"*We're coming!*" Garth shouted, and we quickened our pace descending the stairs.

I half expected a gunman to suddenly appear in the stairwell below us and start shooting, but we made it to the ground floor. With Garth a half step ahead of me and slightly to my right, we walked quickly across the grand foyer toward the entrance to the ballroom. I was talking, loud and fast, as we proceeded under the great arch.

"You men may think you're fighting communism, but the fact of the matter is that the Russians are likely to give you the Order of Lenin for this little caper!"

Ah. No bullets tearing through us yet. We stopped a few feet inside the entrance and surveyed the scene. The sun was just climbing over the horizon, and light was pouring in through the huge bank of windows at the eastern end of the ballroom, to our left. Fourteen men and women, ranging in age from early twenties to middle age and most still in their pajamas and bathrobes, were standing on a paint-spattered tarpaulin, lined up against the wall directly across from us. They were being guarded by three men wearing identical green-plaid ski masks; the men were armed with automatic pistols they definitely hadn't picked up in the local Army & Navy store. One man, easily identifiable from his physique as Gregory Trex, was standing next to Mary, twisting her right arm up behind her back. The gazes of all three men were on us.

They certainly looked like a death squad to me.

"If you love the United States of America, you'd damn well better listen to what I have to say before you start shooting anybody!" I continued quickly in a voice that sounded hopelessly high-pitched and squeaky in my own ears. "You've been set up and used by the very Russians you claim to hate so much. The communists have been making fools of you. If you kill us, they're not only going to get away with it but'll be able to go on making fools of you and the whole nation. You think Jay Acton, the man who's giving you your marching orders, is a super-patriotic American. I'm telling you the son-of-a-bitch is a Russian, and a KGB agent to boot! Without realizing it, you've been acting as a goon squad for the enemies of this country. Give it up *now*! Don't do this thing. If you give us time, my brother and I can prove that Acton is a Russian agent. If you stop the killing now, if you turn yourselves in and cooperate with the authorities, you may be able to strike a deal. If you love your country, you'll lay down your guns and help us nail Jay Acton."

I thought it was rather a nice speech—if not exactly instantly hypnotic, then at least strongly persuasive. However, it hadn't seemed to make much of an impression on my audience, the gunmen, who exchanged glances. It was Gregory Trex—making no effort whatsoever to disguise his voice—who spoke.

"What the hell are you talking about, dwarf? What's this bullshit about Acton giving us orders?"

Hmm. "You're saying he doesn't? You're saying it wasn't Jay Acton who put you up to this?"

"You're fucking crazy."

Trex sounded genuinely confused by the mention of Jay Acton, which tended to genuinely confuse me. The problem was that I didn't have time to be confused. I made an expansive gesture, putting my hands out to my sides, the purpose being to get my right hand as close as possible to the gun in Garth's waistband. Garth began to move slowly across the room, and I moved with him, resting my hand now on the butt of the gun.

Trex, still bending Mary's arm up behind her back, stayed where he was, while the other two men fanned out across the room, one stopping in the center and the other going to the opposite wall; it would make for a hell of a cross fire.

"It doesn't make any difference who gave you the orders, Gregory," I said, tightening my grip on the gun, "because it's obvious that somebody did. You didn't get those weapons on your own."

"Stop there!" the gunman in the center of the room commanded.

We stopped. The figures of the three men blurred in and out of focus, and I squinted to try to keep the ghostly double images away. Sweat was now running into my good left eye, stinging it, and that didn't help at all. If Garth and I were going to die, the man I most wanted to take with us was Gregory Trex, but Trex was still holding Mary close to him. Even if I weren't suffering from double vision, I couldn't be sure of missing the woman if I fired at him.

Almost as if she had been reading my mind, Mary suddenly twisted in Trex's grip, then spat in his face. "Let me go, Gregory! Don't be a fool! You'll never—!"

Trex abruptly released his grip on her arm, spun her around, and drove his fist into her stomach. She cried out, doubled over, and slowly sank to her knees.

"Enough of this bullshit!" the man in the center of the room shouted, and abruptly stripped off his mask. It was the Vietnam vet with the ponytail I'd seen at the art exhibition Friday evening. "We don't need masks! We came here to clean out this nest of communist faggots, so let's get on with it!"

The other two gunmen slowly removed their masks. Trex leered at me, bloodlust gleaming in his milky green eyes. His mouth was half open, and saliva glistened on his small, gapped teeth. I hadn't seen the third gunman before.

It was time, and I began to slowly pull the gun from Garth's waistband. I knew I had no chance of killing all three men before they killed Garth and me, but I was damned well determined to kill Trex.

A balding, middle-aged man abruptly stepped away form the wall and moved toward Trex. "Listen, you—!"

"*Don't!*" I shouted—too late.

The man with the ponytail leveled his automatic pistol on the other man's stomach, pulled the trigger. The bullets caught the middle-aged man in the stomach and torso, ripping him open and hurling him backward. Blood spurted, misted in the air, sprayed over the rest of the shocked, screaming members of the Community of Conciliation.

I grabbed the Colt from Garth's waistband at almost the precise moment when my brother lunged forward, hit the floor, and rolled at the legs of the ponytailed gunman. I crouched down, squinted, and squeezed off a shot at the blurred figure that was Gregory Trex. I heard him scream, saw him grab at his right shoulder as he spun around and fell to the floor. I cursed my poor marksmanship and knew there was no time for a second shot. I leaped to my left, hit the floor, and rolled as a hail of bullets tore through the space where I had just been standing. I had no plan; there was absolutely no cover in the stripped ballroom, and there was no way I could make it out through the archway into the foyer before I was riddled with bullets. It was all instinct now, reflex; I knew I was going to die and was simply determined to elude death until the last possible moment. I was sorry I hadn't had time to say a proper goodbye to my brother.

Then, mixed with the cacophony of screams and automatic weapons fire, there was another sound—the higher-pitched chatter of another, heavier automatic weapon, muffled somewhat, as if the fire was coming from outside the mansion. An instant later there erupted a booming cascade of sound like an explosion of glass, as if the bank of windows at the east end was collapsing. The Colt slipped from my grasp. I stopped rolling, curled up in an instinctive attempt to make myself as small a target as possible; I clamped my arms over my head and waited for bullets to rip into me.

And then the gunfire stopped abruptly, leaving in its wake an echo that reverberated throughout the huge chamber, a hideous counterpoint to the continued screaming of the Community members. Hands gripped my shoulders, and I recognized the touch of my brother.

"Mongo! Mongo, are you hit?!"

I opened my left eye, found myself looking into Garth's face through a film of blood that I knew was coming from the reopened gash over my right eye. But the wound didn't hurt. My head didn't hurt; nothing hurt. Astonishment at finding the Frederickson brothers still alive seemed to be working like a powerful general anesthesia. I wiped the blood away with my shirt sleeve, sat up.

"No," I said. "You?"

"No."

"What the hell happened?"

"We've got a visitor, brother," Garth said in a tone of voice that I thought sounded somewhat cryptic.

"Who?"

"See for yourself," he replied, and moved to one side.

I took Garth's hand and hauled myself to my feet, looked out over the room, and squinted in an effort to focus my vision. The dawn light streaming in through the open space where the windows had been was mixed now with swirling dust and gunsmoke that danced and spun and drifted on the gentle breezes flowing into the ballroom from off the Hudson. A figure moved in the backlit dust and smoke, but I couldn't see who it was. Off to my right, Mary and other Community members were attending to the men and women who had been wounded. The Vietnam veteran with the ponytail was missing not only his ponytail but the half of his head to which it had been attached; he was quite dead, lying in a spreading pool of blood in the center of the room. The third gunman was dead also. Of the death squad members, only Gregory Trex remained alive—thanks to me. The pig-faced young man with the bandaged nose and forehead was writhing on the floor, yelping in pain, clawing at his bullet-ravaged right shoulder. By attempting to kill him but only winging him and sending him to the floor, I had inadvertently saved Gregory Trex's life, protected him from the fate that had befallen his two comrades at the hands of our mysterious rescuer.

This did not please me. Suddenly the identity of the shadowy figure moving in the smoky light was nowhere near as important to me as the rage I felt toward Trex. I pushed Garth's supporting hand away, staggered over to where the wide-eyed Trex was thrashing on the floor, and sat down hard on his chest. There was a strong odor of feces; with the tables turned, with somebody shooting at *him*, the young killer had lost control of his sphincter.

"*Who sent you?*" I screamed into his battered face.

Trex, saliva streaming from his mouth, moved his lips in an effort to speak, but he wasn't making enough progress to suit me. I punched his wounded shoulder, and he screamed; I raised my fist, threatening to punch him again, and he stopped.

"Who ordered you to do this, Trex? Was it Jay Acton?"

He shook his head back and forth, bubbled up some more saliva, and tried to reach across his body to grip his damaged shoulder. I stopped him.

"Who?! You'd better find your voice fast, kiddo, or I'm going to rip your fucking shoulder off! Who sent you?! Who gave you those weapons?!"

". . . hane," he finally managed to croak. "Mr. Culhane. We've been . . . helping him clean the trash off the streets and fight the communists. He said it was the only way left, because the leftists had taken over the government and the courts. He said what we needed was a death squad like they have in other countries. When he found out you were gone, he called me. He said I should get the other two and go after you. He said that you were probably hiding out here and that we should kill everyone because it was time to get serious about what we wanted to do. He said that you two and these people were just like the communists and that the only way to deal with you was to kill you."

"He gave you the guns?"

Trex nodded, then reached up with his left hand and wiped spittle off his chin. "He gave them to us a few weeks ago. He said first we'd kill some of the scum on the streets, like drug dealers, and then we'd go after communists."

"How did Culhane find out so fast that I was gone from the hospital?"

"I don't know. I suppose the police told him. Mosely's scared shitless of Mr. Culhane; he tells him everything."

"Did you people kill Michael Burana and Harry Peal?"

"No."

"Who did? Acton?"

"I don't know."

"I don't believe you," I said, and raised my fist again.

A voice close beside me said, "I think he's telling the truth."

In my seething rage at Gregory Trex, in my need for answers, I had virtually forgotten all about the man who had saved our lives. Now I raised my head, glanced to my left, and found myself looking into the dark eyes and deeply tanned face of Jay Acton. His razor-cut brown hair was covered now by a black seaman's cap; instead of one of his custom-tailored suits, he was dressed in black—boots, jeans, a turtleneck sweater. In his right hand he carried an Uzi automatic rifle. Under his left arm he carried the three automatic pistols originally wielded by the recently disbanded death squad. Garth's Colt was stuck in the waistband of his jeans.

"Damn," I said.

"What the hell have you two been up to?" he asked curtly, glancing back and forth between Garth, who had come over to stand beside him, and me. "Who have you been talking to, and what have you been saying?"

"What have *we* been up to?!" I swallowed hard, again used the sleeve of my shirt to wipe blood away from my eyes. "Listen, you lying, spying, Russian son-of-a-bitch, I—!" I stopped in midsentence when I heard the distant wail of approaching police sirens. "This should be interesting," I said, grabbing Garth's outstretched hand and hauling myself to my feet.

Jay Acton glanced quickly toward the front of the house, then back at us. "If you wait for the police, you'll be taken into custody," he said tersely. "If that happens, the chances are good that you'll both end up dead within seventy-two hours. We have to go."

"Why?" Garth asked, studying Acton through narrowed lids. He pointed at the two dead gunmen, then at the writhing, whimpering man on the floor at my feet. "You put the death squad out of business."

Acton shook his head impatiently, again glanced anxiously toward the front of the house. The sirens were much closer. "These were amateurs," he said quickly, in the same curt tone. "Clumsy boobs manipulated by Culhane to act out Culhane's fantasy of operating a death squad like the political death squads they have in his beloved Guatemala and El Salvador. I know because I put the idea in his head."

I blinked, stared into the other man's glacial black eyes. "*You* put—?!"

"There's no time to explain now," Acton interrupted. "I'm here because a few hours ago somebody tried to kill me—and that person was no amateur. I have reason to believe there's a KGB assassin after me, which means that the same assassin, or assassins, will also be after you now that this attempt has failed. You'll have no chance out in the open. You have to come with me."

"Where?" Garth asked.

The dark-eyed KGB officer with the high cheekbones and strong chin abruptly shoved one of the automatic pistols into my brother's hands. "We have to trust each other now; all our lives depend on it. I need you to tell me precisely what's been going on and to walk me in; you need me to stay alive."

Garth and I glanced at each other, and I could see my own thoughts reflected in his eyes; considering the fact that everyone in the mansion would now be dead if it weren't for Jay Acton, it seemed the man had proved his *bona fides.* "It's your show, Acton," I said.

"Who else knows about me?"

"I do." It was Mary. I hadn't heard her come up, but she was now standing directly behind me, and it was obvious that she'd overheard most of our conversation. "I'm coming with you."

"And we'll take him," Acton said, pointing to Gregory Trex. "He's been witness to a lot of things we'll need to prove—but he'll end up a dead witness if we leave him here."

Garth grunted, stepped over to Trex, and reached down. He grabbed the front of Trex's shirt, rudely hauled him to his feet.

"Let's go," Acton said as he grabbed one of Trex's arms. "Follow me. Down to the river."

Garth grabbed Trex's other arm, and together they half dragged, half carried the thoroughly terrified young man across the glass-strewn floor of the ballroom toward the gaping hole at the far end. Mary offered me her hand. I gratefully took it, and together we followed along through the clouds of sunlit dust and smoke. As I stepped up and over a jagged ridge of glass and dropped to the lawn outside, I thought I heard the police come crashing in at the other end.

Tightly holding on to Mary's hand for support, I stumbled along over the grass down toward the river and the Community's dock. Garth was already removing a canoe and paddles from the wooden rack nearby. Acton abruptly swung the stock of his Uzi around, catching Gregory Trex squarely on the jaw. Trex crumpled to the ground. Acton helped Garth put the canoe into the water, where Mary and I steadied it while they went back to the rack for a second canoe.

I glanced up toward the mansion, but saw no one in the space where the windows had been. Either I had been wrong about hearing the police coming in just as we were leaving, or everyone was too busy attending to the wounded to bother about us, or the Community members—sensing, if not understanding, our need to escape—were providing some kind of distraction.

Garth and Acton lifted the unconscious Trex off the ground and unceremoniously dumped him into the bottom of the canoe Mary and I were holding steady. Acton handed me a paddle and motioned for me to get into the bow, and I did. He got in behind me. Mary climbed into the second canoe, with Garth in the stern, and we shoved off, heading straight out into the river.

I had no idea where we were going, but since I didn't have to steer, it didn't make any difference; my job was simply to paddle, and that's what I did. Every time I dipped my paddle in the water and pulled, pain shot through my entire body, especially my head, but the hurt was bearable; despite me and my circumstances, my body seemed to be healing itself, and I vowed to give it a healthy dose of Scotch as a reward as soon as I got the opportunity. I scooped up a handful of river water to wash the sticky blood from around my eyes, then looked back over my shoulder. Our mini-armada would be clearly visible from the shore, but there was no sign of anyone there to see us. Garth's steady, powerful strokes were keeping the canoe carrying him and Mary a few feet off our stern and slightly to starboard.

Then we passed beneath the looming prow of a three-masted sloop into a veritable thicket of sail- and powerboats that were anchored a hundred to a hundred and fifty yards offshore up and down the river. Acton trailed the edge of his paddle off the port gunwale, and the canoe turned that way, the bow pointing upriver. Now we were hidden from view and would stay that way as long as we continued to thread our way through the anchored boats.

Suddenly I was very, very tired, as if the healing body I had been so pleased with a few moments before had decided that enough was enough and was shutting down for an indefinite period of time. I splashed some more water on my face, and when that didn't help I laid my paddle across the gunwales, leaned on it, and took a series of deep breaths in an attempt to reenergize myself.

"I can handle it, Frederickson," Jay Acton said from behind me. "We're in the clear now. Take it easy."

I nodded, leaned even harder on my paddle. "How did you know we were in the mansion?"

"I didn't; I just knew that Culhane thought you might be, and, if you were, that his boys would kill you, and everyone else in there, so that you wouldn't be able to expose me. I have a tap on his phone."

"What did he tell Trex and the other two?"

"Culhane always talked to Trex, and left Trex to talk to the others. Nothing complicated. He just said you were all communists, naturally, and that it was time for the real patriots in this country to take some drastic action. I don't imagine it took much to get Trex moving; he's been aching to kill Community members anyway, ever since Culhane gave the three of them those automatic pistols."

I half turned in my seat, looked down at the unconscious man sprawled in the bottom of the canoe, sniffed, and wrinkled my nose. "I don't think our boy here would have made out too well in combat. I really wish he hadn't shit in his pants."

Acton grunted. "You and your brother are something else, Frederickson."

"Garth and I owe you our lives. Thanks for what you did back there, Acton."

"You're welcome. But I've told you that I need you alive for my own purposes."

"To explain to you how you were found out?"

"That and more."

"I don't understand. What use can Garth and I be to you?"

"I suggest you rest now. Save your energy. We'll talk later, when we're all together."

"Where are we going?"

"You'll see."

The fact of the matter was that, for the moment at least, I didn't really care where we were going; I was simply happy that Garth and I were alive, that the pain in my head and the double vision had eased somewhat, and that I could rest. Leaning forward on the paddle, I kept nodding off.

When I lifted my head and looked around after yet another brief nap, I was surprised to find that we had cut back out of the pack of anchored boats and were almost ashore. Above us, soaring into the sky, was the scarred, gouged, naked stone face of the abandoned rock quarry.

Suddenly the bow of the canoe scraped against the fine gravel that formed a narrow beach at the base of the mountain. I tried to get out, intending to pull the canoe up on the beach and steady it, but wobbled and sat down hard on the damp gravel. I gripped the gunwales with both hands and tried to pull myself to my feet, but couldn't. Finally I just leaned back on my elbows and supervised as Garth and Acton unloaded the now semiconscious Gregory Trex. With Garth holding his arms and Acton his feet, they sloshed the helpless would-be hunter of communist men, women, and children in the river in an attempt to get some of the stink out of his clothes, then unceremoniously set him down hard on a rock a few yards away from me. His milky green eyes, filled now with shock and terror, kept darting around, as if he were looking for someone to come to his rescue. He kept clutching at his wounded shoulder, but otherwise remained still.

Mary came up, knelt down beside me, and put her arm around me as Garth and Jay Acton waded both canoes back out to chest-deep water, then used sharp-edged rocks to punch holes in their bottoms. As the canoes slowly sank out of sight, I slowly sank my head onto Mary Tree's left breast and promptly fell asleep again.

CHAPTER NINE

Alittle sleep did wonders. I awoke to the tantalizing aroma of coffee with a merely dull headache and only slightly blurred vision. My right eye was beginning to open. With the help of a little bouncing around on a hardwood floor while being shot at, followed by a scenic canoe ride, my condition just kept improving. Talk about physical therapy. My sprained wrist, sore knee, and bruised arm seemed healed. I was a medical marvel.

I touched my head, found it covered with a fresh bandage, as was the gash over my right eye. I threw back the lightweight wool blanket covering me, sat up, and looked around. I'd been laid to rest on an inflated air mattress in a corner of a large cave. A naked light bulb hung on its cord from a steel cleat driven into a crevice in the rock ceiling; the cord snaked down a wall and then around a corner into another, smaller cave where I thought I heard the hum of a gasoline-driven electric generator. Another wire, which appeared to be an aerial, snaked along the ceiling and out of the entrance; it was connected to a large shortwave radio console set up on a plain wooden table directly under the light bulb. Also on the table were a cardboard carton and the new cellular telephone that had been in it. Toward the front of the cave, to one side of the entrance, was a large foot locker, with its lid open. There was also a camp stove, and a pot of coffee was being kept warm over a flaming Sterno can. There was an ample supply of bottled water, pots and pans, kerosene space heaters for colder weather, and even a chemical toilet toward the rear. It looked like the perfect spy's *pied-à-terre*, with virtually all the comforts of home.

And more. When I rose, walked to the front of the cave, and looked in the foot locker, I found an assortment of weapons inside, including a Kalashnikov assault rifle. Also ammunition, electronic eavesdropping equipment that appeared to be state-of-the-art, code pads, a well-stocked medical kit, Styrofoam cups, and a half carton of Campbell's chicken soup.

I took one of the Styrofoam cups, filled it to the brim with steaming black coffee, sipped at it as I made my way out of the cave in search of my spymaster host and his other guests. I found Gregory Trex, his wrists and ankles tied with nylon rope, in a wide rock channel just outside the cave where he had been put to air out. His shirt around his bullet-damaged shoulder had been torn away, and the wound bandaged. He appeared to be in a state of shock; his eyes were dull and unfocused as he looked in my direction, and he didn't speak. His breathing was rapid and shallow; his mouth was half open, and dried saliva flecked his lips and chin. He still stank.

Prolonged exposure to the rapidly deteriorating young man was almost, if not quite, enough to make me feel like a bully for what I'd done to him. It was the kind of thinking, I mused, that could lead to my application for membership in the Community of Conciliation. I gave him a wide berth as I headed toward the mouth of the channel.

I recalled my conversation with Elysius Culhane on Friday evening at the art exhibition. Now I realized that he'd had a lot more on his mind than the desire to pump me for potentially damaging information on President Kevin Shannon; he'd been concerned that my visit to Cairn might somehow be connected to his death squad. As things were turning out, his concern had not been totally unfounded.

At the end of the channel I emerged onto a relatively narrow rock ledge high above the Hudson, close to the top of the mountain. Below, off to the south, I could see the plateau and picnic area where Dan Mosely took me for our chat two days before. To my immediate left was the beginning of a rough, brush-covered trail that appeared to go nowhere, but that I suspected led to other parts of the quarry, and perhaps to the top of the mountain as well.

Still sipping my coffee, I moved off to my right on the ledge, and before long came to a rather deep and wide plateau that had been gouged out of the side of the mountain. Garth and Mary stood across the way, and they seemed to be involved in a heavy conversation. Mary was standing very close to my brother, both of her hands resting on one of his heavily muscled forearms. They definitely looked like an item to me. I sipped some more coffee, loudly cleared my throat; the two of them started, turned, and looked at me.

"The coffee in this establishment is okay," I said, "but I have to tell you that the nursing care sucks."

"You don't need a nurse, Mongo," Garth said, concern in his voice and face as he and Mary quickly walked across the stone to me, put their hands on my shoulders, "you need a goddamn keeper. We thought you'd sleep around the clock. What the hell are you doing walking around?"

"Mongo?" Mary said, frowning in obvious disapproval. "You shouldn't be up. You could have gotten dizzy and fallen off the ledge."

"I'm all right. Where's our KGB friend?"

Garth stepped back, pointed above my head. I turned around, looked up. Jay Acton, his chestnut-brown hair blowing in the breeze coming down off the mountain, was sitting on a ledge about ten feet above my head, staring out over the river. His Uzi was resting across his knees. It was impossible to tell from his impassive features what he was thinking, but from this angle he bore an even more striking resemblance to his father.

"I filled him in on what's been going down, Mongo," Garth said quietly.

"All of it?"

"What you've told me, and what I know."

"Then he knows about Harry Peal?"

"Sure. I told him that's how you got on to him."

"Did he kill him?"

"I don't know."

"What was his reaction when you told him Harry Peal was his father?"

"You're looking at it," Garth said, gesturing toward the man sitting on the ledge above us. "He just turned around and climbed up there. He's been sitting there for about an hour."

Acton looked down, saw me. He abruptly rose and, carrying the Uzi in his left hand, nimbly climbed down through a fissure in the rock connecting the ledge to the plateau on which we stood. He walked up to me, fixed me with the jet-black eyes that were obviously an inheritance from his mother.

"I'm sorry about your friend, Frederickson," he said to me, his voice low, even.

"Yeah," I said, and drained off my coffee. I crumpled the Styrofoam cup, dropped it to my feet. "Did you kill him, Acton? And did you kill your father?"

If the Russian-American was shocked or hurt by my bluntness, he didn't show it. It occurred to me that, whatever he was guilty of, in the hour he had spent alone on the ledge he had somehow made peace with, and perhaps paid homage to, the father he had never known. He stared into my face for a few moments, his features still impassive, then sat down on the stone, setting the Uzi down at his side.

"My mother is still alive," he said in a voice so low that Garth, Mary, and I had to squat down in order to hear him. "She lives in a special residence for retired KGB personnel on the Black Sea. She told me that my father died in the siege of Stalingrad. I grew up in Dayton, Ohio, but I learned later that I was actually born in Kiev, and that my mother and I were smuggled back into the United States when I was still an infant; false identities, papers, and false histories were meticulously prepared, and a home was even provided for us. From the time I could talk it was instilled in me that, although we lived in the United States, I was very different from other American children; I was special, with a very special mission that would gradually be explained to me as I grew older. From a very early age I learned to be secretive. I was bilingual, of course, because my mother was bilingual, and she taught me both languages; but Russian was spoken only in the home, when we were alone, and in Russia. I learned the American version of history in the schools here, and my mother taught me the Russian version—the truth about the class struggle, as she put it. And, of course, there were the indoctrination sessions when I was taken back to the Soviet Union. My mother worked as a professor of music at a community college near Dayton, and part of our cover, or 'legend,' was that we had received a sizeable inheritance from my dead father. There was always money for travel; and when we traveled we almost always ended up in the Soviet Union for variable periods of time. In Russia my mother would meet and plan strategy with her controller while I would attend intensive indoctrination sessions. I was given a great deal of attention from an early age and received special favors. I was given my first 'medal' at the age of eleven. Arrangements were always made to get us in and out of Russia on special travel documents, so that our visits were never recorded in our U.S. passports.

"By the time I graduated from high school in this country I had already had virtually complete training as a KGB operative, if not an officer. I was a committed communist, completely dedicated to my mission, which was to infiltrate the American ultraconservative political movement and eventually move up to a position where I would have power and influence over key figures in that movement, without attracting too much attention to myself. That was my sole assignment. I attended Dartmouth in the late fifties, joined the Young Republicans there, and, years later, helped start up the *Dartmouth Review* with money I'd supposedly made publishing a small, ultraconservative newsletter in New Hampshire. Of course, it was actually Communist party money. I had a lot of what you might describe as editorial input with the *Review*—suggesting pieces and writing a lot of letters to the editor. Articles I'd suggested were responsible for inciting the attacks on the anti-apartheid shanties on campus, and I had a lot of input into the magazine's cruder attacks on black and Jewish professors. Op-ed articles I wrote for various newspapers and newsletters, including my own, on the supposed communist infiltration of the Democratic party and leftist organizations brought me to the attention of a number of important archconservatives at the national level. I turned down offers of editorial positions at the *National Review* and *Washington Times;* again, too public. When PACs got big, I sold my newsletter and took a job with the fund-raisers. Within six months, Elysius Culhane had hired me as a senior staff assistant and speechwriter." Acton paused, laughed drily. "I could have joined the CIA or FBI if I'd wanted to; I was heavily recruited by both agencies while I was at Dartmouth."

I asked, "Why didn't you?"

"Because that wasn't my assignment, and I hadn't been trained for that kind of intelligence work. I had excellent cover for what I was doing, but my legend might not have survived close vetting by an intelligence or counterintelligence agency. Besides, the KGB gets all the information it wants about the CIA from other sources. Infiltrating the right-wing political infrastructure in this country was considered of much greater importance."

Mary, who had been listening to Jay Acton with an increasingly puzzled expression on her face, shook her head. "Why would you want to waste time with a bunch of right-wing loonies and chickenhawks like Elysius Culhane? That seems like very odd company for a communist. I don't understand."

My brother and I had had more than our share of experiences with said right-wing loonies, chickenhawks, and a battalion of religious zealots to boot. I thought I understood perfectly, and I was sure Garth did too.

"It's the perfect cover for a communist agent," Garth said evenly. "The groups would be relatively easy to penetrate, and once you were accepted in your role, no questions would likely ever be asked. The greatest danger would be discovery by an outsider, which is what happened in this case."

"Correct," Acton said in a flat voice, glancing at me.

My squatting position was beginning to hurt my knees, so I sat down on the stone and leaned back on my hands. "You don't understand because you're a liberal," I said to Mary, who still looked thoroughly bewildered. "You're a left-winger. Liberal types like you tend to be intellectual, straight-ahead rationalists. Symbols—things like the flag, 'The Star-Spangled Banner,' and pledges of allegiance—are all vaguely embarrassing to you; you don't think symbols should mean that much to truly thoughtful and patriotic citizens. You think political candidates visiting flag factories and spouting jingoistic rhetoric in halls filled with flags and nasty-looking bronze eagles is an insult to your intelligence, and you try your best to ignore such things.

"What liberals constantly underestimate is the power of those symbols and rhetoric over the minds of average people in this, or any other, country. The right wing never makes that mistake. They understand and are perfectly willing to exploit the fact that masses of citizens, usually a majority, can be relatively easily swayed by the right combination of demagoguery, hot rhetoric, and the manipulation of national symbols. Ultraconservatives tend to be anti-intellectual, which is why *public* education is never one of their primary concerns; in any nation where the electorate is 'numb, dumb, and happy,' as it were, it's easier for demagogues to get elected and then to stay in office. But their weakness—and the reason why it was so easy for Mr. Acton here to gain their trust—is that they're vulnerable to the same weapons they use: language and the manipulation of symbols. The right wing loves pageantry—look at the massive rallies in Nazi Germany—and they love to believe that their lies and deceptions aren't really lies and deceptions. In short, they tend to actually start believing their own bullshit, and if you feed it to them, in return they'll easily accept you as one of them.

"Language mirrors the world we live in; if we use screwed-up language to define reality, if you're always looking to use language to put 'spin control' on something instead of trying to accurately describe it, then you actually end up with a screwed-up reality—at least for you. Alices who misuse language end up eventually living in their own Wonderlands. Lousy language hurts the people who use it, as well as the society they live in; if you use sloppy language, then you end up with sloppy perceptions. So it's easy to fool these people simply by using their corrupted vocabulary; tell them what they want to hear. They'll not only believe what you say, but they'll believe *in you*."

"Precisely," Acton said, nodding his head as he stared at me intently. Now Mary eased herself down next to me. Only Garth remained in a squatting position, absently tracing invisible patterns on the stone in front of him with his index finger. "They use the language of cannibals, which eats up people's perceptions and sensibilities, and sometimes their lives. But the language of cannibals also consumes the people who use it; they become fools, as easily manipulable as their intended victims."

I said, "It's no wonder you were so taken by that painting of Jack Trex's. You knew exactly what he was talking about."

"Yes," Acton replied simply.

"Well, in the country you come from—"

"This is my country too, Frederickson," Acton said in a strong, steady voice. "I felt that way even before I found out that my father was an American."

"I think you're full of shit, Acton; don't try to use cannibal language on us. And as far as that kind of language is concerned, the Russian communists make American right-wingers look like grammar school students. There you have—or used to have—an entire government and bureaucratic infrastructure totally committed to distorting reality with smoke and mirrors."

"Just like this country," Acton replied evenly.

"Except that we have a free press to counter it."

"You won't get an argument from me on that, Frederickson. You might be surprised to know how I really feel about a lot of things—American and Russian."

"I'm sure I'd be astonished. In the meantime, you've been spying on this country since you were a teenager. I'll bet I'd also be astonished to learn how much classified information is leaked by right-wingers inside the government to right-wingers outside it."

"I don't think you'd be astonished at all; obviously, you realize it."

"But your primary task wasn't to gather information, was it, Acton?" It was Garth, who was still squatting with his head down, tracing patterns on the stone with his finger. "Your primary task was to act as a *provocateur*."

"That's right, Garth," Acton said evenly, glancing at my brother. "I see you understand. Provoking extreme or bizarre behavior was—is—the primary task for all of us."

Now Garth looked up. "All of us?"

Acton, a faint smile on his face, glanced first at Mary, then me, then turned his attention back to Garth. "Lady and gentlemen," he said drily, "there are probably almost as many KGB operatives working inside the American right wing as there are Nazi collaborators and sympathizers, and I can assure you there are plenty of them."

Mary, who was showing signs of immensely enjoying herself as the scope and impact of what Jay Acton was describing dawned on her, laughed loudly.

I said, "Jesus Christ."

Garth said, "Are they all like you, Acton? Do they all look and sound American?"

"Not all. Many came in with the Nazis and Nazi collaborators the CIA and State Department brought to this country to use against Russia in the cold war. I can't be sure, but I believe that there are others like me, also—although there can't be many who are actually American-bred; I didn't even know that about myself until Garth told me about my . . . father. The Russians have what are called American Academies set up deep inside the Soviet Union; I know of two of them, because I've been inside them, but there may be more. These are large complexes constructed and designed to imitate small American towns, down to the minutest detail. They are, of course, elaborate schools for spies, and it's considered a great honor to be chosen to go to one. The government selects candidates when they're quite young, and the children literally grow up in these 'American' towns, seeing their parents only once or twice a year, and sometimes not at all. They learn to speak American English without an accent, are surrounded by American pop culture, and so on. The best of the students, as determined by psychological profiles and a vast battery of tests, are smuggled into America when they're in their midteens; legends have been created for them, and they go to live with KGB operatives who are already in place here."

I asked, "Do you know who any of these other people are?"

"No, Mongo—if I may call you Mongo."

"I'd rather you didn't, and I still think you're full of shit."

Acton merely smiled, shrugged. "Nevertheless, what I'm telling you is true. All of us in this operation, at least those at my level, are kept totally insulated from one another for obvious reasons of security; when you have time to reflect on it, you'll see that the precaution is totally logical. However, at our indoctrination sessions in Russia, we are occasionally given progress reports and success stories involving other operatives like ourselves. Being the kind of operative that's called a 'solitary' can be hard on the spirit, and these little information-sharing sessions are designed to keep up our morale. At one session I heard a tape recording of a conservative spokesman calling Ronald Reagan a dupe of the communists because he'd signed an arms treaty with us. That tape was the source of a lot of jokes, because—or so I was told—it was sent to my controller by one of our own people, who is a third-term senator from a western state and who's considered a possibility for a seat on the Supreme Court whenever the conservatives in this country get into power again. If that happens, a KGB officer is going to be helping to interpret your Constitution for you. No, I don't know which senator it is, and no, I don't know the names of the other KGB personnel who occupy high administration positions in various federal agencies. I was just told they're there."

Mary laughed again, even louder.

I said, "Shit."

Garth said, "Who dreamed this thing up, Acton?"

"Three Russian patriots in the NKVD who were eventually murdered by Beria during one of Stalin's purges. Their names wouldn't mean anything to you. The plan came into being in the late forties and early fifties, after the infrastructure of the American Communist party collapsed with the revelations about Stalin's terror campaign and his earlier pact with Hitler. Russia, of course, was collapsing too; Stalin was murdering millions of our citizens, and the entire country was convulsed with terror and paranoia. The American Communist party had become a joke, with most of the membership leaving. There were people in Russia, such as these three NKVD men, who realized that the dream of communism would die unless something was done to tarnish the image of America and the dream it represented; ours was the better dream, but our own leaders were destroying it with their madness. Propaganda wasn't enough, because few people outside Russia believed it, and Stalin was giving the American propagandists a field day. You'd emerged from the war not only a military but an economic giant; as the saying went, most of the rest of the world believed that the streets of America were paved with gold. You had individual freedoms, and we had

Stalin and Beria killing us in droves. Everyone who could was coming to America, and we could only keep our own citizens inside our borders by force and by bringing down the Iron Curtain around the captive nations. It looked as if you would bury the dream of Marxism before it had ever had a chance to flower—unless a way could be found to dilute the ideological strength of the United States.

"And then Joseph McCarthy rose to power, and he was the answer to our planners' prayers. The KGB was astonished at the degree of paranoia, terror, and divisiveness this one man and his followers were able to generate as he searched for wicked communists in American government and the military. Our planners realized that the American right wing would happily decimate American cities, throw people out of work, and in short do just about anything, as long as they believed they were defending America against Russia. We didn't have to subvert or attack; the right wing was all too happy to subvert and attack the fiber of their own country for us. The planners realized that we could actually use this anticommunist atmosphere McCarthy was creating to vastly improve our operations here. McCarthy and the ultraconservative right wing were studied closely. And then our program was instituted. My mother, of course, was one of the pioneers, the first to offer up herself and her son to exile in order to further the communist cause by weakening America. As Garth has correctly pointed out, our primary task was to act as *provocateurs*. We were to infiltrate organizations like the Ku Klux Klan, the American Nazi party, and organizations like Elysius Culhane's would come to be, in order to provoke the organizations' members into the kinds of extreme behavior and rhetoric that would polarize America, divide her from her allies, and tarnish her image in the eyes of the rest of the world. The communists would hide in the last place that anticommunists, and even your counterintelligence people, would think to look: right in the heart of the fascist sector of America.

"Again, we were given success stories to boost our morale. One of our jobs was to make it seem like the Republican party wants to steal the country every time it gets into power. I don't know if this is true, but I was told that Watergate and the subsequent attempt by Nixon and his plumbers to cover it up were instigated—inspired, perhaps, is a better word—by operatives like me, as was the subsequent exposure; Deep Throat may have been a KGB operative, and one of the 'plumbers' may have been also. The same with Iran-Contra. Our people pushed the politicians for the invasion of Grenada because it made Americans look like reckless fools to the rest of the world. Actually our job was—is—easy because it entails simply goading the extreme rightists to do what they want to do anyway. Thus, Elysius Culhane's death squad. He's always *wanted* to control a death squad to quickly and efficiently kill people he thought represented a danger to the country, and in effect I gave him permission to do so by subtly, but repeatedly, telling him what a good idea it was, and then suggesting ways it could be done. I'm not saying that the American government, like the Soviet government, can't do stupid and self-destructive things all on its own; what I'm saying is that some—maybe most—of the more spectacularly stupid and self-destructive behavior of the past few conservative administrations has been inspired in no small part by KGB operatives like myself. The KGB loves it when Americans keep electing conservatives to power; administrations like Kevin Shannon's present much more difficult problems of infiltration and manipulation."

When Acton finished, we were all silent for some time. The KGB operative studied us, looking from one face to another, apparently waiting for some response. I was the one who finally broke the silence.

"You've talked a lot, Acton, but you still haven't answered my question. Did you kill Michael Burana and Harry Peal—your father?"

"No," Acton replied in a flat voice. "I never laid eyes on Michael Burana, and I never knew that he'd discovered my secret. And I didn't kill my father."

I looked at Garth, who nodded to me. "He could be telling the truth about that, Mongo. He cried when I told him who his father was and what had happened." He paused, shifted his gaze to Acton. "Then again, he wouldn't have known who Harry Peal was when he killed him."

"I knew who he was," Acton said quietly. "I didn't know that he was my father, but Harry Peal was always one of my idols."

"Why are you being so hard on him?" Mary asked, looking back and forth between Garth and me. "If it hadn't been for Jay, the three of us wouldn't be alive now."

"The question becomes one of why he saved our lives," Garth replied evenly, gazing steadily at Acton. "If you didn't kill Burana and your father, then who did?"

"I have to assume it was the same man who tried to kill me—a KGB assassin."

"Why would the KGB want you dead?" I asked. "You have to be one of their most important assets."

"I would no longer be of any value at all if I was exposed as a KGB operative. Also, they may have feared that I'd become unreliable; that was always the fear with people like me and the reason we were never given high rank. And in my case, they feared me being caught and telling American intelligence what I'm telling you."

"How did this attack take place?"

"A poison gas grenade was lobbed through my bedroom window at around the same time Garth was driving up from New York to see you in the hospital. If I'd been in bed asleep, I would have died almost instantly, and all an autopsy would have shown was that I died of a heart attack; the grenade itself would have been retrieved. As it happened, I was in the bathroom, with the door closed. I heard the window break and the grenade hitting the floor, and I immediately knew what was happening. I managed to escape through the bathroom window before the gas got to me. I had a spare set of keys taped under my car's bumper. I drove here, got into these clothes. The machine I used to monitor all Culhane's calls is in my home, but there's an electronic hookup to my telephone that I can activate by remote control. I played back the tapes of his most recent conversations, heard what he'd said to Gregory Trex, and realized what had happened. Then I went to the Community of Conciliation mansion to try and head off the death squad."

"If you're not in the business of killing people, why would the KGB give you all the weapons you have up here?"

"The KGB never provided me with anything but communications and wiretapping equipment. I got my weapons from the same places Culhane got his—various arms dealers in the western states and Florida. I trained myself to use them. He supplied the death squad with their weapons."

Garth grunted, said, "What exactly do you want from us, Acton?"

"I want the two of you to walk me in, to get all of us in the hands of people you trust, and who can guarantee our safety. Supposedly you have powerful friends in Washington and elsewhere; Culhane claimed you have a personal relationship with the director of the Defense Intelligence Agency. Is that true?"

"It might be," Garth replied evenly.

"Do you have other friends in the intelligence community, people you trust completely?"

"Maybe."

"We have all the communications equipment we need up here. I would like you to contact whoever can get us safely off this mountain and to Washington, where I'll talk to your counterintelligence people. They'll have to guarantee our safety for an indefinite period of time. Thousands—maybe tens of thousands—of people in federal and state governments, and in conservative political organizations, are going to have to be vetted; and others are going to have to vet the vetters. It won't be as formidable a task as it might sound to flush out the other KGB people like me, because the legends constructed for us aren't as complex as they'd be if we were engaged in ordinary espionage. It was never anticipated that anyone would delve too deeply into our birth records or other background. But it must be done. Only when my story has been accepted by your people, and the process of rooting out the other KGB plants has begun, will the four of us be safe from assassination; the KGB is more likely to leave us alone if there's nothing to be gained by killing us and if our murders could be logically blamed on them. I need the three of you to back up my story and then support me."

Garth and I exchanged glances, and I could see in his eyes that we were thinking the same things. We both looked back at Acton, waited.

"You don't seem too taken with my proposal, gentlemen," Acton continued at last in a slightly wry tone, turning to look at Mary. "Maybe you don't realize how much danger we're all in.

This is the most important and productive operation the KGB has ever mounted. You can be sure that a crack assassin—or maybe even a team of assassins—is searching for us right now. And if we're caught by the police, we die; the people who are after us would be perfectly willing to blow up a police station, or even the town of Cairn, to keep this operation secret and the KGB plants in place. I'm not sure you understand—"

"Okay, you've already played the tune for us, Acton," I interrupted, "and it's a real spooky one. We're all properly impressed with your story. What my brother and I are wondering is if it's true. You've had such success bullshitting Culhane and his friends, maybe you think you can bullshit us and our friends. Maybe there is no KGB assassin, no assassination team; maybe the story about the right wing and the government being infiltrated by a load of carbon-copy Americans manufactured by the KGB is just a fairy tale. Maybe there's just you. Maybe it was you, after all, who murdered Michael and Harry."

"Then why would I save your lives?"

"Because your cute game with Culhane and his lunatic friends and followers was over, no matter what happened to us. You'd listened to Culhane's telephone conversations, so you knew I'd already told Culhane about you, and I'd contacted the head of the FBI's counterintelligence unit, as well as Dan Mosely. While it's true that those people might have done nothing more than conspire to make you disappear back to Russia, that's probably the last thing you wanted, and want. Having lived most of your life in the United States, you didn't find the idea of a Kim Philby existence in Mother Russia all that appealing. You weren't ready to retire, and the only way you could stay on the job would be to find a new way to make yourself useful to your KGB masters. Not only could you cause massive disruption, erosion of morale, and loss of confidence in the government if you had FBI counterintelligence vetting everyone from congressmen to secretaries, but you'd top it off by graciously accepting a job with the CIA. The KGB would flip; they would not only have caused divisiveness and disruption in the United States government, but they'd have a new mole. You might have just a bit of difficulty getting anyone to believe you on your own, so you want Garth and me to help you, to vouch for you. Garth and I just aren't all that anxious to become KGB accomplices—without pay, no less."

Garth abruptly snatched the Uzi from where it lay beside Acton's thigh, then straightened up. "Mongo and I will be happy to walk you in, Acton," he said evenly, "and our friends will guarantee your safety. But we have only your word for all this other business, and we're not about to vouch for you on the basis of that. Quite the contrary; it should be clear to you by now that Mongo is serious about having the murderer of his friend brought to justice, along with Elysius Culhane for making it all possible and for trying to obstruct justice."

"You got that right," I said.

Acton stared impassively at the Uzi in my brother's hand for a few moments, then glanced up into his face. "Your brother is right in some of the things he said," he said quietly and evenly to Garth. "Yes, I want to stay here; I've spent most of my life here, and Russia is an alien culture to me." He paused, looked at me. "But you're wrong when you suggest that I want to penetrate the CIA; I want nothing to do with the CIA. Indeed, I need you and your friends to *protect* me from the CIA. They don't have a good track record when it comes to dealing with defectors. Before they would even consider using me, I'd be endlessly interrogated, drugged, and probably locked away for a good long time while they tried to turn my brain inside out. I don't want to switch sides in the sense that you think of switching sides; I don't want to spy any longer, but I want to be an American—as my father was. I did what I did for ideology. I'm a communist, and probably will be until the day I die. But the Russians themselves have killed the dream of communism as a global system. They can't even take care of themselves. *Glasnost* and *perestroika* came too late. Gorbachev never realized that you can't instill spirit and initiative into the souls of people who were gutted first by the terror of Stalin and then the stagnation under Brezhnev. *This* country is where the action is, and where it will be as long as the fascists can be kept at bay. Ever since the Depression, this country has been adopting precisely those social attitudes and programs that communists like me believe in; the difference is that this country made them work, while Russia never has. Russia and China have had to adopt *capitalist* attitudes and programs in order to survive. The world that I want may not be all that different from the world Robert and Garth Frederickson and Mary Tree want." He paused, smiled. "Who knows? Maybe I'll write a book. Maybe I'll become a politician. If a former grand dragon of the Ku Klux Klan can win office by appealing to one segment of Americans, maybe an ex-KGB operative can win office by appealing to another segment. My ideology is certainly closer to the things this country supposedly stands for than a klansman's."

"Don't count on my vote, Acton," I said.

Mary cleared her throat, peered at me over the tops of her bifocals. "I'm glad you're only speaking for yourself, Mongo."

Acton's smile faded. "But first I have to make sure that we all stay alive."

It was easy enough to see that Acton had won over Mary, had her support and sympathy. I glanced at Garth, who merely shrugged noncommittally.

I said, "It still sounds to me like switching sides, and doing it free of charge."

"It's not free of charge, Frederickson. I'm bringing to you information that can decimate one of the greatest spy operations ever mounted in any country. But then, you still don't believe me when I tell you that the right-wing infrastructure in this country, in and out of government, is riddled with KGB operatives."

"You gave us a nice speech—but it may be the same kind of language you found so effective with Elysius Culhane. You still haven't said anything, or offered any proof, to convince us that you're not the only one."

Acton's response was to sigh, straighten up and stretch, then walk to the edge of the plateau and gaze out over the river. He remained there, his back to us, for nearly five minutes. Finally he turned back, spoke to me.

"You're a tough audience, Frederickson."

"Even if your aim isn't to penetrate our intelligence apparatus, you would still be in a position to feed our government disinformation, and to disrupt."

"Tell me how your friend was killed."

It was Garth who replied. "I've already told you; he was drowned."

Acton shook his head impatiently, and his dark eyes flashed. "Give me the details; tell me everything you know about Michael Burana's activities on the day he was killed."

"He'd gone to see your father to pay his respects," I said, watching Acton's face carefully. I'd already decided that if he was an actor, he was a good one—but then, that was precisely what he had been so thoroughly trained to do. "They hit it off. They got to drinking, and Harry Peal told him about a certain advisor to the right wing who had the Peal family birthmark on his back and shoulder. Then Michael must have come back and confronted you."

Now Acton slowly walked back toward us, stopped when he was standing between Garth and me. Garth switched the Uzi to his other hand, away from Acton, but the KGB operative didn't even look at the weapon. "Would that be standard procedure, Frederickson? Would an FBI agent who'd just learned about a KGB spy in this country confront that spy before reporting the fact to someone and asking for direction and backup?"

I averted my gaze, somewhat grudgingly shook my head. "No, that wouldn't be standard procedure. But Michael was in a very strange place in his head."

"Oh, really?" The faintest trace of a smile had appeared on the other man's lips, but there was no trace of humor in his eyes or voice. "Does that mean that he'd suddenly gone stupid?"

"Look, Acton, I don't know what—"

"Mongo, I'm telling you that Michael Burana never contacted me. I'd never *heard* of Burana until you came to town and started asking questions of Mosely, Culhane, and Mary. Just for the sake of argument, assume I'm telling the truth. If he didn't contact me after learning that I was KGB, then who *did* he contact to report about me?"

He'd found the one weak link in my scenario of what Michael had done, and what had happened to him, on the day he was killed, and hammered it. Attention had to be paid, thought given. If Acton was telling the truth, then the KGB was indeed all over the place—elected officials, advisors to powerful figures, government officials. . . .

"Damn," I said.

Garth stepped around Acton and laid a hand on my shoulder. "Mongo?"

"That fucking Hendricks," I said hoarsely. "Edward J. Hendricks."

Mary was staring at me, her impossibly blue eyes very wide. "Michael's boss?"

"Michael's boss. The head of the FBI's counterintelligence unit. Mary, you said that Michael went into town twice after he came back from talking to Harry Peal, right?"

She nodded.

"Did he say why?"

She shook her head.

"Well, I think I may know why. He went into town to use a pay phone there, because he was afraid the Community's phones might be tapped—as they were. He called Hendricks—the first time to report what he'd found out and probably to ask for an immediate warrant and backup to go and arrest his man here. Then he went back to the mansion to wait for help to arrive. When it didn't, he got impatient and went back into town a second time to ask Hendricks what was happening. What was happening was that Hendricks was sending an assassin after him."

"I really hope this FBI agent isn't one of those powerful friends of yours, Frederickson," Acton said in a flat voice.

"Hardly, Acton. Listen, you said that the people who were doing what you were doing were insulated from one another. If Hendricks is one of you, how would he have been able to call in an assassin?"

Acton shook his head, shrugged. "I don't know. I told you what I was told. It's possible this man is more trusted than I was, or of a higher rank. He may be a control."

"It could be, Mongo," Garth said quietly. "It just could be this man is telling the truth."

"Maybe," I said, looking at my brother. Suddenly my stomach muscles were tight, and I felt slightly short of breath. "There could be a way to find out."

"Not a good idea," Acton said quickly, tersely. "If you call Hendricks and report all this to him, and if Hendricks is what we suspect him to be, then it's true that you'll undoubtedly get the assassin who killed your friend and my father after us. It doesn't mean that we'll survive the encounter. He or she or they will be very good."

"But we've got the drop on him or her or them." ·

"If it's a team, there'll be three. The KGB hit teams usually work in threes."

"I know."

"How are you feeling, Mongo?" Garth asked.

"I feel like nailing Michael and Harry's killer. It may be the only chance we'll get. Agreed, brother?"

Garth held up his hand, raised two fingers. "How many fingers?"

"Six. Let's do it."

"I'd like my weapon back," Acton said to Garth.

Garth shook his head. "You spectate until we see what goes down here." He turned to Mary, who was pale and trembling slightly. "It's going to be all right," he continued, touching the woman's arm. "Do you remember the number, code words, and name I wrote down for you?"

"Yes," Mary replied in a small voice.

"Find a way to get up to the top of the mountain—and be careful climbing. If you hear shooting, you get off the mountain and to a phone just as fast as you can. Get hold of that person we mentioned and tell him what's happening. He'll give you instructions. He'll also make sure that you're safe."

Mary shook her head. Despite her paleness and slight tremor, her voice was firm. "No. I want to stay here with you."

"Mary, there's no need."

"Maybe I have a need. And I want a gun." She paused, took a deep, shuddering breath, then smiled wryly. "My experiences of the past few hours have convinced me that pacifism is not a philosophy that's workable in all situations." She paused, and her smile faded. "I've had friends killed too."

"The three of you are fools," Acton said in disgust. "You're going to get us all killed. You're going up against a professional killer, maybe more than one."

Jay Acton had already amply demonstrated his courage, and he didn't seem afraid now, only thoroughly exasperated. Suddenly I realized that I believed his story. It meant that I was about to use his cellular telephone to dial us up an assassin from the KGB. Talk about home delivery.

"I want a gun, Garth," Mary said in the same firm voice. "There are plenty back up in Jay's cave."

"You've never fired a gun."

"I can certainly point one in the right direction and pull a trigger. You just load it for me and show me where to aim. Please. It's important to me."

To my utter astonishment, Garth nodded his assent, then turned to me. "Mongo, I suggest you go check on the idiot back there, call to pay our respects to Mr. Hendricks, and bring back guns for yourself and Mary. I'll have a talk with our KGB friend here about the best place to set up an ambush."

CHAPTER TEN

It had been impossible to tell from Edward J. Hendricks's tone of voice on the telephone just what he was thinking; but then, considering the fact that I'd had to call him at his Washington office and go through his secretary, he'd had time to get his thoughts together. He had sounded in control, almost subdued, when he came on the line, almost as if he'd been expecting to hear from me, which wouldn't be surprising; a panicked Elysius Culhane would almost certainly have contacted the FBI counterintelligence chief concerning my escape from police custody, and perhaps even about the massacre inside the Community's mansion. Hendricks had listened without interruption while I described the sequence of events that had occurred since I last spoke to him on Sunday afternoon. I told him about Jay Acton's assertion that ultraconservative organizations around the country were riddled with KGB plants, and ventured the opinion that the FBI, with the vast resources of men, data, and equipment at its command, should have little difficulty rooting out these fake Americans now that their existence was known.

Hendricks had chided me gently about my disobedience of his

179

previous order, as he would be expected to do, but then went on to congratulate me on my good fortune, thank me for my display of good citizenship, and tell me that he was sending a heavily armed team of FBI agents from the Bureau's New York City office to take us out of the stone quarry and whisk us off to Washington, where we would be housed in a comfortable and secure facility and provided with protection while the KGB network of *provocateurs* was being dismantled, and until the danger had passed. The FBI would take custody of Gregory Trex, and Hendricks would personally see to it that a federal warrant was issued immediately for Elysius Culhane's arrest on a variety of charges, including one to conceal acts of espionage. I told him we were concerned about being spotted on the mountainside by someone with binoculars, and so wished to stay out of sight in the cave with the electronics gear until our FBI escort arrived to spirit us away. Then I told him exactly how to get to the cave. Hendricks expressed considerable enthusiasm for this idea. The FBI head of counterintelligence assured me that he would have men to us within an hour, and that I shouldn't worry.

Right.

I'd neglected to mention that we had a veritable arsenal at our disposal, but then, what Edward J. Hendricks didn't know couldn't hurt us.

I'd purposely called on the cellular telephone from a position just outside the mouth of the cave, in the stone channel, where I could watch the bound Gregory Trex, and where he could watch and listen to me while I talked. I'd wanted to see his reaction—which I'd assumed would be humiliation and anger—when it was driven home to him that he'd been thoroughly duped and humiliated by the very enemies he hated so much. But Gregory Trex, already thoroughly humiliated when he lost control of his bowels during the firefight in the ballroom of the Community mansion, had hardly displayed any reaction at all; he hadn't even seemed to be listening to me, hadn't seemed to comprehend what had happened. There was dried spittle on his lips and chin, a blank look in his eyes. I suspected Gregory Trex would be serving no time for the murders he helped commit, but would be returned to some kind of institution, where he would spend the rest of his life. He showed no interest in the food or water I'd offered him when I finished my conversation with Hendricks. I'd retrieved two automatic pistols from the foot locker in the cave, checked to make certain that the magazines were full, then gone back to join Garth, Jay Acton, and Mary.

Now we were waiting in ambush; Acton had chosen the site, and it seemed a good one. Here, the rutted main access road had been cut right through the trap rock that comprised most of the mountain, and the machine-scarred rock on both sides of the road formed a deep, narrow channel. In addition, a rockslide about a hundred feet down the mountain blocked the road, preventing further advance by vehicle. It was the route that would certainly be used by any FBI agents, who would be identifiable from the government plates on their cars. There were other roads, like the one leading to the grassy plateau and picnic area, but there was no reason for anyone coming to rescue us to take them. An assassin on his way up would assume that we were all holed up in the cave, as I'd said we'd be, waiting to be shot like fish in a barrel, and so could be expected to come up by this, the route of least resistance. And if an assassin, or team of assassins, tried to come at us from another direction, we felt we had that covered too.

The site was about midway between the hidden cave near the top of the mountain and the base, where Pave Avenue ended at the fork in the access road leading both up to the quarry and down to the river. Acton was with me, on an outcropping of rock on a ledge perhaps seventy or eighty feet above the roadbed. Garth and Mary were on a ledge across the way, closer to the road, screened from view on the ground—but not from us—by a pile of rubble. I could see down to the river, in the unlikely event an attacker came from that direction, and Garth had a clear view of the top of the mountain, if someone came that way. We could both see sections of Pave Avenue and would thus see any vehicles approaching the access road. The down side was all the high ground above us, sculpted ledges left by the machines that had cut the rock, but we'd agreed that it would take a local resident with an intimate knowledge of the mountain and quarry to get into position above us—and then only if the potential sniper knew where we were, which was not possible. We considered it a more than acceptable risk for the position we held.

It was late afternoon, and I estimated that we had about three hours of daylight left—more than enough time for Hendricks's mission of mercy or murder to arrive. But we had to wait considerably less time than that. Less than fifteen minutes after we had come down from the cave and taken up our positions, a late-model gray Cadillac appeared below us on Pave Avenue. It slowed down as it neared the mountain, then disappeared from sight as it made a sharp left turn onto the access road.

"My God," Acton said tightly. "That's Culhane's car."

I glanced at the other man, who looked thoroughly shaken. He looked at me, bewilderment clearly visible in his dark eyes and on his sharp features.

"Surprise, surprise," I said softly, clicking off the safety catch on my machine pistol. "What tangled webs these KGB creatures weave."

"Frederickson," Acton said in the same tight voice, "I don't understand this at all."

"Be quiet. Maybe your former boss is just coming up here for a nice view of the river and a little meditation."

"Frederickson—"

I cut off the KGB operative with a curt wave of my hand as Elysius Culhane's Cadillac came around a bend in the road below us, then braked to a stop on the other side of the rockslide. The right-wing columnist, commentator, and activist had definitely not come to the quarry for the view, and the only subject on which he was meditating was murder.

The engine of the car was turned off, the driver's door opened, and Culhane got out. He was wearing heavy tweed slacks, high-top hiking boots, and a white, quilted hunter's vest festooned with shotgun shells. He tilted his head back and squinted, looking up the side of the mountain in the direction of the cave, then bent over and reached back into the car. What he brought out were a shotgun and an ammunition belt on which hung two hand grenades. He slung the belt over his shoulder, carefully picked his way over the rock rubble blocking the way, then began moving up the road, walking with stiff, nervous strides. I could see the sweat streaming down his face, soaking his shirt and the quilted vest.

I glanced across the way, saw Garth whisper something in Mary's ear. She nodded, then held the gun straight in front of her with both hands, bracing herself with her elbows on the ledge. Garth sidled backward, then disappeared from view around an outcropping of stone. I had a pretty good idea where he was going—down to the road to personally greet Mr. Elysius Culhane, undoubtedly with a fist to the face.

I glanced sideways at Acton. He seemed somehow different. His brow was knitted, and he appeared to be in deep thought as he stared down at the figure moving on the road below us. I wondered what he was thinking.

Culhane was perhaps ten yards from the spot where I expected Garth to step out and rudely greet him when I suddenly heard the sound of running footsteps coming down the road from the opposite direction. Culhane heard them too and stopped dead in his tracks. He crouched slightly, brought the shotgun up to waist-high firing position, and waited.

A few moments later a terrified, haunted-looking Gregory Trex came staggering around a bend in the road. He had obviously found a way to free himself from his bonds, but he had paid a price: both his wrists were bleeding profusely, the flesh shredded by the sharp rocks he must have sawed against to cut through the nylon rope. He'd obviously had nothing on his ruined mind but escape, for he hadn't even thought to take a weapon from the foot locker just inside the cave.

He saw Culhane and abruptly stopped; suddenly his face was wreathed in a childlike smile of elation and relief at the sight of his friend and mentor, the creator and master of the Cairn death squad. He certainly didn't appear to understand the situation, and definitely didn't understand that he, as the only surviving member of the death squad, was not someone Elysius Culhane wanted to remain alive. Then Trex's smile vanished as a thought seemed to occur to him.

"You have to go back, Mr. Culhane!" Trex shouted as he waved his arms in the air and again started down the road. "Something's wrong! I think they've set a trap for you! Go back! Take me with you!"

Culhane hunched his shoulders slightly, glanced quickly, furtively, around him. Then he looked back at the man approaching him, leveled the barrel of the shotgun on Gregory Trex's belly, and pulled the trigger. The slugs from both barrels caught Trex in the pit of the stomach, blew him off his feet and backward even as they doubled him over. The corpse hit the ground, twitched for a few moments, then was still, arms and legs flayed out to either side, blood oozing from the fist-size hole in his stomach and the basketball-size hole in his back.

Culhane again looked around nervously, then broke the smoking barrel of the shotgun and reached for a fresh shell in a pocket of his vest. I moved around to the other side of the boulder where I'd been crouched at the same time as Garth stepped out from behind a column of rock and into the road.

Culhane saw Garth, stiffened, then stutter-stepped backward a yard or so as he fumbled with his shotgun and a shell. *"Who the hell are you?"* he shouted in a whining, high-pitched voice.

"That's my big brother, Culhane!" I shouted at the only slightly blurred figure on the road below me. "He's a very nasty man, with a quick trigger finger! We want you alive to answer questions, but dead will do! Drop the shotgun right now!"

He did. Then he stepped back, bowed his head, and wrapped his arms around his chest, as if he were suddenly cold. Garth walked forward and bent down to pick up the shotgun. As he did so, Culhane was suddenly seized with a spasm of mindless rage and frustration. He threw his head back and screamed, at the same time reaching for one of the grenades dangling from the ammunition belt slung over his chest.

"Don't do it, Culhane!" I screamed at the top of my lungs, knowing that I was too far away to fire on Culhane without risk of killing my brother. *"Garth, look—!"*

It was Mary, directly above Culhane, who opened fire on the man. She was able to let loose one quick burst before the shock of the unfamiliar recoil and shattering noise made her drop the machine pistol. But it was enough, because her aim had been true. Bullets tore into Culhane's head and chest, spinning him around like a top. His involuntary jerking pulled the pin from the grenade he was holding, and it dropped to the ground an instant before he fell on top of it. Garth ran three steps, then dove headlong over a sharp ridge of loose stones a moment before the grenade exploded, painting the flesh, bone, and blood of Elysius Culhane across the sheer stone wall below me.

The echo in the rock cathedral from the chatter of Mary's machine pistol was now joined by the booming echo of the exploding grenade. When the echoes died away, I could hear an approaching siren, very close.

"That's it," I said, half to myself, as I stared down at the carnage below me. Across the way, Garth had climbed back up to the ledge. He helped a very shaken Mary Tree rise to her feet, then gripped her firmly by the elbow as he guided her toward the path leading·down to the road.

A police car, lights flashing and siren wailing, appeared below on Pave Avenue, then disappeared from sight as it made a sharp turn onto the access road.

I turned toward Acton, who was staring down at the corpses of Gregory Trex and Elysius Culhane, confusion and concern clearly etched on his features. "Let's go," I said, pointing with the barrel of my machine pistol toward the cleft in the stone wall behind us that was the entrance to the narrow, rubble-strewn rock chute that led down to the road. "It's over."

Acton looked at me, but he didn't move. "Nothing's changed, Frederickson," he said in a low voice. "Mosely can't give us the protection we need."

I stepped back a few paces and raised the machine pistol slightly—just enough to give the KGB operative pause in the event he was thinking about making any sudden moves. "What's the matter, Acton? Aren't you relieved that we've eliminated your dreaded KGB assassin? I don't understand your problem."

"Something's wrong."

"You're damn right there's something wrong. What's wrong is that you're full of shit. Culhane was no KGB assassin. I saw his face when he found out *you* were KGB, and I thought he was going to have a heart attack. Unless they teach you people to throw up on command, his reaction was no act. It would have made no sense for the *Komitet Gosudarstvennoi Bezopasnosti* to have two of their agents working the same territory, blind to each other, constantly stepping on each other's toes. Nobody has ever confused the KGB with the Keystone Kops. Culhane showed up here because his old buddy Edward J. Hendricks gave him a little courtesy call to warn him that the shit had already hit the fan and that there was no way he could keep the whole story of Culhane's manipulation by the KGB from becoming public. Culhane flipped out. He must have figured that he had one last chance to wipe out all the people who could implicate him in this nightmare and then get away clean, counting on his right-wing buddies to cover up for him. There was never any KGB assassin after us, and there's no massive KGB network inside the ultra-conservative movement—as much as I find the notion enormously entertaining. As Garth and I suspected, there's just you—one very clever, valuable, and enterprising KGB officer looking to make lemonade out of lemons. So let's get out of here. We can all sit down at the Cairn police station and wait for the FBI to arrive."

Jay Acton still didn't move. "Frederickson, we're all dead if we end up in police custody. Somehow, in some way, the KGB will find a way to kill us."

On the road below, Dan Mosely was out of his car, talking to Garth and Mary, apparently getting an explanation of what had happened. At the base of the mountain, three patrol cars were parked across Pave Avenue, blocking off access to the quarry. Mosely looked up, saw me, and waved. I waved back.

"You don't quit, do you?" I said, looking back at Acton. I raised the machine pistol higher, leveled it on his chest. "Get your ass down there. I'll be right behind you. Don't even think of trying to run, because there's no place for you to go."

Acton walked stiffly across the ledge, paused at the fissure, and looked back to me. "You've killed us," he said tersely, then bent down and slipped through the crack in the stone.

"*Hey, Mongo!*" Garth shouted up to me. "*You all right? Can you get down?*"

"*Yeah!*" I shouted back. "*Acton's already on his way! It's going to take me a little longer!*"

I slipped through the fissure, started picking my way down through the sharp rubble in the narrow chute. The adrenaline that had kept me going was now fast draining out of my system, and I suddenly felt as exhausted as I had been in the canoe. My headache was returning, along with more pronounced double vision. I almost tripped on a rock and decided it was time for a breather. I sat down on a pile of crushed rock, took a series of deep breaths while I reflected on how nice it was going to feel to soak in a hot tub and then take to my bed for as long as it took for my body to completely heal.

Jay Acton had certainly been earnest, I thought, a great performer, like his father, but in his own case an actor determined to try to write his own ending to his own play right to the finish. Instead of escaping earlier, as I was certain he could have done, he had opted to save our lives as a necessary first step in trying to lend credibility to a cock-and-bull story that he'd hoped would enable him to burrow his way into the highest echelons of the American counterintelligence apparatus—or, at the very least, to sow a great deal of discord and suspicion.

"Mongo?!"

"I'm coming, Garth! Don't be so goddamn impatient!"

I used the stock of the machine pistol to push myself to my feet, then continued my descent. I came to a spot where there was a cleft in the rock wall to my right, affording me a clear view of the scene below. Acton had arrived and was cuffed, hands behind his back, to the handle on the passenger's door of Mosely's patrol car; he was standing very rigid, staring off down the road. Mosely had taken the automatic weapons from Garth and Mary, laid one on the hood of the car, and was holding the other. I whistled to get their attention, then saluted; Garth and Mosely saluted back, and Mary waved. I stepped around a boulder, continued down.

It was a damn good thing Acton had tried to be clever, I thought, or Garth, Mary, me, and every member of the Community of Conciliation would be dead. Clever, yes, except . . .

Except . . .

I only had another ten or fifteen yards to go in the rock chute before I reached the road, but I abruptly stopped, sat down again, and tried to sort out the problem in logic that had just occurred to me.

Assuming Acton had been believed, a massive vetting operation would have been instituted by the FBI, with every member of Congress, and possibly every official in the government, being obliged to prove they were who they said they were. But the process would have been fairly simple, focusing primarily on birth records and early childhood history; for the vast majority of those being investigated, a copy of a grammar school report card would probably suffice. No KGB operatives would turn up. So what had Jay Acton planned for an encore after he was exposed as a liar? Intelligence work as a double agent? No way. As he had pointed out, the CIA would never trust him, and by now Moscow Centre would certainly have learned that he had been blown.

What could Acton have been planning . . . ?

"*Hey, Mongo?!*"

"Yo! Hold your horses!"

Yet Acton had wanted to get straight to Washington, to an even tighter trap, where it would be proved even faster that he was a liar, and where he would be turned over even faster to the friendly ministrations of the CIA, with their walled-in safe houses, drugs, and other unpleasant interrogation techniques. Calling Hendricks to get home delivery of an assassin had been my idea, not his. He hadn't liked the idea one bit.

"Shit," I said to myself with venom, as I turned and scrambled back up the rock chute to the cleft. I leaned through the opening, whistled and waved.

"*What the hell are you doing, Frederickson?*" Mosely shouted, impatience ringing in his voice. "*I haven't got all day!*"

Indeed. The police manning the patrol cars at the base of the mountain had to be wondering by now why they had been ordered to stay in place on Pave Avenue for so long, perhaps even wondering why their chief had issued such an order in the first place. Maybe.

"Chief, I sprained an ankle! Send Garth and Mary up here to give me a hand, will you?"

Garth started forward, but Mosely abruptly reached out and grabbed his arm, restraining him. Garth wheeled around, them stiffened when he saw the service revolver in Mosely's right hand aimed at his chest. The machine pistol in the man's other hand was raised just slightly, leveled on the ground at Mary's feet.

"*I can't allow that, Mongo!*" Mosely shouted in a strained voice. "*Until we get this business all sorted out, I have to place all of you under arrest! Throw out your weapon, and I'll let your brother come up!"*

I ducked back as sweat suddenly broke out on my face, ran into my eyes. The muscles in my stomach knotted painfully, and I cursed Elysius Culhane anew—not only for being a KGB dupe in the first place, but for then continuing to be their dupe right up to his death, when he had served as a stalking horse to expose any ambush we might have set.

And now what was I supposed to do? I thought, trying to choke back the panic I felt rising in me. Even if I could see straight, which I couldn't, I couldn't fire on Mosely without the risk of hitting Garth and Mary.

"Let's compromise, Chief!" I called, still desperately hoping that I might be wrong about Chief of Police Dan Mosely. "I'm just a little bit nervous after all the commotion we've had up here, and the sight of a lot of cops will make me feel better! Order your men to come up here to join you! And then send McAlpin up here to give me a hand! I'll give him my gun!"

But I wasn't wrong, and now Jay Acton realized what was happening. I heard Acton shouting in Russian, and I poked my head back up in the cleft in time to see Mosely club him with the barrel of his service revolver. Acton's head snapped back, and he sagged, unconscious. Garth started to react, stopped when the other man's gun came up and was pointed at his head. The machine pistol in Mosely's left hand was now aimed directly at Mary's spine.

"Throw out your weapon and come down, Frederickson," the KGB assassin who had masqueraded as an officer of the law said in an only slightly louder than normal speaking voice that nevertheless carried up clearly to me. "Do it right now, or your brother and the woman die."

"Don't do it, Mongo!" Garth called. *"He'll kill us all anyway!"*

"I'm not afraid to die, Mongo!" Mary shouted defiantly in a voice that was strong and steady. *"Do what you have to do!"*

"Don't you think I'm serious, Frederickson?" Mosely snapped. "Don't you think I'll kill them?"

I licked my lips, swallowed hard, trying to think of something—anything—to say to stall for time, and keep the other man from pulling the triggers on the weapons he held on my brother and Mary. "At the first sound of gunfire, those cops down below will be all over here, Mosely. They may be up here any moment, as it is. I think I'll wait."

"But your brother and the woman will be dead."

"So will you, pal. Give it up. Give yourself up to us, and we'll take you in and see if we can't help you cut some kind of deal. This is a standoff, which means you lose. You have absolutely nothing to gain by killing Garth and Mary, because then I'll blow you away."

"Maybe, maybe not," the man who called himself Dan Mosely replied in a perfectly steady voice, as if I had suggested he was in danger of nothing more serious than catching cold. "You've got a head injury, and I'm betting you may not be able to see too clearly. All I need to do is get off one burst up that rock chute you're sitting in, and the ricocheting bullets will do the rest."

"I can see well enough to blow you away with a machine pistol, Mosely. Let it go. What the hell? The KGB makes a point of always getting their own home, so they'll trade for you. Going back to Russia with KGB honors is a hell of a lot better than being dead."

"I won't negotiate, and I won't give up your brother and the woman as a shield while you're sitting up there with a gun on me."

"Is that what we're doing, Mosely? Negotiating?"

"A machine pistol isn't the most accurate weapon in the world at that range, Frederickson. I believe I can kill these two people and escape your burst of fire. Then I'll be the one shooting up that rock chute. I'm going to count to five. If you haven't thrown out your weapon and started down by then, that's exactly what I'm going to do. The police will be told you all managed to shoot each other."

"Nobody's going to believe that, Mosely!"

"They'll have to believe it; there are no other witnesses. I'm the chief of police, remember? *One!*"

"*Don't come down, Mongo!*" Mary shouted, her voice clear and strong. "*He means to kill you too! I'm not afraid to die!*"

"*Two!*"

I leaned out through the cleft, bracing my elbows against the rock, and used both hands to aim the machine pistol at the point where Dan Mosely would be if Garth's body weren't in the way. I felt paralyzed with indecision. Sweat continued to run into my eyes, stinging them, blurring my vision even more.

"Don't let him bullshit you, Mongo!" Garth shouted. *"Just divide by two and shoot the fucker!"*

"Three!"

And I knew that the KGB assassin wasn't bluffing; he fully intended to play out his string to the very end. I desperately wanted to plead with the man to give Garth and Mary a few more seconds of life, perhaps even throw out my weapon to buy those seconds for them. But I knew that giving up my own life, which I would surely be doing if I disarmed myself and stepped out onto the road, would be a futile gesture, and would only ensure that I wouldn't be able to avenge my brother's and Mary's deaths. I sighted down the barrel of the machine pistol and prepared myself to pull the trigger at the moment Mosely pulled the triggers of his weapons, killing Garth and Mary. I anticipated that he would immediately try to dart to his left, toward the stone wall on my side of the road, and then try to come at me. Tears sprang to my eyes; I blinked them away, choked back a sob.

"Four! They're going to die in front of your eyes, Frederickson, if you don't throw out your weapon and come down. If you do, I promise that we'll negotiate. Maybe I'll let them go and—"

Mosely abruptly stopped speaking, started, and then reflexively turned to his left as a flesh-colored artificial leg dropped into the road beside him and bounced high into the air. An instant later there was a sharp crack of a high-powered rifle somewhere above and behind me. A red hole appeared in the center of Mosely's forehead a moment before his head exploded in a cloud of blood, brains, and bone. In death, his fingers tightened on the triggers of the service revolver and machine pistol he held, but Garth had ducked away at the instant the prosthesis of plastic, wood, steel, and leather landed, grabbing Mary around the waist and carrying her to the ground with him. The bullets fired by the dead man flew harmlessly through the air over their heads and clattered in the rocks of the quarry further up the road.

As the echo of the gunfire blended with the sound of fast-approaching police sirens, I glanced up behind me, shielded my eyes against the setting sun, and saw a blurred but unmistakable figure on a rock ledge high above me. Jack Trex, dressed in camouflage fatigues and cap, was sitting on the ledge with his good right leg drawn up and his chin resting on his knee. The empty sleeve of his left trouser leg hung over the edge of the ledge, flapping in a stiff breeze rising off the Hudson. I saluted smartly, and he saluted smartly back.

Garth and Mary were waiting for me in the road at the bottom of the chute. We all embraced, and then Garth pointed at the figure silhouetted against the sky high above us.

"Mongo, who the *hell* is that?"

"Gregory Trex's father," I replied quietly. "That was payback time for one of the men who helped eat up his son."

What looked like the entire Cairn police force, led by Officer McAlpin, came pouring out of the three patrol cars that had screamed to a halt behind Mosely's car on the other side of the rockslide. Guns drawn, they clambered over the loose rock, then fanned out in the road, leveling their guns on us and on the figure high in the quarry. Only then did I realize that I was still holding my machine pistol. I dropped it to the ground at the same time as Jack Trex tossed his .30-30 out over the ledge. The weapon plummeted down through the air like a broken bird, black against the sky and stone, to shatter on the rocks below.

McAlpin holstered his own revolver, indicated to the others that they should do the same, then slowly walked toward us. His almond-colored eyes were filled with horror as he looked around him, and he nervously stroked his droopy mustache. "What the hell happened here?" he asked hoarsely.

Garth walked over to where the artificial limb had landed, bent over, and picked it up. "Mongo will explain it all to you," he said over his shoulder as headed for a break in the stone wall that looked as if it could be the start of a trail to the top of the mountain. "I'm going to see if I can get this man's leg back up to him."

Epilogue

Jack Trex's *The Language of Cannibals* stood propped up, unwrapped, against the trunk of an elm tree down by the river, along with the other wedding gifts.

"I'm a paramedic with the volunteer ambulance corps in Cairn, so after the shooting at the Community's mansion I was on the scene a few minutes after the police. But I ended up a hospital patient myself. When I saw and heard about what had happened, when I found out that my son was a . . . killer, I collapsed. The doctors thought I'd had a heart attack. It wasn't that, but I spent the night in the hospital, under observation. My roommate was one of the Community members who'd been wounded in the shoot-out. She gave me all the details of what had happened, and what she could remember of the conversation between the three of you after Jay here had come to your rescue. She finally told me you'd left just before the police arrived, and that she was pretty sure you'd taken canoes out onto the river and that Gregory was with you. If you'd escaped by way of the river, I knew there was only one place you would have any chance of reaching and hiding out in without being spotted, and that was the quarry. The questions were why you had left the mansion, who or what

193

you were hiding from, and what you hoped to accomplish. And, of course, why you had taken my son. I felt a need to find out what had happened and the reason why you were hiding. I felt responsible for what Gregory had done, since I should have taken steps to straighten him out years ago."

We were sitting at one of a dozen linen-draped tables set up in Jay Trex's riverside yard where the wedding reception, hosted by Cairn's Vietnam veterans, was in progress. Across from us, Jay Acton was leaning back in his lawn chair, practicing chords and idly strumming his father's guitar, which Mary was teaching him to play. Jack Trex seemed to harbor no resentment toward the former KGB operative, indeed seemed to be very fond of him, and I wasn't sure why. Perhaps it had something to do with the fact that it was Elysius Culhane, not Acton, who had stolen his son's soul—and Acton hadn't so much stolen Culhane's soul as probed, twisted, and manipulated the darkness that was already there. Also, the affection might have been due to the fact that Jack Trex was nothing if not patriotic, and it was thanks to Jay Acton that the largest and most insidious KGB operation ever mounted against the United States was being rapidly closed down; we tend to forgive a great deal in those onetime enemies who slip over to our side.

I sipped at my Scotch, said, "You did everything you could for your son, Jack," and wondered if it was true. "Culhane manipulated and stroked him in ways you never could. Gregory was determined to go his own way, and that was the direction in which Culhane steered him. In the end, we all have to be responsible for our own behavior. If it wasn't for you, Garth, Mary, Jay, and I would be dead, Dan Mosely would probably still be Cairn's chief of police, and the KGB would still be using people like Elysius Culhane and your boy to damage the country. You picked one hell of a good time to weigh in."

Jack Trex shrugged his broad shoulders. "Like I said, I felt responsible; I felt I had to *do* something, even if it was only to find you and my son, try to understand just what the situation was, and help you if I could. I guess I was also looking for a way to help Gregory, although I didn't know what help I could be to him any longer. I had the feeling that something very important was at stake, and that's why I dressed in my old uniform. I guess it gave me courage, maybe even a feeling of . . . legitimacy.

"I'd played all over the quarry when I was a kid, so I knew my way around up there. In fact, up there where I was is very close to the site where the veterans have a Watchfire every Memorial Day weekend. There's a trail leading down from the top to the ledge I was on. I didn't want to be seen—by you or the police—and that seemed the best route for me to take to get into the quarry and look around without being spotted. I was already on the ledge, resting and checking out the quarry through my binoculars, when you people came down out of the rocks and took up your positions. I almost called to you then, but I wasn't sure what your reactions would be, and I figured it was just better to wait and see what it was you were up to.

"I saw Elysius Culhane murder my son, and it threw me into a kind of state of shock; it felt like I was paralyzed. I still can't remember clearly what I was thinking while I stared at my son's corpse in the road, but the next thing I knew Dan Mosely was down there with your brother and Mary, Jay was handcuffed to the door of the patrol car, and you were on your way down that rock chute to join them. The rest—well, I couldn't hear everything that was being said, but it didn't look right for Mosely to be holding the guns on Garth and Mary the way he was, and I couldn't understand what all the rest of the cops were doing waiting down at the bottom of the mountain; I know a little something about police procedure, and I knew they wouldn't be there unless Mosely had ordered it. It was clear to me that Mosely wanted you to keep coming down, Mongo, but for some reason you'd changed your mind and were staying put—even if it meant that Mosely was going to shoot your brother and Mary. Nothing Mosely was doing by now looked much like standard police work to me. I'd talked to you, and I knew you were a good man. I figured you had good reasons for what you were doing. Then I heard Mosely starting to count, saw that he intended to kill your brother and Mary, and I made my decision." He paused, smiled faintly, continued, "I was hoping having that leg of mine land next to him might distract him for the half second or so I needed to get a clear shot at him, and it did."

"Thanks for trusting me, Jack," I said quietly.

I had not even been aware that Jay Acton, absorbed as he seemed to be in his guitar playing, had been listening to our conversation. However, he now laid the Gibson gently down on the grass, pulled his chair close to the table, leaned forward on his elbows as he spoke to the Vietnam veteran.

"In the KGB, Jack, there are always watchers watching the watchers, which may explain what Mosely was doing in Cairn. We think now that the KGB, by manipulating the ultra-conservatives under their control, maneuvered to get Dan Mosely, another one of their plants, and a trained assassin, the chief's job primarily because of me. I'd been successful in planting the idea for a death squad in Culhane's mind and then actually getting him to act on it. The KGB considered Culhane's death squad the prototype for right-wing terrorist squads they wanted to see formed all over the country; the squads would, of course, serve Soviet interests whether or not they were ever discovered, since in no case would there be any direct link to the KGB. So this prototype death squad was of immense interest to the KGB, and it turns out that they weren't too pleased with the fact that I was the operative who'd augmented it. I was suspect—all plants are suspect, but some more than others. The truth is that I've been ambivalent about a lot of things, and particularly about my relationship to America, for some time. I didn't know that my superiors were aware of my feelings, but they obviously were. Their answer was to send a trusted KGB officer and assassin to keep an eye on the embryonic death squad, as well as me. Mosely, whose real name was Sergei Kotcheloff, was a product of the American Academy system in the Soviet Union, a system I spoke to Mongo about. He was infiltrated into this country when he was in his early twenties, and part of his legend included a distinguished service record in Vietnam. That part of his false background enabled him to easily get a job with the NYPD, and he used his position as a police officer for twenty years as a cover for his real job, which was to carry out assassinations in and around the metropolitan area as the need, as the KGB saw it, arose. It was Kotcheloff who killed Mongo's friend, and then my father, in an attempt to keep the whole thing from unraveling. When the death squad failed to kill Mongo, he figured he still had a chance to protect the operation if he killed me, to prevent me from talking if I was captured. It seems possible now that Kotcheloff himself, without Culhane ever being aware of it, was giving direct orders—or suggestions—to members of the death squad, but now we'll probably never know for sure."

Jack Trex was hearing the whole story for the first time; I knew it, so I excused myself with a curt nod and rose from the table as Jay Acton proceeded to fill Jack Trex in on the details of everything that had happened since I'd come to Cairn to ask questions about the death of Michael Burana.

I got a fresh drink from the bar set up near the house, then made my way around the perimeter of the yard, nodding to one of the four hulking, grim-faced, no-nonsense Secret Service agents who had been assigned as our bodyguards, and who accompanied us even to the bathroom; their birth records and childhood histories had been examined under a microscope. Down by the rickety dock, my brother, resplendent in the tuxedo he had chosen to wear, was holding the hand of his wife, resplendent in the simple cotton dress and sandals she had chosen to wear, as they spoke with a group of Vietnam veterans and Cairn police officers. Mr. Lippitt, his totally bald head gleaming in the bright sunlight of a perfect autumn afternoon, was standing just behind Garth, beaming like a proud parent as he kept patting my brother on the back.

I had never seen Garth looking so happy—certainly not in the many years that had passed since his poisoning with nitrophenyldienal, and the subtle character changes that had taken place as a result. I dared hope that by marrying the woman of his dreams, Garth would finally escape some of his demons. I knew I was going to sorely miss my brother's presence on the Frederickson and Frederickson premises, but I couldn't have been happier for him.

I paused by the pile of wedding gifts, stared into the haunting depths of Jack Trex's painting as I reflected on the past six weeks that Garth, Mary, Jay Acton, and I spent in the confines of a safe house in Arlington while the KGB operative was debriefed and the machinery to dismantle the massive KGB penetration of a segment of American society was begun. The operation was code-named Operation Cannibal, after Trex's painting.

Edward J. Hendricks had been picked up immediately; under

the loving care of a meticulously vetted joint Operation Cannibal team of CIA-DIA-FBI interrogators, Hendricks had broken and provided valuable information leading to others. He hadn't cared to return to Russia, and in exchange for a promise of a false identity—another false identity, as it were—and relocation under the FBI's Witness Protection Plan, he had agreed to cooperate fully in flushing out the remaining KGB operatives who had penetrated the American right wing.

There had indeed been a senator, who'd managed to get away, and seven representatives, who hadn't. With the eager cooperation of every conservative group in the country, birth records and childhood histories of tens of thousands of people belonging to their organizations were being checked; to date, twenty-eight KGB operatives had been uncovered, and the investigation was continuing. It had been decided that it was in everyone's best interests, and the nation's, to keep publicity surrounding Operation Cannibal to a minimum, and thus far no news organization had tumbled on to just how massive the conspiracy had been, or how much of American foreign policy for the past thirty years had been secretly manipulated by the Soviets. However, I suspected it was only a matter of time before some enterprising reporter got on to the whole story, and I wondered what the electorate's reaction would be when it was realized that 90 percent of everything on the ultraconservative agenda for three decades and more had been considered a godsend by the KGB, and had been actively promoted by the Soviets as a way of keeping the United States off balance, politically weak, and internationally discredited.

Now the Soviet system was crumbling under its own weight, but the collapse owed no thanks to the men who had squandered the lives of countless numbers of people in so many countries, and wasted so much national treasure, pursuing policies of anticommunism that the communists had considered advantageous to them in the long run.

I couldn't help but wonder if it wasn't KGB whisperers who had caught the ears of the people who'd sent America into Vietnam. And, if so, why the Soviets hadn't heeded the very lesson they'd taught us when the specter of Afghanistan beckoned. Could the OSS-CIA have instituted a similar program of plants in Russia after the war? I doubted it, but the very thought was enough to make my head start hurting all over again.

"Mongo?"

I looked up from the painting, was surprised to find my brother standing beside me, an odd, strained, expression on his face; I hadn't heard him come up. Down by the dock, Mr. Lippitt was engaged in animated conversation with the cops and veterans, but Mary was looking at us.

"Are you all right, Garth?"

"I need to talk to you alone."

I nodded toward the river, and we walked together across the lawn, down an incline to a pebble beach. I could feel the presence of two Secret Service agents at our backs, but they remained up on the edge of the lawn, out of earshot.

"I should have asked you before," Garth continued quietly as he picked up a flat stone and skipped it across the water, startling some ducks. "But I knew you'd be honest, and I guess I was afraid I might not like the answer."

"Garth, what the hell are you talking about?"

He turned to face me, swallowed hard, said, "Do you think I'm healthy enough to be doing this thing?"

"What?"

"You know the problems I've had since I was poisoned with that spy dust shit. Do you think I'm doing the right thing? Am I well enough to marry and settle down in Cairn, maybe adopt some kids? I guess maybe I'm looking for a little reassurance."

Suddenly I felt tears well in my eyes. "Of course you're well enough, you idiot. Don't you know you're the most spiritually healthy person I know, outside of Mom? I'm not certain Cairn is ready for you, but you're certainly ready for Cairn. Besides, if Mary ever tells me you're going spooky on her, I'll be right up here to kick your ass."

Garth smiled broadly, and he seemed relieved. "Some people on the town board asked me if I'd be interested in becoming Cairn's chief of police."

"That's great news, Garth," I said evenly. "What did you say?"

"I told them I'd have to confer with you regarding my status with Frederickson and Frederickson."

"Ah, well. I managed to carry on for quite a few years without your assistance, dear brother, and I'm sure I can do it again."

"That's funny; I don't remember you ever being able to manage without my assistance."

"I'll ignore that and continue with what I was going to say. I rather like having you as my partner. We've done all right, and you have enough equity in the brownstone and the business so that you shouldn't have any financial worries if you want to be top cop here—or if you want to do nothing at all except make love and sail all day. On the other hand, Cairn is only an hour away from the city. It isn't a bad commute, and we could even hook up a computer terminal for you here so that you wouldn't have to come in to the office every day. What I'm saying is that you have all the options; I want you to do exactly what you want to do, what will make you happiest."

Garth nodded. "That's what I wanted to hear. I just wanted to make sure it was all right with you if we remained partners and I worked out of Cairn."

"Done."

We walked together back up the incline into Jack Trex's yard, where my brother's bride, at everyone's urging, had borrowed Jay Acton's guitar and was preparing to give an impromptu concert.